The Angelic Darkness

Richard Zimler was born in Manhasset, New York, in 1956. He has a bachelor's degree in Comparative Religion from Duke University and a master's degree in Print Journalism from Stanford University. After working as a journalist and editor in San Francisco for eight years, he moved to Porto, Portugal, in 1990. In 1994 Zimler received a National Endowment for the Arts Fellowship in Fiction. He is currently a professor at the College of Journalism in Porto.

Zimler's first novel, *The Last Kabbalist of Lisbon*, was published by Quetzal Editores in Lisbon in 1996. An immediate best-seller, this historical mystery has been published worldwide. It was named 1998 Book of the Year by Fiona Pitt-Kethley and Francis King, who called Zimler 'an American Umberto Eco'. His second novel, *Unholy Ghosts*, was published in London in 1996.

Zimler's short fiction has been anthologized in several collections, including *The Slow Mirror and Other Stories*, an anthology of contemporary Jewish fiction for which he supplied the title story. Other collections featuring his work include *Voices from Home*, *His 2,700 Kisses*, *Men on Men: 6* and *The Book of Eros*. His short stories and translations have appeared in many British and American magazines, including *London Magazine* and *The Literary Review*. He has translated a great deal of Portuguese prose and poetry into English, including excerpts from the work of José Saramago, who won the 1998 Nobel Prize in Literature.

The Angelic Darkness

Richard Zimler

A

ARCADIA BOOKS

LONDON

Arcadia Books Ltd
15—16 Nassau Street
London WIN 7RE

A catalogue record for this book is available
from the British Library.

ISBN 1—900850—30—3

Typeset in Stempel Garamond and Poetica Chancery by
Discript, London WC2N 4BL
Printed in the United Kingdom by Biddles Ltd, Guildford
Cover photo copyright © Richard Bates

Arcadia Books distributors are as follows:
in the UK and elsewhere in Europe:

Turnaround Publishers Services
Unit 3, Olympia Trading Estate
Coburg Road
London N22 6TZ

in the USA and Canada:
Consortium Book Sales and Distribution, Inc.
1045 Westgate Drive
St Paul, MN 55114—1065

in Australia:
Tower Books
PO Box 213
Brookvale, NSW 2100

in New Zealand:
Addenda
Box 78224
Grey Lynn
Auckland

in South Africa:
Peter Hyde Associates (Pty) Ltd
PO Box 2856
Cape Town 8000

For Alex and my mother, without whom this book
would not have been lived. With thanks to
Gary Pulsifer and Daniela de Groote of
Arcadia Books; Judith Ravenscroft and
Timothy Hyman; Cynthia Cannell; Bob Weil;
Richard Bates; Turnaround Publisher Services;
Michael, Dale, Fiona, Peter and all the
wonderful people at Tower Books;
Alan Davidson; and Jenny Nagle.

Chapter 1

*I*T WAS MY FATHER'S STORY of the Ethiopian baby that I couldn't get out of my head on the night of Tuesday, June 3, 1986. I was sitting up in bed with the lights on, seeing the glimmer in his eyes, hearing the clink of his lighter, and watching the smoky words cascade out of his mouth, wondering if it was right then that my life started to go wrong. Although I couldn't figure out the exact connection, I knew that things had to have skittered off course somewhere, very probably there, because here I was, scared of the dark and shivering alone at two in the morning, without any semblance of a family; my wife, Alexandra, had left me for good that morning.

Not that I hadn't expected Alexandra to leave. We'd been fighting on and off for months – about my need for other women; whether she was suffocating me or belittling me; if she'd listened to what I'd just said; eaten leftover pizza earmarked for me; or purposely pruned the plum trees too severely. Weeks before, I'd risked discussing it all with my younger brother, Jay. I was sure I was no longer in love – after all, I rarely even felt like touching her and the very idea of having sex with her was enough to make me nauseous. It seemed like the most sensible explanation. But I was wrong; Jay said authoritatively that I couldn't stand Alexandra – that I'd become obsessed with our arguments, in fact – because I was *too much in love with her*. Maybe he was right. Or very possibly, he was nuts. But what to do then? As if he were playing at police detective, impersonating his beloved Captain Furillo on *Hill Street Blues* most likely, he told me that I'd better figure out what my motives were.

So I did my best to separate the white light of the explosions that Alex and I produced into a spectrum of my desires and fears, then transferred it all to a colouring book that I could refer to whenever I wanted. Colour incest violet; disapproval, indigo; loss of control, blue; abandonment, green; punishment, yellow. My parents and brother had helped me mix all these dyes. And I was the painter and publisher; I had final responsibility. But it was no fucking help, of course; there were so many more tones contributing to the surface colours of my emotions that I could hardly ever know what was really going on. Besides, it was no one colour (or even two or three), but instead the great white light of our uncontrollable rage that could no longer be quelled and that flash-fired to ashes the last dazed fragments of our marriage.

On that first night alone in the house we'd shared in Pacific Heights for four years, it wasn't the intricacies of my wayward life with Alex that tangled up my thoughts, however, but my long-ago conversation with my father; I kept seeing him grab hold of his cherished silver jug and telling me his story of the Ethiopian baby – only this time the infant's blood was sluicing like new wine over his callused hands.

For years, my dad had kept his jug on the top ledge of my parents' walk-in closet, out of reach, just in front of the small trap-door to our attic. Studded with bevelled coloured glass squares and banded with intricate arabesques, it was always black with tarnish. Even so, my father had forbidden my mother – the designated silver polisher in our house – from touching it. Not to mention Jay and me. It was too valuable to risk being scratched or even smudged, we figured, having been carried back from Ethiopia to Naples when my father was a soldier fighting to extend the Italian Empire back in the 1930s.

Lacking any evidence to the contrary, my brother and I fantasized that the jug was from the sixteenth century, having picked that particular time period because it looked more

archaic and pleasingly imperfect than any of the polished pew-
ter mugs and cups we'd seen in our schoolbooks on colonial
history. Having long ago discovered the capital of Ethiopia on
the beach-ball-sized globe I kept in our bedroom, we guessed
that Dad had bought it at a crumbling antique store in Addis
Ababa. Or maybe he'd looted it, Jay thought with starry-eyed
envy, stolen it from a Thousand and One Nights palace crown-
ing a lonely desert mountain. We figured it was magical, of
course, like Aladdin's lamp.

Then one day when I was ten – back in the summer of
sixty-three, that slow hot postcard-perfect August when we'd
all seen John-John and Caroline running happily along sandy
beaches with their parents, a mere three months before their
own world would be shattered to pieces – I found out what it
really was.

My father called me into my parents' bedroom. He was
standing by his night table, had his big coarse hand inside the
jug, was winking at me as if he really were about to perform a
magic trick. My mouth was probably hanging open; it was the
first time I'd seen his prized possession outside its protective
shrine.

Taking out a small piece of rough brown leather, he motioned me over to him and dangled it in front of my eyes. It
was hanging from a straw-like string, was maybe an inch and a
half long and an inch wide, a bit pimply in spots, as if it might
have been covered with tiny hairs at one time. It looked just
like dried hide, I thought, though I didn't know how I might
know that – maybe from our yearly field trips from
Searingtown School to the Museum of Natural History in
Manhattan. As he jiggled it up and down, arousing my curiosity, Dad's deep-set black eyes began shimmering with pride –
pride mixed with corruption, I've thought in years since. As if
he enjoyed how he was about to soil me.

'Take a look-a this, Billy,' he said in his gruff voice, a slight

Italian accent adding weight to the ends of his words, not like Rossano Brazzi or any of the other Italian actors whose exhausting movies my dad made us watch on TV – much darker, without any trace of charm or comedy.

I turned the hide in my hands, sniffed it. It smelled like dust, a bit sour, too, as if it had been pickled or something. I could tell he really wanted me to ask him what it was. I didn't want to, because I'd already figured out, of course, that this was going to be trouble. When I did, he replied, 'Billy, that little dried *niente* you're holding – that *nothing* – was the future of Ethiopia. Back when it still had a future, I mean.'

He smiled cagily, then sat down on the edge of his bed. My father was just over six feet tall, muscular then, though he would develop a hanging belly and hairy breasts over the next few years. The bed sank with a groan. 'Come here,' he said. 'Now that you're ten, you're old enough to hear about it. Might do you some good. Keep you out of trouble.'

I didn't like sitting next to my father. I never liked being within arm's distance of him. Or smelling his caustic scent of tobacco, which mingled with the Old Spice aftershave.

'Sit, boy,' he said, seeing me hesitate. 'You're such a little *topo* sometimes – a mouse. No one's going to eat you.' He opened his mouth to show me his browned teeth and gold fillings, then laughed; my father found things funny that other people didn't.

After I dropped down next to him, he explained that long before I'd been born he'd been fighting in Ethiopia. This one time, he said, his platoon had been destroying railroad tracks near the coast when some villagers started to protest. The captain in charge ordered the soldiers to kill them. 'Maybe fifty or sixty of them,' Dad said. 'With guns, it's not that hard – doesn't take much time.'

At that, I remember not being able to hold back any longer and trying for an escape: 'Hey, Dad, I'm kinda worried my bike might get stolen,' I said. 'I left it in the driveway. I better go get it.'

He threw his arm across my chest, as he did to keep us from flying forward if we were sitting in the front seat of our Dodge station wagon and had to stop short. 'You just sit still and listen for once, you little *topo*.' After I nodded, he continued: 'So, after we killed them, and just before we dug the pits to bury them ... it was sunset, and there was this group of kids that must have been playing away from the village. They came back wet. Like they'd been swimming. Maybe your age, Billy, though smaller than you.'

I could hear my mother preparing lunch downstairs, the tap-tap-tap of her slicing something on her round cutting board, probably plum tomatoes; I'd seen a thick white rope of mozzarella sitting on the kitchen counter on my way toward the stairs, and my dad liked a big tomato and cheese salad during the summer. I was hoping she'd call us down before this story got much further.

Dad took his pack of Lucky Strike cigarettes from his shirt pocket, stuck one in his mouth, and lit it with his clanky lighter. I was wondering where Jay had escaped to and I was thinking that it was just as well that he was probably playing at one of our neighbours' houses. Maybe my hearing this story would mean that he wouldn't have to. Dad took a greedy puff, then said, 'I'd never killed kids during the war. It was a rule I had. Pure *pecoraggine*. Being ... being yellow. So my friends in our platoon, they wanted to see me kill the kids. When I told them I couldn't, they all laughed. Except the *capitano* – Fortanelli. A big bastard from Torino. *Feroce*, and built like a *rinoceronte*. He hated southern Italians like me – *meridionali, terroni*. He ordered me to kill the kids. You didn't argue with him. You just didn't. So I pointed my gun at the oldest one first, held it out ...' Here, my dad thrust out two fingers with his cigarette in between, then pointed his thumb straight up, making a revolver.

He gave a nasty laugh that didn't seem like a laugh at all. More like the sneer he sometimes gave my brother and me when he thought we were too American. 'So there I was, with my hand shaking. I squeezed the trigger and ... pow! He fell over, half his face blown off. Not like a kid any more. Like a bleeding animal. Black and red all over.'

He was silent for a while, getting back his composure, inhaling hard on his cigarette, as if he were drawing in stubborn memories from it. I could hear my mom opening and closing the refrigerator door. Maybe if I yelled down to her to ask if I could help make lunch, she might agree, and I could dash out before my dad bashed me. When I looked up at him, however, he seemed to understand my thoughts. His shimmering eyes conspired to say, *Just try it!*

'As we were leaving, one of the soldiers discovered a girl giving birth. She'd crawled somewhere outside the village, was lying behind this big thorny bush. She was maybe fifteen, was trying not to scream. Kind of grunting, Billy. I'd never seen anybody giving birth. None of us had, I think. We were just kids ourselves. I was only eighteen, you know. And watching that girl, I had this moment, this ... It was like I was alone in the world with her.' Unable to explain his feelings at that moment, his hands swirled in lazy circles. 'I was like a character in a play or something. I felt like I understood things about life. I mean, there was this baby coming into the world – it was the future for these people, these Ethiopians. And I understood that *their* future belonged to *us* – should belong to us, anyway. I mean, that was our goal in Africa. I realized it was the most important thing – killing them, killing the kids.' He gripped the leather in his fist, the cord dangling down, then opened it in front of my nose. He stood up. He towered over me. 'A few of the men helped the girl have her baby,' he continued. 'Then I killed it and cut this off. *È il suo ...*'

Dad said some other word in Italian I didn't get. It probably meant *ear* or *nose*. Or maybe even *testicles*. Jay speculated a few years later that he'd actually cut off a section of the umbilical cord. That's a word I definitely wouldn't have understood at the time. But we never learned exactly what he'd said.

It was now more than two decades since my dad told me his story, and yet I *still* found myself regretting never having found out for sure. Sitting up in bed, a shivering blanket draped over my shoulders, I was watching my father drop his keepsake back into the mouth of his silver jug, listening to him say matter-of-factly, 'Your mother must have lunch almost ready by now. Go wash your hands, then go downstairs.' He spoke as if the story he'd told me didn't change anything for good, as if we could just go on with our lives.

'What about the girl, Dad?' I asked. 'The girl who gave birth?'

He flapped his hands dismissively and said that she'd screamed like a hyena when they'd killed her newborn, but that they – Africans – don't feel death as deeply as Europeans, so it wasn't so bad.

'And did you kill her, too?'

'Course we did, boy. When we were ready.'

Something about that word, *ready* – now, I began wondering what else he and his friends might have done to the girl. Though maybe it was all a lie. Maybe Italian soldiers never committed any atrocities in Ethiopia and the keepsake was nothing more than animal hide. Maybe he and his friends didn't hunger after trophies like ears and fingers, didn't try to convince themselves that the people they'd just killed were really only animals. And it would have been just like Dad to invent a story to scare me. Though I never bothered asking him; I'd never have believed his reply either way.

But when Dad told me all this, I was only ten, of course, and I wasn't wondering about the connotation of particular words like *when we were ready* or having any heretical doubts about the truth of his story. I *knew* it had happened just as he had told me. And I felt the dry hot wind of an overwhelming sickness pervading me, as if I'd been shipwrecked on an island, as if I'd spend my whole life alone, never have a real family.

As it happens, this feeling of utter loneliness only came back to me twenty-three years later, after my wife's outraged accusations had subsided and she'd withdrawn into the silence of her imminent departure.

Kicking my legs over the side of the bed, holding my head in my hands, I remembered that as my father was walking away, I called after him, 'And what about the jug?' I guess I was hoping that there was some remnant of good in his story, some potential for magic still vibrating inside that tarnished silver.

He turned at the doorway to his walk-in closet. He held it up. 'This?'

I nodded and said, 'Where'd you get it? Did you find it in a cave or something?'

He shrugged. 'I just picked it up somewhere – some store. It's nothing. It's what's inside that means something, that's important.'

That's important ... I knew now that he was right, because here I was speculating that the break-up of my marriage might even somehow have its origins in that dangling swatch of stolen flesh, in the years of future life cut away from a child I never knew. And I was convinced, too, just as when I was a kid, that my only friend was the light filling the room from a bulb above my head, that if I were to flip a switch and cede to the darkness lurking inside my own house, that I, too, might be murdered.

Why my fear had always taken this form – was linked to the dark, I mean – I couldn't say. The few friends to whom I'd ever mentioned it usually intimated that it represented years of repression — that what I really wanted was for the horned witches inside my closet and psychopaths under my bed to reach out for me and lead me off into their embracing darkness. You could've fooled me. But, as I found out while trying to discover the motives behind the failure of my marriage, the First Law of Self-Sleuthing might very well be: *who the hell really knows for sure why we do anything?*

∞

So there I was on my first night alone in quite some time, inside the house I'd shared with Alex since just before our wedding, learning once again that every creak was the jungle drumbeat of my impending doom. Listening for ghostly whispers through my closed door, leaning forward as if to eavesdrop upon my own timid imaginings, I realized in an instant of icy clarity that I was the very same person who continually took this posture of terror in childhood. Or at least I was his descendant — somewhat larger but equally panicked.

My first instant of pure naked fear was touched off by the groan of a lamp downstairs. I recalled with despair my skittish mother informing me years before that such noises were symptomatic of 'the house settling.' *Settling into what?* I'd always wondered. *And for how long would we descend?*

As a kid, I always constructed night-time protection out of my two pillows; when the first was placed horizontally under my head and the other arranged vertically against the border of the bed, they formed the bricks of a magic wall that no murderer could ever breach. I normally arranged my blue fur pussycat at the corner of the two pillows and, despite fears of carbon dioxide poisoning, occasionally draped a blanket roof — or in summer a sheet — over my head.

These days, I figure that the witch in the closet was my mother and the murderer under the bed, my father. Most people who've met them tend to think I'm exaggerating wildly, but then, we never really get to know other people's parents.

9

At least not what they're like with the doors closed and locked.

My fear became so bad one summer – I was fifteen, I believe – that I would unfailingly burst up out of dreams of criminal evil into a confining darkness, my whole body poised for imminent death. Although the towel I kept by my bed could soak up my sweat, neither it nor my electric light could dispel the stalking eyes of the grotesque monsters who inhabited my nightmares. It was impossible for me to fall asleep again until the appearance of the sun. Often I would tiptoe into my parents' room wrapped in a protective blanket, nuzzle myself into the green lounge chair onto which my father tossed his stained undershirts, and watch my mother and father sleep all night long. Dad was pretty overweight by then, having taken a desk job the year before as sales manager for Perucci Brothers Construction, where he'd previously been a foreman. He'd also grown a stubby moustache that made him look a bit like Oliver Hardy. He wheezed when he slept. My mother was small and dishevelled, had droopy eyes and a bald spot at the top of her head where she'd pulled out her hair. She curled into a ball while she slept. Both of them would turn occasionally under the covers but rarely wake up. In fact, I can't remember them ever spotting me there. Maybe they did – I'm not sure they would have cared. Anyway, I'd sit there listening for creaks and rumbles, expecting the first footstep of my murderer at any moment. I would count and count. I'd be up in the tens of thousands when oblique rays of blessed sunlight would finally pierce their venetian blinds, and I'd trudge with relief back to my room to fall instantly asleep.

With my new-found penchant for looking at things in inverted ways, I'd now wager that instead of coming into my parents' room for comfort, I was really keeping an eye on them to make sure they wouldn't do me in while I slept.

With Alexandra gone, however, these insights didn't help much. And when I did finally talk myself into slipping under the covers and turning off the lights, I tossed and turned over a frigid sheet, fighting the urge to build my pillow fortress again. I was amazed that I was now thirty-two years old and that I was less upset about her leaving than about my fear of the dark. I fantasized about telling Jay what had happened, pictured him standing there frowning at me as I detailed Alexandra's accusations and my own motions for the defence, as if he were sure that I didn't have a clue what our arguments were really about. I don't know why I picked him for my imaginary conversation; after all, I had been given ample reasons not to trust him over the last ten years. Maybe I figured that he was just the right person to make me feel even worse about my life. Anyway, in my imaginings with him, out popped my certainty that Alexandra was never coming back and that if I wanted her to return, which I wasn't sure I did, it was really only to dispel my fear of living alone – which most frequently came down to my fear of the dark. I said that maybe what I really needed was a tenant to share my house in the mean time, explaining to Jay that the layout of rooms would make it easy to live with some-one and still maintain my privacy. I added that I needed the extra income if Alexandra wasn't going to pay half our mort-gage any more. 'It's a practical solution,' I concluded.

'Yeah, it sure is,' he replied eagerly. But I could see him thinking I was a moron.

'Maybe ... maybe it won't work, after all,' I added. 'Maybe it won't get to the root of my problem.'

'No, it probably won't,' Jay nodded.

He seemed happy about that, so I took a deep breath and rushed him out my fantasy front door.

Looking hopelessly for a warm spot inside the icy sheets, I thought for a while about how hard it is to effect real change. Then Jay, like my own personal homunculus, was back inside my head, and I told him, 'I think that maybe I'm going to try to find a tenant as soon as I can.'

'Go ahead. If you think *that's* going to work, be my guest.'

He was so smug. And *be my guest* was an expression my mother would have used against me. Which made me angry. And knowing that I desperately needed someone else's presence in the house, I came swiftly to the conclusion that I was damn well going to look for someone to live with. Only I also wanted to wait a little while in order to be certain that letting a stranger inside the crumbling walls of my life was the right thing to do.

I didn't need great patience. My second night alone in the house, I imagined that slumbering spirits, awakened by each rustling of leaves in the garden, would blame me for their being disturbed. So I buried my head at the corner of my pillow fortress and slept in and out of dreams of feral animals and strangers who had somehow stolen into the house. In the worst of my nightmares, a lizard-faced taxi driver was sitting on the back of the white couch in my living-room. In the panic of my first waking moments, I sensed this reptilian thing downstairs, looking up covetously at the closed door to my bedroom. I crept forward to this barrier between us, turned the handle ever so carefully – so as not to create any noise that would give away my position – and caressed it open. I turned on the light...

The living-room was empty. The front door was locked and latched. Same with the back entrance and the door to the spare rooms.

And yet my heart was thumping.

I got no sleep the rest of that night. My father's voice kept coming to me. He was telling me how soldiers get used to the blood. 'To the *puzzo* of death, too – the stink,' he was saying. 'You even like it – like it *a hell of a lot*. Because it means you're still alive.' With a wink, he added, 'But that's a kind of secret.'

Back in bed, I began picturing Alexandra lying on the

futon in the spare room at my brother's house; I was pretty sure that was where she'd gone. I wondered how she was faring, if she maintained symmetry by thinking of me. But mostly I waited for spirits. Now and again, I tried to figure out from what depths I'd conjured them up, why my fears took this form.

That night firmed my resolve. After work the next day, I listed the back rooms of my house with a flat-finding service on Divisadero Street.

I saw four prospective tenants on Friday. All of them were awful. I passed the entire weekend haunted by nefarious spirits, stopped shaving and bathing. On Monday, I told the people at work that I was growing a beard. Who knows what they thought of my odour. The only person I told about my split with Alexandra was Jessica. She'd met Alex a few times at the office, once for a movie. She also knew a little about my trysts with other women. We'd even joked about them. So the break-up wouldn't be the biggest shock in the world. And unlike the rest of the vultures at work, she wouldn't dig her beak into me for scraps she could pass along to her friends.

Jessica's got sad black eyes, a large nose that she claims to have inherited from her Sicilian grandmother, thick brown hair cropped like a porcupine.

'That explains your ... your less than professional state,' she said when I told her about my separation from Alexandra. 'So when did it happen? Did she just walk out on you? No tears ... no note?'

'A few days ago. We argued. The usual — my affairs, women. She said she couldn't take it any more, that she'd been building up to this ... "like a pyramid on which she'd finally placed the last stone," she said.'

'A pyramid?'

'It's just Alex — her metaphors. An English teacher she loved once told her it was an effective way of communicating.

And Alex loves to be effective. Her best ... God, once she said that all my emotions were like the sewage in a cesspool – hidden way underground, decomposing, putrid, unavailable to the living.'

Jessica laughed.

I smiled; it did seem strangely funny now. 'You know, we didn't always get along,' I sighed. 'But I thought we'd go on for a longer time than this.'

My words conjured up a silence founded in failure. I gestured that Jessica was free to leave. She shifted her position, shrugged. 'Yeah – we all think like that,' she observed. 'But she'll probably come back.'

'No.'

'You don't think so?'

'Not this time. She turned into a bigger mummy than I'd ever seen before – stiff, rigid, hard. No way. She's taken a lot of her stuff already. And we already agreed that I could stay in the house indefinitely. No way she's coming back – no way.'

Jessica came forward out of the doorway and bent down in front of me, peering at me with those big eyes of hers as if I were a hurt kid. 'It's hard,' she said with a mothering pout. She rubbed my shoulder. 'I know. But wait and see what happens. Maybe you're wrong. Lots of things can happen in life.'

I didn't want to tell her that maybe I didn't want Alex back. 'I suppose anything's possible,' I replied.

She stood back up and sighed, 'Life,' as if it implied a series of inevitable disappointments. I felt she understood me till she added, 'Maybe it has a positive side, you know.'

Jessica waited for my acknowledgment. I demurred; I was wondering if finding a positive side to everything was a late-twentieth-century disease or if it had been released into the world during some earlier age. Maybe women were particularly susceptible to it; unflagging optimism had been one of Alex's most exasperating qualities as well.

'So what's the positive side?' I asked, giving in to my fate.

'This way, you'll know if you really want her or not,' Jessica declared.

I nodded rather than press the issue.

'And besides,' she twinkled, 'this way you can screw other women without feeling any guilt!'

I rolled my eyes. 'You think so, Jessica?'

'Sure. That's the way it was for me after the divorce. Now I sleep with anyone I want without having to worry a bit that I'm hurting anyone.'

'Except yourself,' I said.

'Ooh, that's heavy.' Jessica giggled and strutted back into the doorway, blew me a kiss, and gave me a thumbs-up sign. 'Go for it!' she said.

That was the last confessional experiment I tried. The only person I really wanted to talk to was Alex herself. Part of me wanted to assuage my guilt with stories of how well she was doing and another little dark part of me wanted her to have sagging eyes and tear tracks on her cheeks, of course – dishevelled hair, maybe a nightgown on in the middle of the day. During one of these cruel daydreams, I realized with a start it was my mother I was describing. *I was hoping she had turned into my mother!* Pretty damn strange.

∞

That week, it began to get really difficult for me to face going home after work. At the time, I had an office on the thirty-fourth floor of One Post Street, just one more tower inside the growing steel and glass sprawl of downtown San Francisco, was editing a bi-monthly magazine for employees of a Fortune 500 corporation. So I'd hibernate there till maybe seven in the evening, then get a little tipsy on gin and tonics at a sleazy bar on Mission called the Belfry. When my stomach began crying out for food, I'd walk home on Sutter Street through the Tenderloin, San Francisco's senseless-crime district. Any other neighbourhood would have provided a contrast to my mood, you see. But not the Tenderloin. It advertised depression. I mean, those transient hotels with the horrible neon signs out front. God, they always made me think of old people having to put up with sludge in their sinks and cockroaches in their beds after fifty years of sweating it out on some assembly line. Where's the justice in that? And the whores ... I was fascinated and repulsed by them at the same time. Never visited any, you see. I guess that would have dispelled the magic. But for me, they were representatives from another world, a bit like elves. Or maybe more to the point, like those witches I used to imagine. I'd watch them teasing one another, compare their ludicrously snug outfits, marvel at the way they pranced around in spiked heels like prosaic Tina Turners, all the while wondering what they thought about, what sex meant for them. I'd marvel at my missing obsessions, too, my lack of libido. I couldn't figure out where it had gone of late. Then I'd continue on home. Once there, I'd look around as if on patrol, whisper with bravado to myself *this ain't so bad*, flip on the TV, and boil some ziti. By then, the San Francisco sunset of pink and gold had usually splashed itself across the big bay window. I'd sit on the couch and eat. I'd think of Alex being gone a lot, of course. But I was pervaded by a companionable loneliness, the I-know-I'm-feeling-sorry-for-myself-but-it-feels-too-good-to-stop sort that I'd felt as a kid when I was punished and sent to my room.

One thing I began to understand for certain, however: the downfall of my marriage had banished me to the isolated, solitary world that I'd originally built for myself as a child.

I'd come home to the landscape that was my birthright.

All this is not to say that part of me didn't know that I was letting my home decay into a pig-pen of self-pity. But I figured a little wallowing didn't matter. For despite even my most indulgent intentions, my comfortable home would fade each night with the descent of dusk. In the dark, I'd turn around into a house I no longer trusted, with closets that just might be hiding killers who could be incited to murder by the slightest noise.

I saw two more people interested in my spare rooms at the end of the week: a giant nature girl wearing a Mexican poncho and a walnut-faced grandpa with tufted eyebrows. They brought out my nastiness and loneliness. I ushered them quickly out of the house as if they were exiles from a Nathanael West novel.

Then, on Monday, June 16, thirteen days after Alexandra had left, I started to cry convulsively – for hours at a time. And for no particular reason; my tears were simply beyond my control. I knew then that I was very little changed from the shy college freshman who'd been exiled from sexuality and the thirteen-year-old boy who'd been trapped inside a world of abusive adults; for several days each time, I'd entered a horizonless landscape composed only of tears.

It was as if – during these two periods of my life – the rusty armour bequeathed to me by my father had cracked.

In my calmer moments, I now considered that maybe I would be subject to such displays of fragility every few years until my death; they were like repetitive phrases in the long slow symphony that was my life.

Yet there was a difference this time; now, there was the added realization that this world was just a moment's loss of balance away.

Thankfully, however, I was also able to remember that I'd already gone beyond what my parents had planned for me in just being able to love Alexandra. If I never accomplished anything else, I'd surpassed my grandest dreams and escaped maybe the biggest of their snares.

At times, I considered calling a few friends just to talk. Or even my Benedict Arnold brother Jay; after all, he had known me longer than anyone. But I sensed that the time for shoulders to cry on had passed, and I didn't want to risk having to speak with Alex if I called my brother.

While I was trying to keep my tears from forming an untraversable moat around me, an intriguing man left a message on my recording machine. I know for sure that it was Wednesday the eighteenth of June because, months later, when I finally got home from the hospital, I saved the calendar on which I'd written all my appointment notes in the hopes of reconstructing this extraordinary sequence of events.

It was the man's undefined accent that made me curious; I'm a sucker for foreigners, probably because you can't really understand all they're saying and end up giving them the benefit of the doubt that it's intelligent. Or perhaps because learning that other countries didn't just exist as coloured shapes on maps was important for me. His name was Peter something. I couldn't quite get it. He sounded as if the recording machine confused him. I liked that.

I returned his call right away, and he asked in an enthusiastic voice if he could come by that evening. In my mind, I made a mad list of excuses for why he couldn't come, but I was somehow able to see that even a crying spell in front of him might be absurdly amusing. In the end, I agreed that we should meet.

Chapter 2

ETER ARRIVED THAT EVENING during a russet and crimson sunset, stepped inside the house with a cautious smile. I found it endearing because it didn't seem to come to him easily. That surprised me because he was handsome, and I'd thought that all good-looking men had been taught to smile as soon as they had learned to walk – maybe sooner. He had shoulder-length dark brown hair, grey, wintry eyes, pale smooth cheeks, and a trace of aristocratic judgment in his stern lips. He stood very upright, like a dancer. Perhaps he was thirty-five, perhaps a bit older. Of course, I was immediately envious of his looks, gripped by that boundless jealousy of mine traceable to the fragments of my soul trampled and crushed by my parents. But I was also honestly curious about him, too. I've always wondered what it would have been like to have been born beautiful. These speculations were originally even the source of my fascination for Alexandra. She and Peter both had a natural elegance that seemed to call for photographs, to transcend time – that evidenced fulfilled possibilities. Yet where her good looks had been those of a woman forever aloof, his were those of a flamenco dancer – of repressed passion.

It was intimidating, and I feared that his looks were a sword against which I would never find a shield.

When Peter bowed slightly, a lock of his smooth brown hair fell sloppily onto his forehead. He twisted it back over his ear with a graceful motion and looked up with a nervous smile. That's when I noticed how coolly metallic his eyes were. I caught myself wondering if Alex would have been attracted to him. He opened his mouth once and tugged down on his right ear lobe. He noticed my curiosity. 'Sinuses...' he said. 'My Achilles' heel.'

'With me, it's my elbows. They ache when it rains or gets too muggy out. From playing too much tackle football as a kid.' I offered my hand. 'Bill Ticino.'

'Peter Castanheira.' We shook hands. I felt his warm touch for a long time afterward, as if he'd deposited something on my palm – not the contagion my father used to leave behind, but a lingering heat of some sort. As I motioned him to the couch, he twitched his long, straight nose like a rabbit and sniffed at the air. I realized with perverse pleasure that I must have stunk from days without bathing. My God, I couldn't even smell myself any more!

'Thank you for seeing me,' he said, again with an untraceable accent, one that added a border of vowels to the ends of his words. With shoulders back and head held high, he walked like a military officer from another century to the couch and sat down, crossing his legs. I was amused. I wondered about his age again. The crow's-feet spreading out from his eyes like delicate spokes told me he might even have been as old as forty-five.

'So, you read about the room today?' I asked.

Peter nodded and leaned forward, sniffed at the air again, and spoke slowly, considering his words. Barely controlled enthusiasm lit his eyes. 'Yes, oh yes,' he said.

Three words. They shouldn't have meant much to me. Yet the way he pronounced them, awkwardly, with the effort of translation, made me feel comfortable.

'I'm eager to find something around here that is pleasing and not too expensive,' he added, speaking his words carefully.

I smiled, wanting him to feel at ease. 'Have you been in San Francisco long?' I asked.

'Just a few months.'

'Your English is very good,' I observed.

'Thank you.' He shrugged. 'I'm afraid I'm a little rusty.'

'So you've been here before?'

'No, South Africa for a short time, studying.'

'What'd you study?' I asked.

'History.'

'European?'

'European and African mostly. Portuguese is my speciality.'

I took it as a favourable coincidence that I was reading a book about the Spanish Inquisition at the time. I said, 'I'm just reading about a period in Iberian history – the Inquisition. Unless you're into torture, it wasn't really a good time to be around.'

'Yes, it has...' Peter looked up, searching for words. 'It has made a big difference in Portugal. It's a very homogeneous country now. Though, of course, we all have Arab and Jewish blood. I'm sure I must.'

'Then maybe we're related,' I smiled. 'I'm part Jewish. On my mother's side. My father's Italian, *very* Italian. He was a soldier for Mussolini when he was young. His family was from the area around Naples. Maybe it's all that volcanic earth. It's made all my relatives pretty crusty and mean. They're like a pack of wild dogs. They eat their children if they get too hungry. At least my father and his relatives do.'

'I know Naples a little,' he replied. 'I was there once. Crowded. Too many people living too close together for my taste. Maybe it's the impossibility for encounters with wide-open spaces that makes people so very hard. People need to be able to lose themselves to be happy.'

We sat considering his words, and I realized we were comfortable enough with each other to let silence descend without rushing to pierce it. When he continued, he said, 'I hope to learn some American history while I'm here. I don't know much. Only about Walt Whitman really.'

'Whitman?'

'Oh yes,' he said in that awkward way of his. He folded his arms and took an upright posture of enthusiasm that seemed natural to him. 'I think he must have been a great man. His verses are so moving – the poems about nursing soldiers wounded in your Civil War, about befriending them, hearing their stories, healing them ... Coming to people's aid is the most important thing, I think. It's why we're here ... I mean, why we're born. I hope to go to New Jersey, to Camden, and see his home. I'd like to be in the same space he once inhabited.'

His words, his grace, his strange pronunciations were propelling me toward the realization that I had the tenant I wanted. But there was the problem of his good looks. I was hesitant to voice an incantation that would join our paths together. I stalled. 'So you're Portuguese,' I said.

'Yes, well, my father was Portuguese. And I grew up in a Portuguese colony – in Africa.'

I wondered why he didn't name his particular country of origin and offered the fake smile I'd perfected after years with Alexandra.

'Angola actually,' he answered, as if he'd heard my unspoken criticism. 'But later, we ... I moved to Brazil.'

That was the first time I thought about the possibility that Peter had more than the usual ability to anticipate conversation. Then, I dismissed it as a welcome sensitivity, and we continued talking in words that searched for connections in our personal histories. Peter said he was a clerk at the Brazilian consulate, worked mainly on trade and business agreements. He recounted stories of visas and travel. When silence came to us, words caught in my throat; I was captured by a desire, a clutching need, to understand how I had reached this very moment in my life.

Peter surveyed the room, nodding at the maps on the walls and the globe in the corner, then gestured toward the reproduction of a Sienese fresco framed just behind him. I'd brought it back from Italy a decade earlier. It was a depiction of a

Tuscan cavalier riding a magnificently caparisoned horse under a sky painted the blue of lapis lazuli. Peter fixed exacting eyes on me. He seemed to be searching for something so private that it would never enter the world, to be invading a stronghold so protected that I couldn't even give it a name. To break the impasse, I pointed to the painted sky above the Tuscan rider and said, 'I love that particular shade of blue. I think it might be the only reason I love frescoes.' I knew that wasn't true but wanted to impress upon him my love of colour for some reason.

'And your maps?' he asked.

'Oh, I like maps a lot, too,' I replied. 'Especially old ones. I collect them. I had only a couple of friends when I was growing up. Just my brother, Jay, and an old neighbour who gave me my first maps. He gave me some of the ones on the walls.'

'Obviously he gave you presents he valued,' Peter remarked. 'And things that maybe you needed.'

'Needed?'

'Maps ... Why would he give you maps? That's the question, no? Maybe so that you would know that there was a world outside your isolated little home. And also so you'd know that there were signposts you could follow to help you get to ... to a particular destination. If only you could decipher them, that is. He was opening a door for you, we might say.'

'I never thought of it that way,' I replied. I shrugged and added, 'Anyway, he was a good man, and he was the only person I ever knew when I was young who really wanted what was best for me. But he died before I really got to know him. A heart attack.'

Peter gave me a nod that seemed to mark the end of a dream that had long disturbed me, and I found I was able to speak freely for the first time since breaking up with Alex. I talked mostly about my initial trip to Italy, when suddenly, in a magical instant, I realized there was a world separate from

America. It was a revelation centred upon the discovery that there was much beyond the English language and its ways of thinking. I'd never really listened to my father speak Italian, you see. With him, it was a language of slaps across the face and crude Fascist slogans. Mussolini was never far away. But on making rudimentary conversations with Roman shop-keepers and fruit sellers, however, on talking with all those people who put adjectives after nouns, the prop walls of my despotic suburban house had fallen away. Revealed to me was a previously hidden landscape of castles and olive fields and peasants. It seemed to afford the possibility of an infinite variety of adventures way beyond America.

When I finished my stories, Peter said, 'Coming to a foreign country can be an unsettling discovery as well, no? Like me looking for another place to live, now. It's part of the adventure you speak of ... I mean, that you've been talking about, but it also means going in ... entering where one has never passed before.'

I nodded, thinking of our parallel paths. 'So do you like being here?' I asked.

'San Francisco? Oh, it seems quite nice – it's very pastel-coloured, and I like that. And with the hills, you can see all around. You never forget you're surrounded by emptiness. I think more about death here than in other cities I've known.'

That was the second clear indication to me that Peter was a little strange. He started to speak of his mother. She'd died nearly thirty years earlier, but he'd recently begun dreaming of her again. 'My mother appears to me here, and I think it has something to do with the city and its locale,' he said.

I smiled to conceal my doubt, felt suddenly dislocated, as if I were floating above myself. I closed my eyes and breathed deeply. 'So where is it you're currently living?' I asked.

'With a friend. His house. But I've been truly wanting to leave. I've been with him, my ... my friend too long.'

The word *friend*, so carefully chosen by Peter, made me wonder about his being gay. I was thinking about how to ask him and said in the meantime, 'It's hard not to have your own place.'

He nodded.

I leaned back to dispel any notion of accusation or threat and said, 'It doesn't matter about you renting the rooms, but I'd just like to know if you're gay.'

'No, you've misunderstood,' he replied. 'Because of my English, maybe. My friend is more like a surrogate father of sorts. We're very close, too close even. Me and my friend, we've...' Peter looked into my eyes as if he couldn't explain. 'It's just not right any more,' he continued. 'He still wants me to stay. But I can't. And besides...' He smiled awkwardly, remembering something that maybe couldn't be expressed, then laughed for no reason I could figure out.

'In any event, it's too cold in Sea Cliff, in that whole northwestern edge of San Francisco,' he said. 'Too much fog. Though normally I don't mind the fog, the mist. Reminds me of old epic tales. Epic poems. One in particular that I know in which there is a great fog that someone has to cross to reach his goal. I'll tell it to you sometime.'

'I take it you like poetry?' I asked.

'Very much. I was raised to be a poet of sorts – my mother loved Rilke, I was told – and to recite epics, to tell stories. Storytelling is still a tradition among some of the native peoples of Angola.'

An awkward silence descended on us and chilled me, so I asked, 'Would you like to see the rooms now?'

'Yes, yes ... very much.' His words seemed to express a youthful excitement, and I wondered if he were really younger than I'd thought. I led him through the kitchen back to what had been our guest room, explaining the layout of the house as we walked. Once, as I turned to note his impression, his face seemed suddenly feminine. It was the glare of the lighting I suppose. But his cheeks were perfectly smooth, and his eyelashes long and delicate. I had remarked such lashes on other Portuguese people I had known. But his were extraordinary, disturbing. I thought of fern tendrils or butterfly wings, although those metaphors were obviously wrong. Then he turned and his stubble appeared again. I recalled those silly plastic pictures that change when you tilt them.

Gesturing around the guest room, I said, 'I know it's small, but it's nice and sunny – cheerful.' I pointed to the window and its view of the overgrown yard rising gently up toward the back of a neighbour's Victorian house.

Peter swivelled around slowly, nodded, then pointed to the circular opening for the spiral staircase in the corner. 'The other room, he is downstairs?' he asked.

'Exactly, and it's the same size as this one. We had it added on – I mean, my wife and I ... we're separated now and ... Anyway, we had it added on a few years ago. Kind of a false basement, which my wife used to work in. You or whoever takes the room is free to use it. But there's not much light because the windows are small. It does have a door giving out into the yard, so that whoever takes these rooms can enter and leave separately. At least, that's what I intended.'

I led the way down. It was dusk, and with each step I began to sense that there was a cold presence in the grey darkness below. And that it was seeking entry into my body. Alex's desk was in the corner, and in the lyre-shaped back of her chair, I imagined a gaunt face smiling. For an instant, I thought I saw this apparition rise and stare at me with silver eyes set inside skeletal sockets. I reached out for the light switch. The face vanished. But the sight of papers and books piled high on Alex's desk made me sink toward despair. I knew that the pressure building at the back of my head meant that a storm of tears was approaching fast. I ached for the stagnant isolation of my bedroom. 'Not much to see,' I said. 'My wife used to work down here.'

Peter bit his lip nervously, tugged on his ear lobe again. 'I could live here,' he whispered hesitantly. 'Oh yes.' He surveyed the room, and his eyes twinkled. He turned to me and gave me a full smile, his first. He said, 'It's very nice, isn't it?'

I nodded.

He spoke as if to translate his previous words: 'I like it very much . . . very much.'

I gestured him toward the stairs. As he grasped the railing, I said, 'I had expected the person who takes the rooms to sleep upstairs, but if you like, I suppose you could bring the bed down here.'

He stared at me, and the joy in his eyes was gone. Why, I didn't know. And I don't know how long I stood just watching his grave expression, but when I awoke to myself, I realized with a start that I was inside my body. Had I been outside of it for a moment? The tension gripping the back of my head was gone, and my tears had been diverted. Peter was passing by me and about to head up the stairs. There was a sense that some frenzied motion inside me had ceased for the first time in my life. Maybe I'd even lost consciousness for a few moments.

Back in the living-room, Peter sat down stiffly, on the brown couch that Alexandra had arranged, along with the rough white burlap couch, into the shape of an L. I sat on the white one and nestled into the comfort of the corner, surrounding myself with all the colourful pillows we'd brought back from a group tour to Istanbul. I tried to decide if I wanted him to take the rooms. He seemed responsible and intelligent, sensitive and strange – all of which were in his favour. But I was jealous of his beauty and power.

He sensed my dilemma. Staring down at the faded Persian carpet between us, his hands between his legs, his fingertips touching, flexing, he wanted to talk but was afraid to. We sat that way through maybe thirty seconds of silence, and suddenly, as if in a dream, I felt time slowing to a stop. I realized that all my fears were just veiling what I already knew: that I desperately wanted him to move in. And it was more than that. It was as if it were already decided: he would move in. The gods had decreed it.

'I don't know what else to tell you,' I began. 'You know the rent from the listing, and it wouldn't go up very much in the near future. I'd like to add, though, that this is something of an experiment for me. I'm recently separated, as I said, and there's an outside chance I'll decide that sharing the house isn't for me. I'd give you a few weeks' notice of course, but there is a possibility that I'd ask you to leave after a month or so.'

'That would be a shame. Of course, it's your house and your decision. But I like the rooms very much.' Peter nodded sadly. Then he leaned forward. 'I probably should have mentioned it before, but I was nervous ... am nervous. I ... I have a pet ... a bird ... a hoopoe.'

'A hoopoe! Are you serious?'

Before Peter could answer, the phone rang. I cursed and excused myself, then screened the call. 'Hello, this is Bill. I'm not here right now, but...' When the tape finished, there was a beep, and then came the dulcet sound of Alex's voice, pleasant but treacherous – like herself, in other words. I drew a deep breath, grasped the receiver. 'Hi,' I said.

'Is that you or the machine again?' she asked impatiently.

'It's me.'

'I didn't think you'd be home. How are you?'

Her voice was already confined to a glassy domain I would never again enter. 'Okay, how are you?'

'Fine, I'm over at your brother's.'

Peter faced away from me as I talked. A desperate urge to

get off the phone tugged at me. To Alex, I said, 'I figured you'd go there.'

Silence. I wondered for an instant if, even in spite of her cruel metaphors for my love, the pause meant that she'd want to recommence our life together. The very possibility chilled me. I was panicked that she'd demand the house back.

She spoke now in a fatigued voice designed to elicit sympathy: 'Listen, we need to set a time when I can come pick up some things.'

'That's fine,' I answered.

The two of us sounded like weary prizefighters who'd fought their last fight. It was almost comic.

She said, 'How 'bout if I drop by tomorrow evening, around six? You'll be home?'

'Yes.'

'Good, well, that's just super … it's set then. It'll be really good to get my things.'

She spoke with a false eagerness. I remained silent. She was trying to regain the familiar persona of a polished woman on whom even the most tenacious depression could never get a good solid grip. As usual, it seemed that she wanted to present only the patina of her ornamental surface to me, to prove that even our pain couldn't crack such a glistening barrier. Yet I hit on the right response; as her words passed through the silence I let fall between us, I was sure that she, too, could see in herself the shattered glass produced in our white-light explosion. It was why she refused to speak. I wanted to shriek at her: 'Wounds, Alexandra, blood and pain and hurt!' But it wasn't necessary. We both knew it. I could see her damning the hollow world between us, damning us both.

As a dare more than anything else, she finally asked in an angry voice, 'So, do you want to talk about anything? I really don't think it would do much good.'

I seemed to be miles and years away from her. 'No, not

now,' I replied. 'And someone's here anyway.' I wanted to mention that in order to do away with any notion I was collapsing without her.

Big mistake. My words propelled Alexandra from her pit of abasement to the very top of her cliff of suspicion.

'Who?' she demanded.

I looked for how to put it. 'A prospective tenant.'

'To *live* with you?!'

'Yeah, just for a while.'

She chose to misunderstand and jumped down from her cliff to confront me as the radiant Goddess of Victims. 'It's wonderful you've found someone to replace me so quickly,' she began. 'Tell me, is it someone I know – some *piece* you were fucking before we broke up ... or is this opening night?'

I turned to hide my frustration from Peter, for here, deep in the land of repetition, where children magically re-create their parents' lives, I understood the nature of my failure; I had become a fledgling version of my father – a scheming betrayer, a destroyer of souls. 'Neither,' I whispered. 'It's a man ... just a man. A real tenant.'

Her rage tumbled over the truth she now perceived and headed for anything it could find. 'It's half my house!' she screamed. 'Just because I said I'm not living there any more doesn't mean you can find someone to move in without my permission. It's only been ten days or something, you selfish fucking pig!'

I sighed theatrically, let silence reveal two paths to me. Along the first, the older of the two, lay the yellowing script my parents had prepared so long ago. With its help, I would go on arguing with ever-increasing ferocity, and we would end up clawing at each other for the rest of our lives. Along the other path – the new one, without a single footprint from my family – was implanted the white flag of peaceful surrender. I turned back toward Peter and saw him standing by the globe, rubbing a finger over Africa. He would be remembering Angola, I knew. I gripped the white flag, held it over my head, and said, 'Alex, I understand – I'm sorry about springing this on you. But I'd really like someone here right now. I've been having a lot of problems sleeping and it would really help.'

Silence again as she metamorphosed. 'He'd take the back rooms?' she asked.

I resented having to continue waving my flag, but decided it didn't matter. Everything was too screwed up to correct right now. Maybe someday ... 'Yeah, is it okay?'

'Well, I'd have appreciated you letting me know that it's what you wanted to do.'

I decided not to point out that she hadn't called me with where she was, and that if my brother Jay hadn't left a message on my phone machine I wouldn't even have known for sure that she was with him. 'Sorry,' I said.

'Okay, then. I'll pick up the stuff I want tomorrow evening. I've got my key.'

We said goodbye as if a business transaction had been completed. Peter looked at me. He was biting his lip nervously, seemed to be searching for words. I walked back to the white couch. 'My wife – resolving things,' I explained. 'Thank God, we never had children.' I sat down, lifted a pillow onto my lap, and gripped it.

He dropped down opposite me again. I turned away from him; a heavy sadness suddenly took away my voice. I realized that my emotions were out of control. They were rising and falling within me without any reason. It was as if a shadow of myself were spinning a prize wheel inside me with random segments for my emotions. Wherever it stopped was the emotion I'd feel for the moment. And now that Alexandra was coming over, what would I feel? Anger? Envy? Contempt? Whatever the case, she'd probably leave me with my face pressed against the wood of my closed bedroom door, tears sliding across my cheeks.

Though maybe, if I really worked at it, I could somehow regain the stoic composure which I'd always regarded as my most valuable badge of survival.

'So, what were we talking about?' I asked Peter, trying to focus on him for a moment and show that I wasn't temporarily insane.

'My bird, my hoopoe,' he replied gently.

'Yeah, I completely forgot. But it's a good omen, you know. I was a crazed bird-watcher as a kid. I went everywhere looking for them. I wanted to be able to fly. I still occasionally dream of birds. Once, I even dreamed that God was a big old owl with glowing red eyes. Alex, my wife, thought I was completely nuts.' I whispered *hoopoe* to myself as if it were a sacred word. 'Some of my fondest memories are of seeing birds I never thought I'd see,' I continued. 'Rose-breasted grosbeaks, yellow-headed blackbirds, golden-crowned...' I cut myself off; I realized that anxiety was making me babble. 'But yours...' I added. 'A hoopoe is pretty, isn't it? Kind of tannish, with a big crest.'

'That's right.'

'Do you keep it in a cage?' I asked.

'Of course,' he replied. 'But ... but occasionally I do let her out into my room. She likes to sit on my shoulder when I read.'

'When you read?' I laughed.

'That's right.'

'Well, as long as she doesn't make a mess,' I shrugged. 'Or make loud piercing calls in the early morning.'

'Never,' Peter confirmed, shaking his head, smiling shyly.

To me, this timidity seemed so out of place on him. I sensed that it would take me some time to discover the reasons for his obvious vulnerability, to find his hidden demons. But so much the better. It would be a longer adventure for us both.

'She's very well behaved,' he noted. 'And she likes people.'

'Good.'

I watched myself from above for a moment, as I did whenever it seemed as if something I'd remember for the rest of my life was occurring. 'You can have the room if you like,' I said.

Peter tilted his head toward the floor to hide his eyes and grinned. When he raised his glance, he showed me a touching look of thanks. I felt inexplicably close to him.

'Thank God,' he whispered. He jumped up suddenly. His eyes were glassy. 'It's wonderful. Just wonderful! When can I move in?'

I shrugged. 'As soon as you like, I guess.' As I listened to my words, I returned to my body and felt my tears coming for no reason whatsoever. The wheel had been spun again inside me. I was really scared of starting on another life.

∞

I was able to keep from crying till Peter was out the door. I have absolutely no idea what I last said to him or how he responded. Then I went to bed and kept a lookout for creatures moving silently in the darkness. I was thinking then that this would be their final evening in my house. I was hoping that they wouldn't realize that it was their last chance to do me harm. I slept when I could.

∞

Peter moved in the next evening. He came to the door at sundown with two leather suitcases in his right hand. His left arm was circled around a brass cage whose spokes curved to a point at least six feet from the base. Inside, perched regally on a wooden bar, was the hoopoe. It was stunning, about a foot long. The first thing I noticed was the crown of inch-long feathers. They were fawn-coloured but tipped with black. It was as if a divine calligrapher had run his brush across the crown's points in a final burst of inspiration. The bird had the beak of a clown – thin and curved downward, fully as long in proportion to its body as a hummingbird's. Its feet were gnarled and ancient-looking. It was both awkward and beautiful at the same time, compact, energetic. It was a life so very small and yet so complete. Its piercing eyes were grey-green. Strangely, they looked like Peter's.

'Can I help you with something?' I asked.

Peter let me take the cage. His hands were trembling.

'You okay?' I asked.

He sighed. 'It's having to move,' he replied with a shiver. 'I've never ... I've haven't been with someone I ... I never knew very well. Since after my mother died. You, I mean. And I've just had a ... a ... oh God, my English has disappeared.' He gritted his teeth, breathed deeply. 'I've just had a big, big argument.'

'I'm sorry, but it'll be fine here,' I assured him. 'And I don't require perfect English.' The hoopoe was now facing me, and I noticed how very thin it was. It seemed happy though. 'Take your bird's lead,' I advised him. 'It seems to trust me. It looks perfectly comfortable, in fact.'

'Oh, she has an easier time with people than I do,' Peter replied. 'And she's an optimist by nature.'

I shared a smile with him, then nodded toward the bird. 'It looks so thin,' I said. 'It's not dieting?'

'No, no. She eats just fine.'

'Not anorexic? I'd hate to have to worry about an anorexic bird.'

'No, no,' Peter answered as if I'd been serious. 'She eats fine.'

I figured that he was too nervous to find anything even slightly funny. As I carried the cage to his room, I realized the bird was still staring at me, blinking now and again with the tiniest eyelids. I stared back, unnerved.

'Does it always watch people?' I asked.

'No, she only notices those she likes – or who are in need of watching,' he replied with a cagey smile.

'Am I in need of watching?' I inquired.

'I guess we'll see, no?'

I laughed. 'So she's a "she"?'

'Yes.'

'How old?'

'I'm not sure.' The bird turned to Peter for an instant, and they shared a look. 'Twelve, in our years, I think.'

The hoopoe looked back at me. I asked, 'Does she always help you with your answers?'

'No, it wasn't really her, I was just trying to remember.'

'I wasn't serious,' I said. But I think I had been. After all, I'd been responding to spirits of late. And there was something weird between the bird and him no matter what anyone said. As I continued to watch the hoopoe, I wondered what she could be thinking, what kind of communication could take place between her and Peter – or her and me, for that matter.

We entered Peter's upstairs room. 'And what's her name?' I asked.

'Mary.' He took back the cage and set it on the ground.

'A bird named Mary?!'

'Maria, actually.'

'Maria,' I repeated silently to myself with a nod toward Peter, thinking it a ridiculous name for a bird. 'After the Virgin Mary?' I asked.

'Oh dear, no,' he replied.

'After someone else?'

'No one in . . . well, my mother.'

I had the urge to ask about that. I mean, it didn't seem terribly normal to name a bird after your mother. Or flattering, for that matter. But I thought it best to leave all mysteries behind for the time being. I told him to get me if he needed anything, then headed to the living-room. I was wondering how the spirits would take his presence. I began daydreaming, saw myself on a country road flanked by the sea on one side and a thick forest of chestnut trees on the other. Maybe I'd dreamed this scene the night before. Had I been in Italy? In my mental picture, Peter was standing atop a blanket of brown leaves. He was lit in a scattered light. Maria was hopping on the ground next to him, rummaging. When she looked up at me expectantly, Peter glanced at me as well. All was quiet. But the air felt weighted. It was as if a monstrous creature were about to awaken from slumber, and I would soon see that Peter and Maria were actually standing on his back. In the mean time, I had my choice: I could enter the forest and join Peter, take that risk, or forever stay behind.

Chapter 3

I WAS SIPPING TEA in the living-room, immersed in my book on the Spanish Inquisition, when Alexandra arrived. It had been exactly sixteen days since I'd seen her last. Dressed in a tan woollen business suit, she stepped inside lugging her ancient Gucci suitcase, wearing a face as hard as a hazelnut. It was a persona that only tears could penetrate. But I wasn't about to cry. It was also the persona that had once preyed upon my sexual obsession so successfully, yet that drama now lay deeply buried.

Jay was with her, that much I should have guessed. He'd cut his dirty blond hair very short and left a fashionable Don Johnson-ish stubble on his cheeks. His hands had been stashed safely in the pockets of his jeans, and his blue braces gave him the aw-shucks good looks he cultivated of late.

'Hello, Bill, I'm here now,' Alex said. Her voice was flat. I half expected her to reach out and shake my hand. But she held the suitcase in front of her for protection and began to rock back and forth.

I studied her: shimmering brown hair falling to her shoulders; knowing blue eyes; tense slender hands. In short, the same Alex, the beautiful untouchable Venus risen from her cold depths.

Only one sign of weakness: the swollen pouches under her eyes.

I was suddenly pervaded by the presentiment that she was forever consigned to my past.

'Hi,' I replied. I shrugged my apology that I couldn't say more.

Jay fixed me with a mischievous grin. 'You look like hell,' he observed.

I rubbed my hand across my stubble and back through my oily hair. 'Thanks, Jay,' I said.

Alexandra pulled her suitcase around to her hip. 'I'll just get some things from our bedroom.'

I nodded. She marched past me, as impenetrable as one of those reflective pieces of coal Jay and I used to find in our Long Island back yard. I thought: *give her a few million years without love and she'd become a perfect diamond.*

'So how you doing?' Jay whispered conspiratorially as Alex reached our bedroom.

I wasn't sure what to say after two weeks of spirits. 'Okay, I guess.'

I sat on the white couch and surrounded myself with pillows again. Jay sat watching me sip from my mug as if expecting a confession. As Alex closed the door upstairs, he said, 'You haven't returned my calls.'

'I just didn't feel like talking about it,' I replied. 'Besides, you left the message that Alex was with you. That's all I really needed to know.'

'Does it bother you, Bill, that she's staying with me?'

I didn't answer right away because I was startled by how much older he had become in only a few weeks. My tears, or maybe the spirits, had cleansed my eyes. I realized that I'd been seeing him as my little brother for too long. Here he was, an adult. A man. God, I was thirty-two, and only two months away from my next birthday. That made him thirty-one. And I'd soon be divorced, too. How very strange.

'So does it bother you or not?' he repeated.

'I don't know,' I replied.

He fingered the elastic in his braces like some backwoods farmer. In a hurt voice, he said, 'So I only get to rely on you when something's wrong? Is that the way it is? You don't trust me?'

'I trust you,' I replied. But I didn't. On the contrary, I feared his judgments. I said, 'You want to talk, let's talk.'

'Is it over between you and Alex?'

A few minutes earlier, I might have said I wasn't sure. But now a *yes* came to my lips as if they could pronounce no other verdict.

'Is that okay?' he asked.

I shrugged. 'More or less. It's fine sometimes. Like now. Then sometimes, I get a little frightened.'

'Frightened?'

I sighed as I considered whether or not to hide the truth. I laughed to diminish its importance. Then I said, 'Of the dark.'

'Like when we were kids?' he asked.

'Uh-hum.' It all seemed tiresome, and I jumped up to play with my globe. Out of the corner of my eye I could see Jay following me with a long face. He was the watcher. Like my mother. All the times I'd failed to live up to their expectations were in those studied looks.

'The old scars come out when new traumas present themselves,' Jay observed.

I feared that he'd start talking about our parents, and I couldn't bear walking through that maze right now. Jay and I used to sometimes look for an imaginary central point where things started going really wrong with our family, and we'd always just ended up getting lost in the search. So I started hunting on the globe for something much easier to find: Peter's home country.

Angola was coloured sky blue, but was called Portuguese West Africa. I touched Luanda.

'So what are you going to do about it – I mean, your fear of the dark?' Jay asked.

'Alex didn't tell you, I suppose – I got a tenant.'

'A tenant? So you and Alex really have decided to go your separate ways, haven't you?'

I nodded as if he should have figured that one out a while ago.

'Is your tenant anyone I know?'

'No, it's just a guy named Peter.' I spun the globe around and imagined the Earth turning at the same moment, all of us being whisked through space, then flying off in different directions.

'A faggot?' he inquired.

I frowned. 'I can't believe you still talk like that. It's really ugly.'

'Well, is he?' he insisted.

'He's straight,' I said.

'You have that in writing? This *is* San Francisco, Bill.'

I spun the globe again. How I wished I could escape my family forever.

He stood up, walked to me, and stopped the spinning globe with his flattened hand. 'You know, you're the one who's got problems, not me,' he said in a condescending voice.

I pushed past him to the couch and sat down. He made me so very tired. Just looking at his face was an uphill climb for my emotions.

He was watching me again, his expression amused, knowing.

'Please stop staring at me!' I begged.

He looped his thumbs around his braces and fixed me with his look of wisdom about to be imparted. 'Try not to take this badly,' he said, 'because I don't mean it that way. But in some things you're really a bit weak.'

'Weak?'

'Why did you always have to tell Alexandra what you were up to? She would have been happy not knowing. Women don't want to know. They like living in the dark.'

'Maybe you're right,' I replied. 'I don't pretend to know much about anything at all any more. But the thing is, I wouldn't have been happy lying to her. I can't live like that.'

He pointed an angry finger at me. 'Cut the shit! You could live like that. We all can.' The finger began wagging insistently at me. 'You just have to practice. And that's why you're weak – you refused to even give it a try.' He shook his head at me, then flapped his hands just the way my dad used to when he wanted us to think we were puny. He said, 'Anyway, I guess if you haven't figured all this out by now, you never will.'

'No, probably not,' I answered, knowing there was a lot I could add to that, but suspecting that I might end up screaming like a banshee if I started arguing with him. Besides, a part of me was hoping that he would give up on me for good. I was beginning to come to the conclusion, in fact, that using every opportunity to show my brother that I was a lost cause should be my strategy with him in the future.

'So, this tenant of yours, he's got the back room I suppose,' Jay said.

I nodded. He sat next to me. After a few minutes, he patted my back, afraid to really touch me. I wanted him to leave my life forever. Trying to effect a truce, he smiled and said, 'Hey, you'll be fine. All you really need right now is a shower.'

'I suppose so. And *you* could use a shave.'

'My whiskers are stylish,' he noted.

We sat together, now as distant brothers. I thought of us as kids, our fights about leaving the light on in the room. I wanted it on, he didn't. Finally, after a few weeks of petty and ferocious fights, I'd mustered the courage to be honest enough to explain why I needed the light. He had looked at me with the elongated face he gave when pondering what had never oc-curred to him before, brushed my cheek with his hand, and said, 'I'm sorry, I didn't know. We'll have the light then.'

It was as simple as that when Jay was a kid. His compassion took over his whole mind and body, and nothing, but nothing – not even our father with his slaps and insults – could make him veer from the right thing to do once he'd seen the truth. In that sense, he had been stronger than me or most anyone I knew.

And yet, it had all disappeared, almost without a trace, when he reached adulthood. Without warning, he became the heir of all my father's selfishness and acidic wrath.

Or maybe there had been warnings. Maybe I hadn't wanted to notice.

In any event, he took over my father's covert world of grudges, plots, sarcastic smirks.

He acted as if I were his rival, vying for the one empty seat left on the lifeboat fleeing our unwanted past.

I've often wondered how things like that happen, how even ties of true affection can become so ephemeral. How beauty just disappears, how two brothers end up as secret enemies.

Considering that now, I began remembering how I used to protect him from our father, how I'd even got a broken wrist once for my efforts. Jay, while kicking his soccer ball around the back yard, had accidentally knocked off a branch from one of Dad's beloved fig trees. Not knowing what else to do, I snapped another branch right off, then told my father we'd been playing soccer; I knew he'd come after me first, as the older kid, as the one who should have known better. I must have been twelve or thirteen. I remember Dad grimacing with rage, picking me up in a kind of bear hug, and throwing me into the wall. I don't think he meant to hurt me. He probably just wanted to scare me. I thrust my hands out to keep my head from smashing into this poster of melting clocks by Salvador Dalí that Jay and I had framed in glass and put up in our bedroom. And that's when I heard my right wrist crack.

All that for nothing, of course. Because here we were years later, my brother and I, without any genuine solidarity between us.

'Everything's going to be okay if you don't panic,' Jay

suddenly said. 'You've just got to keep yourself together. Is your tenant here now?'

'Yeah.'

'What's his name again?'

'Peter.'

'What's he do?'

'He works for the Brazilian consulate.'

'He's Brazilian?'

'Actually...' I stopped my explanation when I heard Alex open the bedroom door.

She came trudging down the stairs lugging her suitcase. She dropped it onto the floor by the front door with a thud.

I forced a smile. Alex flared her nostrils, kicked back her head, and took a deep breath. It was what she did when she was too peeved to talk. She glanced at Jay, then at me, as hard as a nut again. 'Thanks for the help carrying it,' she said.

That was dart number one, aimed straight for my ganglion of guilt.

My brother rolled his eyes, stood up, and asked, 'What about the rest of it – those papers you wanted?'

Alex turned toward me, determined. 'I'll need to disturb your tenant ... if he's here.'

'He's here – I'll go with you,' I replied.

'Not necessary,' she noted dryly.

I tossed my own dart in a perfect arc toward her heart. 'For him, not you,' I said. Bull's-eye. Alex's shell suddenly cracked. Tears caught in her lashes.

'We'll all go,' Jay said, to make peace. 'Why just introduce one of us when we can intimidate him as a pair?'

'Fine,' I nodded.

I led them to the back of the house, realizing I'd forgotten to clean her desk. I hoped that Peter hadn't touched it. She might explode, send bits of shrapnel all over the house, maybe even injure someone seriously. I knocked at his door.

'I'm coming,' Peter answered.

I heard him switch on the light. The door opened. He was wearing jeans and a billowy yellow shirt. As I spoke to him, I noticed Maria sitting regally in her cage in the middle of the room. Just outside her cage door was a white candle flickering on top of a marble cube. Overwhelmed by the electric light, the flame looked weak, hopeless.

I wondered if Peter had been holding some sort of arcane religious ceremony.

'Sorry to bother you,' I said, then introduced Jay and Alex. 'She needs to pick up some things from the bottom room if that's okay.'

'Of course.' Peter shook Alex's hand, then Jay's. When he smoothed his hair behind his ears, the light caught him at that angle which made him look soft. Again, I noticed his delicate eyelashes. How strange they were.

'Nice to meet you,' Alex said. She offered him the hostess smile that she'd perfected after years of marriage. 'Hope you'll like *our* house.'

'I do already,' he replied with a slight bow of thanks.

I stepped into the room to expedite matters. Alex followed, and spotted the bird. 'Ooh, who's this little one?' she asked. She knelt at the cage and peered in with unbounded curiosity. A remembrance of our love formed a leaden weight in my chest. When it began rising toward my eyes as tears, I whispered to myself, *Not now* ...

'Maria, my bird,' Peter answered.

'She's gorgeous,' Alex said. She stared at the hoopoe, gave a smiling glance up at Peter. My brother came up behind her to look at Maria, too. When Alexandra popped up, she hit him. 'Whoops,' she laughed. She held Jay's arm. 'Sorry, you okay?'

Jay smiled good-naturedly. 'No problem,' he said. He turned to Peter, amused. 'What gave you the idea of having a bird as a pet?' he asked.

Peter offered my brother his shy smile and said, 'I've always needed birds. And after all these years, this one's not really a pet. She's my family.'

'Whatever gets you through the night,' Jay offered.

It was the glib expression he used whenever he was faced with behaviour he found abnormal. The curious thing was, his words were a lie; he didn't share their connotation of open-mindedness in the least.

Alexandra grinned at the bird as if proud to be sharing the same space with her.

The three of them looked like idiot children waiting for lines from an Ionesco play, and it was all I could do to keep from screaming.

Alex suddenly turned to me and frowned. 'If it's okay with you, I'll get my things now.'

'Fine.'

She lifted her eyebrows at me as a signal that I should pay special attention to her next move, then looked ever-so-sincerely at Peter and brushed his arm. 'Thank you for letting me see Maria,' she said. 'You're really lucky to have such a beautiful friend.'

Alex wanted me to know that she was already recovered enough from our split to be gracious – even charming – with other people. As she descended the stairs, I caught myself wondering if she found Peter handsome. Yet she probably hadn't even seen him, was just taking advantage of his presence.

Jay and I waited upstairs with Peter. While my brother tested Peter's patience with stories about what he called the 'rough-and-tumble world' of trading stocks at the Pacific Exchange, I listened for the scream that would signify that something had been moved on Alex's desk. My mouth was really dry, covered with fuzz, as if I were coming down with the flu. My head throbbed madly.

'So you like my brother's house ... your rooms?' Jay asked

Peter politely. He patted my shoulder at the same time, and we looked at each other. I could see him thinking: *don't just stand there panicking, make conversation!*

Peter replied, 'Yes, I'd like to move the bed downstairs though.'

'Why's that?' Jay asked.

'It's a little too bright up here.'

My brother looked at me, puzzled, then back at Peter. 'You prefer the dark?'

'No, not prefer – not all the time. But to sleep in, of course, and well, to think in sometimes. I don't like electric lights very much – they're too noisy. And ... oh, what's the word ...?' Peter scrunched his eyelids tightly together, made fists, then burst them both open and continued, '...Candles, right? Sometimes I seem to forget the easiest words. Candles ... they have string, you light them?' He pointed to the one on the marble cube.

'Yes, candles,' Jay agreed.

'I can never have enough. They let you think and breathe. They will be my accompaniment downstairs. Oh yes, candles are wonderful.'

'Yes, I suppose they are,' my brother replied, looking at me with a prompting face again. I could hear him thinking: *did you have to pick a foreign lunatic for a tenant?*

But I didn't want to participate in any conversation at that moment; listening to Alex's rustlings downstairs again, from a place deep inside my body, I was remembering the first time I saw her. It was during those few minutes that I'd realized how much my sexual obsession had to do with *my* needs and not any woman's.

I recalled Alex had been sitting at a window table at Sweets Café on Fillmore Street. Wrapped in a charcoal grey business suit, her hair tightly drawn into French braids, she looked like the ice goddess of my dreams, a woman who'd been trained for years to keep her thoughts a secret, her desires in shadows. She looked as if nobody had ever had a good up-close whiff of her inner ocean, not even the handful of pathetic schmucks for whom she'd unlocked her bedroom door. And if my cock didn't get hard right away, it was only because I was waiting for some silent signal of complicity on her part, a twinge of animal fear in her eyes, a squirming need to straighten her skirt or dab her lips with her napkin. But she didn't move a muscle. Which was even better. Because what I wanted then, of course, was to fuck that perfect composure out of her with the kind of sex that would make her give up all her reserve, all her years of constraint, in a single instant.

And so I stopped on the sidewalk and stared at her, watched her sip her cappuccino with my hands crossed over my chest, hoping everything about me was saying, That's right, take a good look. Because I want to split you right in two – right here, right now; want to break you with a thud that they'll hear all the way back home in the North Pole; want to grab on to that buried passion of yours and unearth it – screaming and kicking – from that goddamn braided sarcophagus you've built around it.

But the secret that I was only just then beginning to understand was that I ached not only to fuck a whole new life into her, into this new woman whom I walked up to a few moments later and asked to talk, but into myself as well – to fuck my way through the armour around my own sadly neglected warmth, hit ground zero of my numbed emotional core with one last plunge and release some new and better version of myself.

When we heard Alex's footsteps on the stairs, Jay and Peter ceased their conversation. She rose hugging a stack of papers, looking bothered. 'Okay,' she said. 'That's it for now, Jay.'

The clipped sound of her voice made me suddenly realize

that my tears over the past few days had cleared not only my vision of Jay and myself, but her as well. What a contrast this was. Now, she was just an exhausted woman, not a fallen goddess. And if the truth be told, I'd never even come close to releasing her passion, to unearthing her sarcophagus. It was buried too far down for me to get to. And I'd failed myself, too. For I, too, had remained empty, had lost rebirth with each missed opportunity to free what was trapped inside her.

The sad joke was that Alex and I were crippled twins hobbling along over our separate desert landscapes, stepping carefully over the cracked outcroppings of emotions which we'd buried long ago in order to survive our families. Maybe we'd got married precisely because there was no risk in the other person confronting us directly with our lack of life.

Such couplings must happen all the time.

Jay, Alexandra, and I said goodbye to Peter. As he closed his door, his grey eyes tensed and hardened. He seemed to want something from me alone. It was as if he were hoping to discover in my glance a secret from my childhood that we could guard together.

Alex marched us back to the living-room: one, two, one, two ... By the front door, she turned, pressed her fingertips into her temples, and gave me the hassled look that said: if you so much as sneeze the wrong way, I'm going to scream. I suspected that her moods were changing as rapidly and as inexplicably as mine. She said, 'So, I'll call you when I've got a place and arrange to get the rest of my stuff. I'll draw up a list of how I'd like to divide things ... if that's okay, of course?'

No way was I going to risk her wrath. 'It's just perfect, Alex,' I replied.

She eyed me for an opening. 'You know,' she observed, 'it's really lucky we kept our bank accounts separate all these years.'

Her dart grazed the edges of my guilt. She was implying,

of course, that I was never committed enough. Alex had never accepted that it was important for me to measure my own economic progress.

'Yeah, it sure is lucky.'

She met my reserve with her own calm. Jay sensed the gnashing of teeth and picked up her suitcase. 'Well, kids, off we go,' he said. He gave my shoulder a pat, and I nodded a falsely grateful smile toward him.

Alex and I were left facing each other. I saw a woman I didn't know, a woman I didn't want to touch. She was consigned forever to the past.

I looked at both of us from above, came back to my body, and shrugged. 'Sorry,' I said. I wanted to say something more. I wanted to say: I began sleeping with other women because I needed more. Maybe I was too cowardly to tell you that. Maybe I thought it would be cruel asking you for something you couldn't give me.

But I swallowed my words because I wasn't sure that what I was thinking was true. Maybe I'd just been a bastard.

She smiled weakly. 'I'm sorry, too.'

We shared a last look of kinship. It penetrated as an ache through my chest. My journey with Alex was over. I wasn't even going to cross over to her side of the road and kiss her goodbye. I couldn't. It was as if my feet had rooted to the fibres of the rug. Apparently, from here on out, it was every man for himself. And she, too, wasn't about to abandon her side of the road. Her face elongated in pain. Then she turned with a jerk and marched out. Jay looked back at me, frowned as if I were an idiot, and said, 'I'll call you.'

I watched his hand pull the door closed. The room seemed to hold its breath. My body stiffened; invisible spirits were surrounding me. I began talking to myself, and I was saying, *just hold on . . .*

I rushed to Peter's room, stopped in front of the barrier of his door. I came upon the excuse of apologizing again for disturbing him. I realized that I was going nuts. I knocked. He opened the door and smiled. Maria was out of her cage now, standing by the lighted candle.

'Just wanted to see if everything was all right with you,' I said.

'Yes, just fine.'

'And Maria?' I asked.

'She's happy to be here.'

'Good.'

Silence. Peter sensed my anxiety. In an encouraging voice, he said, 'I have noticed in the cabinets that you like tea. I was thinking in preparing some. Would you like a cup?'

I smiled at his awkward English. 'Yeah sure, that would be great.'

Peter took a tin of tea and a colourful belt from atop his dresser. I followed him into the kitchen. He lowered the belt onto the table. 'See what you make of this,' he said.

While he filled the kettle, I studied the belt. It was light and fragile, like rice paper. It had been painted on both sides with brightly coloured dots forming floral and animal designs. Red and green diamond-shaped petals hid blue and yellow animals. There were elephants, tigers, mongooses, and dolphins, and they all possessed human, almond-shaped eyes. Their long lashes resembled Peter's. It was naïve and pleasing. I wondered where it had come from. But there was no buckle. 'I don't know what it is,' I said. 'Is it purely decorative?'

'In a sense.' Peter put two blue mugs down on the table. 'It's from India.' He sat opposite me and held the belt up, squinted at it. His lips puckered and his nose twitched. He sniffed at it. 'It was given to me by a close friend,' he said. 'She was born in Goa. Do you know it?'

'On the west coast, south of Bombay, isn't it?'

'I should have known – all your maps.' He explained that

Goa had been a Portuguese colony until its takeover by the Indian army in 1961. 'It had been Portuguese for many centuries,' he went on. 'It was maintained for the spice trade – among other things. My friend's grandfather went there just before the First World War. He was a missionary of sorts. But his real concern was medical care. His speciality was parasitic diseases. I think sometimes that he saw them as, I don't know, metaphors maybe – for unhealthy thoughts. He just couldn't bear that people's bodies would get destroyed by such horrible creatures. In his own way, he believed he'd been put on the Earth to do battle against the demons that invade our bodies.'

The kettle was beginning to rattle. Peter gestured for me to leave it be. 'Please, let me make it,' he said as if I would be doing him a great favour.

It was calming for me to listen to his voice, his accent, to feel his protection. I said, 'Thank you for talking to me.'

Peter nodded and waved away my need to express gratitude. He stood up and leaned against the oven to wait for the water to boil. He continued his story: 'The grandfather, at the sight of a tick or a louse, any parasite at all, he'd lift up his glasses onto his forehead...' Peter leaned toward me and mimicked the careful movements of the grandfather hunting for a tick, then continued, 'And he'd stare at the creature as if he were looking at the devil himself. My friend said this look, this maddening look in his eyes, his bulging dark eyes ... It used to give her...' He clenched his fists. 'What's the word ... ?' He turned away while searching his memory, then stared at me. '...Is it chicken skin?'

I nodded my understanding, and for the first time in weeks felt safe in the world, as if unwelcome strangers had only now just left my house. I'm pretty sure it was because I liked nothing better than witnessing other people's enthusiasm, to see their faces, hands, and hearts bloom with life. And here was Peter coming alive for me. I felt like laughing with relief.

'And so,' he continued, 'when the grandfather had removed the tick from a dog, or a louse from a child's...' Peter tapped his finger at the top of his head. 'The word?' he asked.

'Scalp,' I offered.

'Scalp, of course. So he would flip his glasses back over his eyes and once again become the kindly man who ... who my friend Mara got to know later on, who'd sit her on his lap and read her stories, teach her English and what he knew of the Indian tongues so that she could accompany him on trips. But this time I'm talking about now – it's many years before Mara was born.

'Anyway, Mara said that when her grandfather set up his clinic, he and his colleagues were most often met with mistrust. It was very difficult to convince villagers to be treated for parasitic diseases. Especially the ones whose symptoms they'd been ... been habituated to...' He shook his head. 'You don't say "habituated to", do you?' He frowned.

'No. We say, "got used to",' I corrected.

'Yes, they'd got used to their discomfort – over many years. And of course, they were not nearly as bad as the cholera and smallpox, which took their lives. Not nearly as debilitating. So, despite certain successes, people remained sceptical. Especially because the parasites and their symptoms returned as soon as they disobeyed the grandfather's counsel – when they ate infected food, undercooked food. Or when they drank spoiled water.

'It was an orphan boy, Miguel, of mixed Turkish, Indian, and Portuguese blood...' Peter showed me his shy smile. 'The Portuguese, you see, have never been ... how shall I put it ... have never been bashful about making children with indigenous populations.' The kettle suddenly began to whistle. Peter poured water into the teapot, letting it warm the porcelain for about half a minute, then spilled the water back out into the sink. After ladling three heaping teaspoons of tea into the pot, he added some newly boiled water, then turned off the gas. His face was that of a man performing a serious ritual, and I suspected that he picked up his love of a proper cup of tea during his time in South Africa. He swirled the water around the pot a few times and placed it on the table between us. He sat down. 'Let's let it steep a few minutes,' he requested, and I nodded my agreement.

He opened his hands to me as if about to discuss the inexplicable. 'This boy, Miguel, he worked in the clinic. And by all accounts, he was a most beautiful young man.' Peter shook his head and closed his eyes in remembrance. 'Yes, most beautiful.' He looked at me sadly now and waved his hand through the air as if summoning dancers to begin. 'Mothers would smile as they caressed his hair. Even other children would stand back from him as if in the company of a blessed being. The grandfather, too – he was drawn to the boy and befriended him with gifts of paints and paper. You see, Miguel was also an artist. Natural-born, I think you say.'

'That's right,' I nodded.

'Upon getting to know the boy better, however, the grandfather discovered that he was often without energy. And plagued by this very bad abdominal pain. He verified in Miguel's faeces that he did indeed have a worm in his belly. He gave the boy some medicine to loosen its hold on his intestines. And one day, to the astonishment of all present, he pulled from the boy's behind a great tapeworm. It just kept coming out of there. It ended up being two meters long. Imagine! The grandfather was, of course, filled with rage for the creature, the devil he had pulled from the innocent child.' Peter glared at me and clenched his fists. 'And he would have destroyed it, you see, in one of his ritual burnings but for the boy. Because Miguel was both disgusted and enchanted by the monstrous worm that had lived inside his body. He asked to keep it. The grandfather, who found that he loved the boy, could not deny his wish.

When Miguel had fully recovered, he set at once to decorating the worm. And he did it in a style that reflected his love of nature. The grandfather varnished it to save it from deterioration.

'This fantastically decorated worm, this magic worm, as it was called by the people in Miguel's village, it became a sensation – a relic of sorts. There were many people so taken with the story and the chance of decorating their own – or of having Miguel decorate it for them – that they willingly agreed to take the antiparasitic drugs administered by the grandfather.'

Peter picked up the decorated worm and held it out for me to examine. 'Miguel was later adopted by the grandfather, married an Iranian woman from Isfahan, and had one child, my friend Mara. Later, they moved to Brazil. Mara gave me this piece of her father's worm. Of course, after so many years, it had deteriorated a bit by the time I got it.'

He grinned, and I suddenly saw the beauty of a little boy in Peter's openness – of Miguel himself, perhaps. I saw, too, that his allure was nothing that I needed to be jealous of. He tilted his head to the side to ask for words from me and took the worm back. 'Mara's here in San Francisco, too,' he added. 'It's one of the reasons we ... I came. She married an American, but she's divorced now. I'm sure you'll meet her.'

'I'd like to,' I replied. I nodded toward the worm. 'It's amazing – absolutely amazing.' But what I felt was a mixture of awe and what ... clarity? It had to do with Peter, and as he poured our tea, I watched him with eyes that sought an understanding of my own feelings of kinship for him. We listened to cars passing from inside the solitude that follows stories told, letting the wisps of steam from our cups warm our faces. And it was suddenly obvious that for the first time I was seeing him as a person separate from my feelings, whether jealousy or curiosity or anxiety. I easily forgot how much trouble I had separating people from my own thoughts. But here was Peter, an entity unto himself, someone who told stories, who had a pet bird,

and who came from Angola. Even more important, he was a
person with a past, with emotions and ideas and remembrances
of pain and love that were not my own, that might not be anything like my own.

Chapter 4

PETER'S STORY OF THE MAGIC WORM was the start of our friendship. That weekend, we introduced each other to our hobbies and loves as a way of easing each other into our separate lives. I showed him my maps and bird books; played CDs for him by Franco Battiato, Umberto Tozzi and other Italian rock stars; lent him two of my favourite novels to read, *Christ Stopped at Eboli* and *Sirius*. He didn't have many possessions, but he let me take a look at an old Portuguese atlas he had with bright colours and antiquated names. I listened to his tapes of Amalia Rodrigues, Portugal's most renowned traditional singer. I didn't like her voice at first. She sang with constant urgency. Later I grew to love her. How silly you are when you see or hear something for the first time. And he played pieces for me on the upright piano in our living-room, which Alex had stopped using a couple of years earlier — mostly harpsichord compositions. He had a flair for Renaissance music, and his fingers were agile and certain. When he found out that I'd studied music theory in college, he explained that he favoured melodies which employed the Dorian and Arabian minor scales. 'They never seem to begin or end,' he observed. He demonstrated what he meant on the piano, playing serpentine melodies linked by pedal points and lustred with augmented intervals that seemed to stretch treacherously across space. Occasionally, he sang, too, in a haunting voice with almost no vibrato. It was an ancient, peasant voice, unstudied but pure, like a Baroque recorder rather than a modern flute.

My Honda was in the shop to have a cracked window replaced, so that Sunday morning I rented a car at Avis on Van Ness so that we could drive around the hills of Berkeley. I must have been a bit giddy, because I chose a lime-green

Pontiac. It was a huge, hulking thing, like something built for dropping the kids off at the neighbourhood bowling alley. I guess I wanted Peter to know America, and cruising over the Bay Bridge inside a lime-green Pontiac seemed like a pretty good place to start. I took him to eat lunch at Cha Am, the first Thai restaurant I remember opening in the Bay Area, and I was crazy for their pad thai noodles. Also, Peter had asked about a good used bookstore, and I figured we could go to Moe's on Telegraph Avenue.

We had our first tense moments just about right away, however.

'Bridges are good for you,' he said to me as we zoomed past Treasure Island, lowering his window, letting the wind whip his hair.

'Good for me, how?'

'I mean for us, for me. I find them quite ... I don't know. I think they've always represented potential for change to me – for being able to move from one place to another. That's always been decisive for me. Going from Angola to Brazil and now America, I mean. But also the ... the potential of being able to change my life around, my person...' He looked at me, puzzled. 'Do you use the word *person* in English like that?'

'No, not any more. I think we used to – last century. But I get what you mean.'

'The bridges make it kind of exciting being here. They're intricate things. So musical – like all these notes turned into great metallic structures. Like alchemy maybe.'

I was sure that Peter was adopting one of Alexandra's favourite tactics, trying to impress me with how appreciative of the world he was (ergo, how dense to beauty I was). So I assumed a teacherly tone, as if to disabuse him of a delusion.

'Peter, bridges are just steel pillars – pillars and cables and roadways,' I said. An ancient Chevy in front of us, all banged up and rusty, was crawling along at about forty-five, so as I braked I added, 'Roadways with too many morons out for a Sunday drive.'

Peter cocked his head like a dog hearing a strange sound and looked at me for a deeper meaning behind my words. I had the feeling that he was trying to place me inside his universe. I thought of square pegs in round holes. He said, 'I find that interpreting the world poetically is much more ... more useful.' Then – and this is the weird thing – as if understanding perfectly well exactly what I'd been thinking, he added, 'And I'm not talking about beauty at all. I'm talking about meaning. Prose is just too clumsy for that particular job. It's like poetry that's had too much to drink and can barely stay awake.'

I gave him one of the frowns I'd picked long ago from my mother's extensive repertoire and said, 'I don't get it.'

'So you don't want to change, do you?' he said.

'Change? What's this got to do with me changing?' I checked the lane to my left to make sure it was free, then swerved in.

'It's just that you talk as if you don't really want to move on to anywhere else. Or do anything different. Even after going ... going separate from Alexandra.'

As I passed the Chevy, I flashed a look of contempt at the gnarly old man. Oblivious, he was leaning forward into the steering wheel as if every inch he moved in might save his life. I hit the gas and sped ahead, then shifted back into our old lane. 'It really doesn't matter what I want,' I said. 'Because I've seen very little evidence that I can change. I was with Alexandra for six years – if you consider the two years we were with each other before we got married. And I don't think either of us changed at all. Certainly not for the better.'

'Except that you're undoubtedly more cynical than you were.'

'Maybe that – but what's the difference?' I shrugged to diminish its importance; I had a very bad feeling about where this was leading.

'What about Alexandra, then? Wouldn't you have liked her to keep modifying herself?'

'Modifying?'

'You know – doing new things, making unexpected comments. Putting out branches and roots – turning into a flowering plant. Or sprouting fins like a tropical fish. Iridescent ones. Or growing feathers. Wouldn't you like a wife like Maria?'

I looked over at him sceptically. 'Like Maria?'

'With feathers, I mean. Imagine sleeping beside a creature like that. Imagine creating life inside a lovely little bird like her.'

'I think Maria would be a bit tiny for me. Our children would be ugly, too – all beak, really skinny. And in the middle of the night, I might just roll over and squash her.'

Peter half-smiled, as if he might have found my comments amusing under other circumstances, then lowered his window all the way and let the full force of the wind hit him square in the face. After a while, he said, 'The Bay Area smells good, doesn't it?'

I nodded. I was hoping he'd keep quiet because I was feeling more and more obliged to ruin the day for the both of us.

After a few minutes of silence, he said, 'I meant a woman with feathers,' he added. 'Not a bird.'

'I tend to be satisfied with women just the way they are.' Even as I said that, I realized I was being dishonest; I'd never been really satisfied with my wife or anyone else. Forging deeper into the land of lies, I added, 'And Alexandra was fine as she was. I didn't want her to change for me. That would have been wrong.'

Opening his eyes wide with surprise, he asked, 'Excuse my curiosity, but who told you that?'

'I don't know. No one told me. But why should she have wanted to change for me?'

'Because she was married to you. Isn't that a good enough

reason? Wouldn't that have been a good enough reason for you to change – for her, I mean.'

So this was where he was headed! 'You shouldn't want to mould other people to fit your needs,' I said authoritatively. 'They're who they are.'

He should have rolled his eyes at my cliché, but he said patiently, 'Not mould – change. And voluntarily.' Witnessing another of my inherited frowns, sensing I wasn't going to go any further with this discussion of how Alexandra and I might have chosen a happy ending, he shrugged and said, 'Anyway, feathers are pretty. Blue ones. Or emerald green – the colour isn't terribly important. Though I think, having met her, that Alexandra would want pink and red and yellow – really hot colours. Though she'd probably never admit it.'

'Peter, this conversation ... I really don't know what you're talking about. I'm lost. Besides, you don't know anything about Alex. Not a thing. She's not what you think,' I said aggressively.

'You're right. But still, at the very least, wings would be nice.'

Maybe he was trying to be amusing. Or maybe it was some sort of pun in Portuguese. The best I could do was nod; he was speaking a language I couldn't understand at all.

'You'd have a hard time believing just how much I've changed,' he said. He smiled shyly, raised his window. Running his hands back through his hair, he stretched like a cat, as if glad to feel himself alive in that moment.

'So why don't I see any colourful feathers on you?' I asked with a forced smile, trying to make up a bit for having shown my temper.

'Mine are mostly black anyway. Like a raven.'

'A raven?'

'Or crow.'

'And invisible, I suppose?'

'Not completely. But you have to look really closely to see them.'

I'd been watching the road for this last part of the conversation, and when I glanced over at him, I was expecting to see a grin. But we'd just reached the other shore of the Bay and he was staring out his window at the hills, his shoulders hunched, hands scrunched happily between his legs, breath making eager clouds of moisture on the glass. It was as if he were an excited little kid who'd already completely forgotten our awkward words.

'It's pretty, isn't it?' I said.

'I enjoy going new places,' he replied. 'Thank you for taking me.' He gave me a generous smile, then continued watching the landscape.

I waited a little while. 'So just how have you changed so much?'

He turned back to me, rubbed his hands together as if he were cold. His played nervously with the mother-of-pearl buttons on his grey silk shirt. 'In lots of ways.'

'Like . . . ?'

'Like, I don't know . . .' He squirmed in his seat. 'You're putting me on the spot.' He lifted his right hand and gestured as if shaking a tiny bell. 'I feel like I'm . . . hanging . . . or dangling in space. You've caught me.' He smiled as if to apologize.

Instead of finding his embarrassment endearing, I was offended that he didn't want to tell me. After some silence during which I could feel my teeth grinding, I said, 'White.'

'What?' he asked.

'Alexandra would want white feathers. Pure white.'

Peter nodded and was about to reply, but I twisted on the radio to cut him off. I just couldn't hear one more word about my marriage. I knew I was being an asshole, but I couldn't control myself. Phil Collins was singing 'You Can't Hurry Love'. Despite the downer lyrics, he sounded altogether too happy, as if all the engineers in the studio were snapping their fingers while he was making the record. I flipped the dial around, settled by default on 'Higher Love'. Steve Winwood sounded depressed. I liked that.

Peter spoke above the music: 'Like getting in this car with you and driving – I never would have done that even six months ago.'

He looked out the window again, but this time to escape my probing. I was beginning to understand that it wasn't easy for him to be out in the world. 'Why wouldn't you have come with me six months ago?' I asked.

He looked me dead in the eye. 'I wouldn't have trusted a man like you.'

'Like me?' I gripped the steering wheel tight. I was ready to burst with anger now, and though a quickly receding part of me knew I was being nuts, I felt as if he'd ambushed me, that I needed to go on the offensive very quickly. 'So what's wrong with me?' I demanded, wanting to shout, Just what have I done *now!*, as if I were being accused of wilful treachery for the umpteenth time.

'Nothing. That's not what I meant.' He grimaced out of self-irritation and shook his head. 'I'm sorry. It's partially my English again. I hate this language stuff. It's just that I wouldn't have trusted anyone I didn't know for a long time. Someone American – from a different country, with different ideas. I'm learning to stop being so cautious like I always was, to reveal things about myself.'

'I assure you, I'm not the least bit dangerous,' I said, now feeling bad that I'd upset him. Yet I was being less than candid, once again; I was obviously more out of control than I'd been in many years, maybe ever. And I had been dangerous – to my marriage, most of all.

Peter played with his shirt buttons some more and spoke about needing to be cautious around Americans, but I wasn't paying much attention. I kept my mouth shut; I was worried that something would pop out that I wanted to keep inside – something about my halfhearted attempts to keep from sleeping with other women, or my fear of Jay's judgments, or even my failure to be of any comfort to my mother since my father's death five years earlier. When we got to Berkeley, I took the Marin exit, drove across the sun-drenched flats toward the range of dry hills that surrounds the East Bay, then shifted into first gear coming off the Arlington Circle and barrelled straight up the slope to Grizzly Peak Boulevard.

Following the roadway across the panoramic landscape there was a bit like flying a thousand feet up. I felt free enough to apologize to Peter. 'Since Alex left I've been a bit aggressive about the least little things,' I explained. 'It's weird. I'm sorry.'

'It's okay,' he said. 'We're just getting to know each other. It's okay.'

We parked the car on a packed-dirt turnout bordered on its southern and western ridges by a grove of tall eucalyptus trees. Spreading out toward the horizon was the green and brown circuit-board of Berkeley and Oakland streets. Further off was the Bay, a jade-green inner sea meeting the open ocean at the Golden Gate Bridge. In the white city itself, in San Francisco, ribbons of fog were rolling over and down the Twin Peaks, casting up smoky wisps into the great blue sky. '*Puxa*,' Peter exclaimed.

'What's that mean?'

'Wow.'

I laughed; he didn't seem like the kind of person who'd say wow.

As he walked toward the grassy edge of the ridge we were perched on, he picked up a tiny branch of finely reticulated pine needles from the ground. He closed his eyes, rubbed the luxury of its foliage down across his neck and up over his face.

He breathed in deeply, curled his head down and then up in a great arc. Then he licked the needles.

'You okay?' I asked.

He looked around in a circle, clearly trying to spot something, then walked straight into the eucalyptus grove to our left.

'Peter!' I called after him.

He began to run as if to get away from me. I rushed after him, calling his name.

He raced down a slope overgrown with ferns, then up a small hillock. He was able to run much faster than I would have thought. I followed as best I could. After a few moments, he reached a low wall of opaque glass bricks separating the woods from the grounds of a square wooden house with an enormous redwood deck all the way around. On the roof, perched on the tip of a metal standard, was a weather vane of a caped troubadour blowing a great golden trumpet back toward Berkeley.

Peter went climbing over the wall.

'Hey, you can't do that!' I called, my heart doing a sudden dive toward panic.

But he'd already dropped over to the other side, was walking across the scruffy lawn up toward the house.

I climbed over, too. I didn't call out for fear of being heard by the owners. I walked stealthily toward Peter. He was rubbing his hand over the trunk of what I thought then was a kind of pine tree, its long delicate branches hanging with needles and looking like weary arms. A small segment must have broken off and blown to the turnout along the road. There'd been a brief rain shower a few days earlier – it had probably happened then.

'What do you think you're doing?' I whispered to him. 'We've got to get out of here.'

When he turned to me, tears were running down his cheeks.

'Jesus, Peter – what's wrong?'

'There's a street along the water in Luanda – a street that's lined with cassuarina trees,' he whispered, his voice gone. 'I haven't seen one in ... in, I don't know, in many years. You can't believe how this takes me ... how this takes me back to then.'

'Peter, listen,' I said gently, glancing at the back windows of the house, 'we should get out of here. This is America. People have guns and things.'

'I grew up in the shade of these trees,' he said. 'Do you know what that means?'

I shook my head. A scrub jay landed about ten feet away, went hopping along the ground toward Peter. 'Shoo,' I whispered, flapping my hand, and the bird took wing.

I could hear a car's tires screeching along a curve, from the road we should have been cruising on by now.

'It means I'll never feel completely at home with any other tree for shade,' Peter said.

'Look, I'm sorry that makes you sad. But we've got to get out of here.'

He wiped his eyes. 'It doesn't make me sad. It makes me happy.'

'So you're crying because you're happy to have discovered that you'll never feel at home with another tree?'

'That's right.' I must have looked puzzled, because he added, 'Why wouldn't it make me happy to find out more about myself, about the way I see the world?'

I didn't try to make a reply, because he'd surprised me with that answer. I gazed instead at his sad eyes, wanting to help. For a moment, it was as if the world were swivelling slowly around the two of us. We were alone, enshrouded in silence. Everything else had receded – the house and the woods, even the sky. I reached out to steady myself, but gripped only air. I was afraid of falling, but the next thing I knew, I was perfectly steady and looking back at myself bordered by a bluish-white light.

Maybe I'd lost consciousness again for an instant, because I remember that I was next looking down into my hands, shocked to find them empty; I had the feeling that I'd been holding on to the cassuarina branch that Peter had found at the turnout, as if it could somehow prevent me from falling.

Peter was now patting the trunk of the tree.

'Come on,' I said, jittery. 'Please, we've got to leave.'

He was about to start off when he looked down at his left leg. So did I. There was a banana slug on his trouser cuff – puce green, glistening. They're pretty common in the Bay Area, and this one was easily five inches long. Its antennae were moving as if in slow motion, as if trying in vain to figure out what strange world it had happened upon. It was ugly as hell.

Peter reached down for it. I guess because he'd licked the cassuarina needles I whisper-screamed, 'Don't eat it!'

He lifted it off his leg and held it in the palm of his hand. 'I wasn't going to eat it,' he said. 'I've never seen such a big one. Though we've got lots of slugs in Angola and Brazil.'

'I'm sure you do, but...' I heard tapping. A white-haired man was peering out at us now through a window at the back of the house, patting the glass. When he saw that I'd noticed him, he furrowed his brows and motioned for us to leave. Those wild Italian gesticulations I get when I'm anxious came to me. 'Peter, it's time to go. Please, we've got to go right this second.'

He placed the slug down carefully on the grass. 'Go on,' he said to it in an encouraging voice.

The door to the redwood deck opened and the man appeared. He had tufted eyebrows and shoulder-length white hair. He was bare-chested. He looked really angry and was raising his arm as if to start yelling.

'We're leaving,' I called. 'Sorry to bother you. My friend spotted something he hadn't seen in years. A tree. A cassuarina tree. But we're going now.'

What an idiot I must have sounded like! But we got lucky; the man didn't say a word, just gathered his hair into a pony-tail as he watched us leave.

We climbed over the wall, walked down the first slope and up the second to the car. I was really annoyed with Peter. I wanted to shout something punishing at him, but as I was brushing myself off, he said, 'Gastropods have always liked me an awful lot.'

His face was so earnest . . . I burst out laughing.

'Snails, slugs – even ones that live in the sea,' he explained. 'They all like me. I don't know why. Once, my mother and I were at the beach in Angola, and she sat me down in a shady spot, then must have fallen asleep herself. I was very tiny. Maybe one or two. She was right next to me. When she awoke, I was covered with snails. She said there were hundreds, cover-ing every inch of me, though I'm sure she was exaggerating. She got a real fright – started smacking them off me. But ap-parently, I hadn't minded in the least.'

'That's really creepy,' I said, but I also figured that this was just a family fable. Probably, two or three snails had made their way up the edges of his baby blanket and his mother got a bit carried away telling the relatives.

In any event, I was coming to the conclusion that it was a lot safer to be with Peter in a city; we drove to Telegraph Avenue so he could look for used books.

I left him alone at Moe's, agreed to meet at the Caffè Mediterraneum across the street in an hour. I took a walk up Telegraph Avenue to the University of California. As always, the street was lined with vendors selling jewellery, ceramics, tie-dyed T-shirts, drug paraphernalia. There were students everywhere, of course, lugging backpacks, laughing, wolfing down slices of pizza and giant chocolate chip cookies. But what I noticed most was all the discarded junk on the sidewalks – candy wrappers, old sneakers, ice-cream cups. And the homeless people sitting in storefronts, their hair matted, dirty as garbage cans. Things seemed to be falling apart – and not just for me. Maybe the 1990s would be better, I was thinking.

I paused at one table to look at a T-shirt that said USA OUT OF CENTRAL AMERICA. The silk-screened image was of a dead little kid, naked, lying in a pool of blood. I had my own reasons, of course, for finding it difficult to turn away from this particular image.

Peter met me an hour later at the Mediterraneum. We were sitting at one of the tables near the window. Next to us were two Rastafarians with sprays of long reddish dreadlocks. I ordered us both banana milk shakes.

He'd bought three books: a biography of John Brown called *To Purge This Land with Blood*, a really old leather-bound edition of Whitman's *Leaves of Grass* (which cost him thirty-five dollars) and John Newton's *Journal of a Slave Trader*. I'd never heard of John Newton. Neither had he. Apparently, it was an account of his work picking up slaves in West Africa, then selling them in the American South.

'There seems to be a theme here,' I told Peter.

'What's that?'

'Slavery – America in the nineteenth century.'

'If slavery hadn't ended here in America, it would have been impossible to end elsewhere. It made all the difference to civilization – metaphorically speaking.'

'Metaphorically speaking?'

He took a sip of his shake, licked the milk moustache from his lips with a swirling tongue. 'Where there's even one person who's a slave, that possibility remains open for all of us, in every area of our lives. Some people have known that since the beginning.'

'Like who, for instance?'

'Moses. He didn't have to struggle against slavery. He was a nobleman – an Egyptian nobleman. But he did. Because he knew that civilization couldn't ... couldn't keep going forward without an end to slavery. For people to believe in themselves, in their own destiny, he knew that the Red Sea had to part, that the slave ships had to be sunk behind him once and for all. For me to be here with you, for you and I to be...' He shook his head, displeased with himself. 'English grammar is a nightmare – is it you and I or you and me?'

'I've no idea.'

'Well, in any case, for us to be sitting here believing we have choices in our lives, he knew that we needed to end the slave trade.' He took another gulp.

'Moses knew about you and me?' I asked.

'He knew what he was doing for us – then and now. A lot of us have known for a long time what we needed to do.'

'For us?'

'For all of us who want to free language from its traditional restrictions.'

'Jesus, Peter, what's language got to do with anything?'

'Everything,' he said. 'If we can free language, then we can conceive of being free ourselves.'

I didn't get what Peter was saying. Maybe I still don't, though sometimes I imagine a small crack opening in my usual way of thinking and giving me a hurried glimpse of a world ruled by language – by words, even individual letters. But the important thing at the time was that I was beginning to realize that he was, in some fundamental way, very different from anyone I'd ever met.

Chapter 5

*A*T THE END of our second full week together, Peter took me to a huge pawnshop on Harrison Street, where I learned a lot more about what made him tick. I know it was Saturday, July 5, because on getting up that morning I'd finally remembered to flip over the hummingbird calendar hanging in the kitchen to the new month. It's curious how some small gestures like this you remember distinctly for years afterward.

The pawnshop had more objects in one place than I'd ever seen in my life: case after case of pocket watches and filigree jewellery, Scottish woollen blankets, water buffalo-hide chairs, antique pistols, mangy zebra-skin rugs, pipes, cigarette cases, cocaine spoons, Roadrunner and Speedy glasses, typewriters, undernourished ficuses, life-size posters of The Who and Marilyn Monroe and Bela Lugosi as Dracula. Everything was tossed together as if there'd been an earthquake just before our arrival. And everywhere dust, acres of dust, dust from the days of the Gold Rush, from the Conquistadores, from Mesopotamia even, dust that had driven allergic cavemen insane, dust from the Big Bang. It made me ill. And it sickened me further to consider all the objects humanity had produced and thrown out since the beginning of so-called civilization.

Peter loved it. 'Isn't it incredible?' he asked me when we first arrived.

I saw a major headache coming on. 'Yeah, incredible,' I moaned. He searched through trunks and poured over cases and closed his eyes while rummaging as if trying to guess what his hands were about to discover. He knew one of the owners, an obese man with a bristly moustache – the kind my father had and that makes men look like pimps. His name was

Mr Thalburg. He showed us objects from the back room that weren't for the eyes of transient customers. We saw a hookah from Turkey inset with coral, turquoise, and lapis lazuli; painted Easter eggs from Hungary that smelled like liniment because of the camphor-wood trunk they'd been kept in; and an enamel box of the most spectacular emerald jewellery I'd ever seen. There were earrings and brooches and necklaces with quarter-sized cabochon stones, flawed, but magnificent. Peter held a choker of emeralds and diamonds in his hand and nearly swooned. His eyes radiated a magnetism that seemed to draw him to the minerals, and he stared without speaking as if trying to decipher a mystery.

I thought of the magic worm, and I realized that this man was fascinated by objects as I never would be. It was wonderful to see. But when we left, I vowed that I wouldn't be back till they cleaned up.

At such moments of solidarity between us, it did occur to me that Peter might indeed be gay, that he might have lied to me out of shyness or fear. But I didn't think so. I felt his strangeness was something deeper, beyond sexuality. And there were many indications that his secret difference was indeed profound. For one thing, there was his sense of smell. That twitching I'd noticed when I first met him happened all the time, and at the slightest odour, he'd swivel his head like an owl and stick his nose in the air till he spotted the source.

'Did you just eat a banana?' he asked me the Saturday after he moved in, a full two hours after I'd munched one down.

I laid my book about the Inquisition on my lap. 'Why?' I asked.

'It smells.'

I was stunned, felt as if Alexandra had returned. 'Sorry,' I said. 'But you might have to get used to it. I like bananas and you can bet I'm going to continue eating them.'

Peter grimaced and clenched his fists. 'It's my English,' he said in despair. 'I only meant that I could smell it, not that it ... that it smelled bad.'

I apologized. And realized once again that not everyone was a witch or ogre trying to hurt me; there were human beings out there without fangs, warts on their noses, or an appetite for their own children. And Peter, I was coming to learn, was one of them.

He apologized, too, though he didn't have to.

Then there was his love of flowers. Bouquets and even outdoor plants had to harmonize in their smells and colours for him to be satisfied. 'I arrange the scents I want, the petals, just as a writer should arrange words for their meanings and sound,' he told me.

'It's poetry, then?' I asked.

'What else could flowers be? If God were to write verse, wouldn't His poems be delphiniums and dahlias?'

Hard to argue with that. Or with the arrangements that he began to place around our living-room. I remember that that first week he put dead oak-tree branches and bursting sunflowers together into a black vase on the mantelpiece. It was like a metaphor for life and death.

The next week, he replaced them with fleshy calla lily leaves, fully three feet long, with dead spider mums that looked like miniature wilted brooms.

I thought maybe that he'd learned ikebana in Brazil.

'No,' he told me, 'it's just a system of my own.'

From time to time I'd bring him home the wildest flowers I could find from a Polk Street florist that stocked protea and other exotic cuttings. He was so excited to get them under his nose that he'd often forget to thank me till hours later.

'Plants are less detached than we think,' he once told me. 'Certainly, they are more responsive than most people. And their company relaxes me.'

Occasionally, we'd watch the hummingbirds buzzing around the honeysuckle in the yard, and he'd move his eyes over the little trumpets from which they fed as if reading the poems of God that he believed in.

∞

Peter could also smell things that even dogs would have trouble detecting. I didn't believe him at first. 'It has no smell,' I said once after he'd offered me a stem of violet orchids to sniff.

'It most *certainly* does,' he answered.

'It doesn't.'

'But it does!' He shook his head and glared at me. 'You are all alike – what you can't smell, doesn't exist,' he said.

I wasn't sure who 'you' was, but was put off by his aggression. Yet I also empathized with his hurt at not being believed. He skulked off. I came to him and apologized. That's when he touched me for the first time since our initial handshake. He held my shoulder for a moment and said, 'It's okay. I have to get used to it. It's just a small thing really.'

'But you spoke honestly, and I should have believed you,' I replied.

After that, I can't remember what either of us said. I was concentrating on the feel of his touch on my shoulder. His fingertips seemed as if they were meant to attract a dispersed energy, to serve as a lightning rod for an unseen force. I was suddenly anxious about our physical connection. I wondered what gave him this power or if it were simply a product of my own imagination.

Hours after he removed his hand, I still felt the pressure of his touch on my skin.

Some days later, on the Sunday after we visited the pawn-shop, he offered me the beginnings of an explanation for this energy. I'd found him in the kitchen eating pink and white rose petals atop steamed brown rice. He responded to my puzzlement by saying: 'I'm a vegetarian.'

'But rose petals?'

'They're part of a ritual. Please don't get upset. I know I take some getting used to. But my eccentricities are my way of making sense out of impressions ... out of disparate impressions. They help me connect what is difficult to put together ... to reconcile. Rose petals, other things I eat and do, are a way of receiving a certain blessing, an energy. Of keeping me sensitive if you like.'

I was lost in a post-Alexandra world where such occult possibilities didn't seem worth challenging. Maybe that was a good thing, because later I began to realize that the price Peter paid for his sensitivity was vulnerability – particularly to the written word, it seemed. For instance, he had just purchased a book on Nazi doctors working in the death camps, and he could only read a few pages before he'd begin pacing the room with an anxious, desolate face. Sometimes, he'd mumble angry words to himself in Portuguese. It was easy to see he was just barely controlling rage. It was scary. But he'd always return to his book. I asked him why he didn't just let it be.

'I owe it to myself and to the victims,' he replied. 'I always try to find out more about the Nazis and the others.'

'What others?' I asked.

'Oh, there are always others,' he replied, as if it were obvious.

'Like who?'

He grunted, jerked around to face me straight on as if suddenly breaking free from rigid hands. 'Like the damn Turks in 1915! Killed a million Armenians! You Americans would give it a try, too, given half the chance. That's why...' He stopped and folded his arms, looked away as if remembering to keep a secret.

After that, I let the subject drop. If he wanted Nazi doctors, he could have them. After all, I'd always been obsessed with my own particular demons as well.

And then there was his relationship with Maria. One night, during our third week together, I came downstairs for some juice at maybe two in the morning. As I passed his open door, I could see him sitting on the floor surrounded by lit candles. Maria was outside of her cage, facing him. They were staring at each other inside jumping shadows. It was as if they were communicating in silence. I peered in the doorway. Peter glanced up at me. Maria looked at me, too. It was the eeriest thing. I felt as if I were being watched by two spirits in animal form.

Peter broke the spell with a smile and asked if I was okay. I nodded and left.

That scene provoked fear in me for the first time since his arrival. Maybe in consequence, I began to sleep fitfully again. In the middle of the night, I awoke a few times in a darkness composed of cold regret. I thought about how, by sleeping with other women, I'd popped the fairy-tale bubble that Alexandra and I had been living in. I worried, too, that she wouldn't recover, for she needed a man almost as much as I needed a woman. Without one, she knew she'd risk turning permanently into a wooden soldier. She'd simply march around the Financial District within those damn business suits of hers, those accursed mummy wraps, thinking that that was all there could be to life. Or maybe, like my mother, she'd melt into a crazy little gob of feminine despair that you'd have to scrape off the ground. I couldn't tell which way she'd go. But she'd never be able to maintain her delicately balanced composure without a man. Or maybe I was just kidding myself, glorifying men and our importance. Maybe she'd be fine.

During this period of insomnia, I sat up in bed just before dawn one weekday night and was looking out the window, glad to have escaped a bad dream. I was comforted by arcs of light glistening on the leaves of my plum trees. In between the topmost branches, a luminescent full moon shone behind wisps of clouds flying in the night wind. It was stunning. A revelation came to me: the Earth has a moon. How strange that seemed. It was tens of thousands of miles away, and it was reflecting the warmth of a hidden star into my eyes, stimulating my rods and cones, sending an impulse across my optic nerve to my brain and registering ... a moon. If we thought about that process all day long, we'd never move on to anything else. Though we'd certainly believe in miracles. Anyway, the sheer glory of a surprising universe made me feel safe. Then, suddenly, I saw the silhouette of a bird perched on one of the branches as if atop a ship's prow. Maria? Moonlight glimmered off her crown. I stood up, walked to the window. It was her all right. Just staring at me with her tiny eyes. She blinked once. So did I. Then I felt Peter's presence behind me. I stood still, chilled, holding my breath, picturing him there, waiting. I gathered my courage. Turned ...

There was nothing. Just a shadowed room. I looked back out the window. Maria was gone.

∞

In the morning, Peter was sipping freshly brewed coffee in the kitchen when I got downstairs. I said, 'Was that Maria I saw outside last night?'

He jerked back his head, looked up as if he were evaluating my physical appearance. 'I sometimes let her out of the cage at night,' he replied. 'It's possible that she went outside.'

I sat opposite him and frowned, wanting to be angry, but unable to muster more than irritation. 'You should have told me,' I said.

'Yes, I suppose you're right. But she does no harm when she's outside, I can assure you. And it gives her an opportunity to explore her new neighbourhood.'

We left it at that and drank our coffee from within separate silences. The discomfort that I felt in his presence slowly swelled as I sat there until I sensed that below his handsome face, beyond the sensitivities to flowers and objects, there just might be something sinister and ugly. I even felt that there might be something capable of murder inside him – of murdering me, to be more to the point. At the time, I suspected this presentiment of danger was only a crazy construct built of my own past associations. I dismissed it as part of the legacy of my parents' unexpressed wishes. Until he told me his next story. Then, I wasn't so sure about anything. It was a Saturday morning, almost four weeks after he moved in. I remember, because his tale disturbed me so much I counted the days before our first month together would be up; I decided it would be fair to give him notice after a month that I didn't want him in my house any longer.

I'd come downstairs after changing the sheets on my bed and found him in the kitchen holding a necklace, counting its freshwater pearls and nuggets of turquoise as you would a string of rosary beads. He was lost in that magic communion he seemed to have with objects.

'You don't wear that necklace to work, I hope,' I said on entering. I was trying to be amusing.

Startled, he showed me his embarrassed smile. 'No, no, oh no, I don't. It's to look at, to touch.'

As I took a glass of orange juice, I watched him running the stones through his fingers. He was mouthing words to himself.

He offered the necklace to me. I sat down. 'You like it?' he inquired.

Taking it in my hands, I could see that it was fashioned of turquoise and ivory rather than pearls. 'It's very pretty,' I said. I handed it back to him. 'Where's it from?'

'Brazil, from a friend of mine. She won't wear it any longer. So she gave it to me when I asked for it.'

Peter puffed out his lips and shrugged. 'Anyway, Bill, that's really another story.'

I sat down opposite him, wary but curious. Morning sunlight

warmed the table between us. At that moment, I couldn't imagine evil having any power in the world. 'Go ahead,' I said.

'You really want to hear?'

When I nodded, Peter laid the necklace on the table.

He explained in a fragile voice how his friend Cecilia had been tortured by the Brazilian military. 'She entered the University of São Paulo in 1967,' he began, 'when the country was still in the grip of a military dictatorship. She was petite, olive-complexioned, and terribly sensuous. With great big blue eyes like the sky. When she was wet from the beach, with her long auburn hair clinging to her back and shoulders, she was irresistible. At the time, she was studying art, was experimenting with traditional Native American paints on her figurative ceramic sculptures. Anyway, she decided to go to work for a small underground student newspaper called *The Sentinel*, where she wrote editorials calling for strikes and protests against the regime in power. When the dictatorship started really cracking down against any and all opposition – this is in 1969 – she was arrested by soldiers from the Military Police, taken to an old sugar refinery near Santos, and tortured. Imaginary crimes were shocked out of her by electrodes attached to her breasts and genitals, and a military court sentenced her to two years in prison. When she was released in September of 1971, I was there to meet her. She told me right away that the beatings, rapes, and electric shocks had caused the birth of a demon inside her. "A creature – a perverted dwarf ... *um anão perverso*", she called it.'

Peter made a fist and surrounded it with his other hand. 'She pictured this dwarf inside her body like one of those smaller boxes that hides inside its parent box. And it was horrible because he forced her to do things – this invisible creature.'

Peter breathed deeply, smoothed his hair behind his ears with his palms to steady himself.

'What kinds of things?' I asked.

'Oh, he forced her to do little things at first – to count the steps to the university, to put her clothes on in the same order every day – compulsive things. And all with the understanding that if she didn't follow his directions, he would kill her. These compulsive habits turned out to be a kind of ... education ... of training for something greater the dwarf had in mind – revenge on the man Cecilia knew only as the Lieutenant.

'In prison, this Lieutenant had pretended friendship, had offered protection from the other soldiers.' Peter stared at me menacingly and said, 'After befriending her, however, he raped her, raped her brutally. Then he offered her to the other men as you would a glass of wine.'

Peter leaned forward and whispered, 'Each morning, the dwarf would breathe in her ear that she must go and wait for the Lieutenant at the headquarters for the Military Police in downtown São Paulo. She obeyed, of course, frightened but fearing for her life should she mount a revolt.

'Then, a month after her release, she spotted him there, standing on the marble steps leading to the main entrance. He was talking to another officer. He was a thin man with a bulbous nose and black beads for eyes, his mouth a contemptuous streak. His uniform was impeccably pressed. He had medals adorning his chest. As he descended toward Cecilia, she felt herself grow faint. But the creature living inside her steadied her.' Peter raised his eyebrows and whispered, 'The dwarf breathed instructions in her ear again, and she knew exactly what she would have to do.

'With her heart racing, she rushed toward the Lieutenant. The dwarf stifled her urge to scream. She walked very upright, neatened her hair. The creature told her, "You must look perfect." She asked him if the Lieutenant would believe her, and he assured her that he would. "A man like that ... to do what he did to you ... he would have to believe that torture might excite a woman, just as it excites him."

'The creature kept her calm. To get the Lieutenant's attention, she brushed against him as she passed. He stared into her eyes. She nodded with modesty and grace.

"Do I know you?" the Lieutenant asked.

'The dwarf pushed Cecilia aside and spoke for her: "You questioned me in prison." Cecilia wanted to take a knife from her handbag and plunge it into her torturer's chest, but the creature ordered her to play the scene out till its conclusion.

'The Lieutenant didn't blush or hesitate. "Yes, yes," he said, grinning, clearly recalling the pleasure of offering her to the other military men for rape. "I see you've been released."

"Yes."

"And how are you doing?" He looked her up and down. "You look elegant, still in your prime."

'The creature said to be gracious. "Thank you," Cecilia replied.

"You live in town?"

"Yes, near here. I have a studio apartment. It's quite nice."

'Cecilia sensed that the Lieutenant was about to bid her goodbye. The creature moved her hand to her purse for a cigarette. "Do you have a light?" she asked.

'When he lifted his gold lighter, the dwarf told her to caress her hand against his. She did as he ordered. She and the Lieutenant looked knowingly into each other's eyes. He laughed. "It seems that you enjoyed our encounter in prison," he observed.

'The dwarf said to smile demurely. Cecilia did.

"And are you a busy lady?" he asked.

"No. Not at all busy for the right man."

"Dinner then sometime?"

"Yes, why don't you come by my apartment? Tonight even. I'll make something special. I'm a good cook." The creature instructed her to lick her lips and smile invitingly. She reached for a pen and a slip of paper from her handbag to write her address. They made an appointment for that night. The Lieutenant looked her up and down once more, grinned at the pleasure to come, and marched off.'

Peter breathed deeply. 'Cecilia felt faint,' he continued. 'For the creature had suddenly disappeared. She staggered home, wondering what was happening.

'But the dwarf, with all his power, reappeared at her home when she recalled the Lieutenant's face. He picked up the book on how to commit suicide that she'd bought after her release and selected a recipe for bringing on death. She shopped for the necessary ingredients in a local pharmacy and market.

'That night, Cecilia and her creature prepared *moqueca*, a spicy Brazilian dish, to hide the flavour of the strychnine-based poison. The Lieutenant arrived a little late, dressed in his uniform, smelling of aftershave, holding a bottle of Chilean wine. The dwarf told Cecilia just how to welcome him. She was charming. She thanked him for the wine with a smile of servitude, asked him to please open it. She brought crystal glasses to him. He poured the wine. The creature told her to worship him with her gaze. She obeyed.

'Then she brought the food to the table and sat down with a coy smile. He sat next to her, felt her thigh, caressed her as if in possession of her already, licked his lips. "I've been thinking about you since this afternoon," he remarked. "I knew you'd enjoy being taken by a man who knows how to treat a woman."

'The creature forced Cecilia to acknowledge this as a compliment and calmed her fears. The Lieutenant ate his meal, watching Cecilia as if putting off the pleasure to come in order to make it so much the sweeter. Cecilia, of course ... she picked delicately at her food, as was proper for a woman who'd enjoy being abused.

'After the meal, she brought him a glass of French brandy.' Peter sipped from an imaginary glass. 'He took it to her couch and patted the pillow next to him for her to sit. When she did, he stroked his hands across her thighs. With a grunt, he suddenly tore open her skirt. She gasped, but stifled a scream under the warnings of the dwarf. Cecilia was wearing an undergarment, of course. The Lieutenant laughed. He said, "In prison, you didn't need any of these. But I rather like them – one more layer to pull off."

'The dwarf ordered Cecilia to show a trembling smile so as to excite her torturer. The Lieutenant slipped his cold hands beneath her panties, gripped her pubic hair, pulled till she felt tears in her eyes.' Peter raised his fist, grinned wickedly. 'He tore a tuft of hair from her and lifted it as a prize, sampling it in his fingers as a connoisseur might fondle raw silk. The creature whispered in her ear to show panic and pleasure.

'It was then that the Lieutenant reached to his abdomen and jerked himself upright. His face twisted with pain.

'The dwarf prompted Cecilia to ask, "Is something wrong? Are you all right?"

'"It's my stomach," he replied.

'"It must be the spices. Just a moment. I'll get you some mineral water."

'She stood up, turned on the stereo, and raised the volume on a symphony.

'"What are you doing?" the Lieutenant demanded.

'Cecilia walked calmly to the kitchen. The creature told her to wait there. She heard staggered footfalls, a glass knocked to the floor. When she peered out from the kitchen, she saw the Lieutenant kneeling. His eyes were opened wide in fear. He cried for help. But the creature whispered, "Do not go to him yet!" Only when the shouts ended did she leave the kitchen. Then, the Lieutenant was near death. She dragged him into the bathroom and lifted him into the bathtub.'

Peter gathered himself behind closed eyes. I was suddenly aware of how distant my body felt. Sunlight wavered over the kitchen table as if threatening to leave. I had the disquieting impression that Cecilia's house was my own. Peter spoke: 'It was there, as life drained from the Lieutenant, that she hacked him to pieces. The dwarf instructed her to put his body parts into plastic bags and to carry them on successive nights to the kiln at the university's pottery studio, to which she already had a key.' He lifted the necklace, swirled it down into the palm of his left hand and closed his fist around it. 'Except for the Lieutenant's teeth. The dwarf knew that they might not burn to ash and could possibly be used to identify him with the help of dental records. So Cecilia knocked his teeth out with a hammer, washed them, put them into her purse, and, on the advice of the creature, brought them to a jeweller who had also been tortured by the Brazilian military. She requested that he put them into his tumbler and polish them to ivory beads. She asked for them to be strung into a necklace with her favourite stone, turquoise.

'The jeweller fashioned a testament to Cecilia's revenge, and over the next several months, she wore the necklace every day at the insistence of her dwarf. For the creature did not disappear with the Lieutenant's destruction. Instead, he swelled with pride and grew demanding in little ways once again. Cecilia's friends all remarked how well the necklace suited her blue eyes, however. They had no idea of its origin and whispered among themselves that she seemed to have recovered from her traumas.

'Eventually, years later, my friend Mara and I helped Cecilia to free herself from the dwarf. Then, the necklace became something unpleasant for her. She could no longer even look at it and asked me to take it away.'

Peter noted the story's completion with a tilt of his head. He opened his fist around the necklace and dropped it onto the table between us. I stared at the polished teeth, impelled to speak. I began to say something about torture, in fact. But when I looked into Peter's eyes, the image of a dwarf swelling inside him – inside all of us – turned me toward silence. That's when I began thinking that I might ask him to leave. Finally, I whispered, 'It's horrible.'

'Yes, the necklace terrifies me as well,' Peter replied.

'Then why the hell do you keep it around?!' I demanded.

'As an amulet, I suppose. When I hold it, let my fingers enter the history of the beads, I feel sentiments I wouldn't feel in other situations.'

'Yeah, like revulsion,' I suggested.

'And other things – fear, remorse, rage ... I don't want to lose those feelings.' Peter gazed out the window as if looking for something on the horizon, then turned back to me. 'I have a great fear of becoming dead.' He searched for words. 'Not true death ... numbness ... a kind of deadening. Is that the word you would use?'

I nodded.

'I don't know why.' He shook his head and stared beyond me. 'No, I don't know the reason, but you could say the necklace protects me in some way.' He picked it up again and began running the stones through his fingers like rosary beads once again. 'It is something healing. At least for me.' He nodded gravely. 'And you, what do you use to protect yourself?'

A memory of Alexandra lying in bed came to me. 'I think I used to use my wife,' I answered. 'She was my insulation.' I laughed to diminish its importance. 'Her very body insulated me against my fears – even my fear of being alone at night.'

'That bothers you?' Peter asked.

'I suppose.'

'And now that she's gone?'

He was coming too close to my secrets. Was that the real reason I suddenly wanted him to leave? 'Everything's more or less fine,' I lied. 'And one of these days, I'll find someone new to protect me.' We shared a silence in which regret for having hidden the truth plagued me. I sighed and said, 'You're a strange guy, Peter.'

'Why?'

Now that I had spoken up, I wanted to recede from him. 'I'm not sure,' I answered.

At that, we heard Maria squawk. Was it meant as an interruption of our conversation? Such bizarre thoughts I was having of late.

Peter got to his feet. 'I've got to check on Maria,' he announced.

'And I've got work to do.'

Peter started off, then turned back to me with a look of consternation. 'One last thing,' he said.

'What?'

'Follow me for a moment.'

We walked to his room. I kept my distance. From his dresser, he took an inch-thick triangle of wood, about the size of a belt buckle, and handed it to me. Writing had been etched crudely on one of its sides. Tiny filaments were tied from the point of the triangle around its base.

'Take this amulet and leave it next to you when you sleep. See what it does,' he said.

When I formed a fist around the wood, my fingers tingled, as if they were in contact with something tainted. I said, 'Nothing bad I hope.'

'No. I don't think this one will produce anything unpleasant.'

'Others then?' I asked.

'Oh yes. I've got things that would give you nightmares for sure.' He smiled furtively. 'But I believe you already have enough problems sleeping without my help.'

He spoke as if challenging me to dispute his words. Walking out of his room, a sense of being controlled by him stiffened my legs. I had the strange impression that time did not exist for me – that past and present and future were one.

I considered that I was becoming mired – even trapped – inside Peter's imagination.

Upstairs, as I examined the wood, I was aware for the first time that the suppressed rage I sensed in him was attractive to me. I wanted him to lose control, for the dwarf inside him to confront me. Maybe I even wanted him to hurt me just as my father had.

I ran my fingertip over the wood. It was dry, old, smooth. I now saw that the base of the triangle – maybe three inches in length – was badly charred. A notch in the point of the triangle held the filaments in place. Upon closer study, I realized that they were actually grey hairs. As for the etched writing, I recognized the names 'Victor' and 'Sarah.' They were incorporated into three sentences in a Germanic language, I thought – though later, I was unable to find anything resembling any of the words in my German dictionary. A Star of David was also etched below the last line.

Chapter 6

A T BEDTIME, I put Peter's triangular piece of wood on my night table. His presence downstairs guarded me from spirits and tears, and I drifted off to sleep. About four hours later, however, I burst awake. The window was wide open. Maybe I'd got up and opened it during the night without being aware of it. A cold wind was blowing. It was just after three in the morning. I rubbed my hands across the hollow of icy sheets around my body, considering how strange it was that only a few weeks before a warm person had been beside me.

I closed the window, jumped back in bed. I told myself that Alexandra would blossom away from me; she was self-confident, sure of her talents. Yet I had destroyed her lifelong wish to live happily ever after. And I didn't know why I had done it.

In the morning, as I sat propped up against my pillow, I remembered it was a dream about Peter that had made me wake up in the night. He was in my living-room, turning my globe, searching for a landmark that would show up as a symbol. It was as if there'd be a pin with a flag marking this special spot on the Earth. Maria was standing on his shoulder, was also staring at the globe. I could see that they were surveying Eastern Europe – Poland, Austria, Hungary. Budapest appeared as if I were flying over it. I don't know how I knew it was that city, but I did. There were eighteenth-century Baroque buildings, tree-lined avenues, a jade-coloured river. Outside the city walls, I could see Peter running across wetlands, jumping effortlessly over a series of low wooden fences, each of which resembled the rickety frame around my parents' garden. Then I was standing beside Peter. He was holding Maria on his outstretched hand and asking me to feed her. I looked through my pockets, turned them inside out, but couldn't find the food that I thought was there.

Disquieted by these images, I jumped up out of bed and shaved for the first time in a week. It helped; I felt as if I'd been grated down to a purer, smoother undercoating of myself. I was thankful, too, that it was Sunday. When I came downstairs, I found that Peter was already gone. I was relieved. A sudden urge to heighten my solitude by hiking through the woods gripped me. So after coffee, I drove to Mount Tamalpais, up near the ranger station. Towering redwoods and oaks greeted me. Butterflies fluttered over fields of high brown grasses. I hiked down to Stinson Beach, memories intersecting with turns in the trail. At a deli, I bought some Genoa salami, cheese, and a French bread. I remembered the egg salad sandwiches my mother prepared for the family when once we took a trip to Jones Beach on Long Island's southern shore. Jay and I had been very little. It was before my mother's agoraphobia had set in and she stopped leaving the house. Her sandwiches had got sand in them. But who couldn't put up with a little crunch to be together as a family? And at the beach, no less!

When I came home in the late afternoon, Peter was still out. I fell asleep while watching television. Afterward, I made myself a strong cup of tea and popped open my book on the Inquisition, discovering right away that it had been the custom on the island of Majorca, right up until the Spanish Revolution of 1931, to discriminate in every facet of life against the Chuetas, impoverished residents whose forefathers had converted to Catholicism from Judaism more than five centuries before.

While reading of a secret plan by a small group of them to escape Majorca in 1688, I heard Peter's key turn in the door. I was seated at the kitchen table. He came into the room and stood over me. After some pleasantries, he asked me what I'd dreamt the night before.

'Not much,' I said, closing my book, figuring that the

outcome of the Chuetas' escape attempt would have to wait. Then I told him.

'Not bad,' he observed.

'Not bad, what?'

'You've got an affinity for this, I think.'

'An affinity for what?' I asked. 'Peter, you tend to talk in riddles. Are you aware of that?'

'What I mean is, you seem to have an affinity for being influenced to have dreams about particular things.'

'So what's the story with the wood?'

He pulled on his ear and replied, 'I'd like you to keep it a few days before we talk about it.'

'Really? Are you sure?' I was concerned that my dreams might become populated by threatening spirits – much like my waking life.

'Yes, I'm quite sure,' he answered.

I nodded my agreement. It seemed strange, but my interest in him at that moment had to do once again with the power of his beauty. Like Alexandra's elegance, it fascinated me.

Peter asked what I was planning to do that night. 'Nothing,' I grumbled.

'Like to get some dessert with me?' he asked. He gave me a boyish smile of enthusiasm.

I figured that I should keep a certain distance from him, but I was lonely all of a sudden. I nodded and stood up. He opened his mouth, tugged on his ear again, and sniffed. He gave me a peeved look. 'My sinuses have decided to drown me slowly from within,' he said.

'No better?'

He shook his head. I gave him a decongestant pill – at his request, one without any antihistamine. He said, 'An antihistamine would make me slip into fantasy in a matter of moments. Just a slight shift in gears...' He ended his thought with a shrug.

'Just a slight shift of gears and what?' I asked.

'I live across a thin veil from my dreams,' he replied. 'Any slight wind can make the veil lift.'

'And when it does, what happens?'

'I disappear!'

At the time, I dismissed this remark of Peter's as simply indicative of his flair for mystery. I wonder, sometimes, if the way things ended up would have been significantly changed if I'd paid more attention.

∞

We decided to sit in a café in North Beach till we thought of something else to do.

As we drove in my car east on Broadway, I saw that it was one of those San Francisco nights when the ether between spaces is blown away: faraway street lights shone like stars, the dark of the sky went on forever, and people seemed small but lovely – imperfect and maybe purposeless, but nevertheless tender and good. I loved the city at that moment and wondered what caused this clarifying wind that blessed the Bay Area.

It seemed to me just then that the First Law of Self-Sleuthing might just as well be applied to the whole world.

We got tea at the Caffè Verdi. Peter sniffed at a piece of marble cake for a long while before he ate it. I sipped my orange juice and watched people walking down Columbus Avenue. I had the eerie sensation that they all had the same destination awaiting them down by the Transamerica building. Maybe because of this seeming journey, I thought of death framing my life. Such a small life it was; a limit approaching zero.

I could see in Peter's quiet eyes that he felt relaxed sitting with me. There was no dwarf controlling his movements just then. Maybe there never had been.

When we left the café, we walked north on Columbus. The cool air dispersed memories of Jay and myself that had begun to plague me. Curiously, however, what filled the gloomy hollow inside me were passages from my book on the Inquisition, maybe because looking at Peter's handsome, silent profile, it was easy for me to imagine him provoking the jealousy and wrath of fanatical, small-minded bishops. The charge against him would have been sorcery, of course. And I seemed to know where he'd have got into trouble. Out of the blue, I told him, 'Majorcans of Jewish ancestry weren't allowed to hold public office, practice certain professions, or even be buried in the main part of the local cemetery for five centuries. All the way from the early fifteenth century when they were forced to convert to Catholicism until 1931. And they were routinely tortured over a lot of that time. Some tried to escape, of course – like in 1688. I've been reading about that attempt. Don't you think it's incredible?'

'Yes, the Chuetas,' he replied. 'It *is* incredible. It's without a doubt the worst instance of prejudice in Spain. Being caught between worlds – it wasn't easy.'

'How did you know what they were called?' I asked.

'I have to know a lot about Spain, too – for my studies of Portuguese history. Their cultures were intimately tied together for many centuries.'

'Have you ever been to Majorca?' I asked.

'No.'

'Are you sure?'

'Yes. Why?'

'I don't know – I had a sudden feeling. You told me when we first met that you thought you might have a Jewish background.'

'My mother may have been. She was adopted. But I only found that out after she died when I discovered some papers she'd kept hidden. Her original name had been Kretchmer – I've been told that ... that there are both Jews and Christians with that name. My father, he was Portuguese. From the Algarve, the southernmost province. From the town of Tavira.

His name was José Pereira dos Santos Castanheira. He was a Catholic, but with that name it's probable that he had Jewish ancestors. Lots of times Jews took the names of trees upon conversion. *Pereira* means *pear tree*, and *castanheira* is the female version of *chestnut tree*. But there's really no way of knowing for sure.'

'I never knew anything about how people like the Chuetas were treated,' I said. 'How prisoners of the Inquisition had all their property stolen by the Church. It's almost like it's a secret. Even though the information is all out there. It's as if we don't want to know. People don't want to admit that certain things happen.'

We crossed the street and walked down the sidewalk fringing Washington Square. In front of the white towers of the Church of St. Peter and Paul, Peter said, 'Yes, we've really got our work cut out for us.'

'Our work cut out?'

'Well, let me see if I can ... let me tell you something about Angola. It happened when I was living back there, when I was a kid. We had this neighbour who often had his servant beaten on his hands. By the police. They'd come around to discipline him.' He motioned me to sit with him on one of the park benches. After we'd made ourselves comfortable, he continued: 'So the first time I saw them hit the palms of his hands with a rod, I became so enraged and frustrated that I began to cry. The next time, I stood on the fence that separated our houses and screamed all the curses I knew at my neighbour. In Portuguese, of course.'

He laughed, full of pleasure in his courage as a boy. He said, 'I called him wonderful things – *camelo, puta de merda* – camel, shit-filled whore. *Camel* is really bad ... really insulting in Portuguese, you see.' We both laughed, and Peter added, 'When I couldn't think of anything else to say, I even called him *hipotenusa* – hypotenuse. I called him anything I could think of to make him stop. He was a filthy man – ignorant, evil. *Hipotenusa* angered him more than the others because he hadn't a clue as to what it meant. He came over to the fence and told me that little kids shouldn't be calling elders bad names and impeding the work of the police.' Peter glared in remembrance. 'When he told me to be quiet, I spit in his face.'

It sounded like something my brother Jay would have done when he was little – before he changed. I asked what happened next.

'Oh, he was furious. He told my mother about me, thinking I'd receive a beating. But my mother, of course, she knew I was right. Though my spitting was somewhat too uncivilized for her. She shook her head at me and observed, as she often did, that I was part angel, part devil. She told the horrible neighbour that I was right, however. Nothing happened to me in the end.'

'Was the servant beaten ever again?'

'Oh, of course. Angola back then – of course. It took a war against Portugal to change all that. And then things got even worse with our civil war. People have been killing each other for fifteen years over there. Though nobody in America knows. You're right about people not wanting to. To change that, we've got a lot of work to do – everywhere. That's what I meant about having our work cut out for us.'

'We'll never change things, Peter. People are always going to kill each other.'

'If … if we could only change language … But to do that, we'd have to allow all our children to think in terms of verse. Kids need to listen closely to the sound of what they say, to imagine the texture … the feel of their words inside the people they talk to.'

'You're crazy,' I laughed.

He shook his head at me, displeased by my incredulity. 'Bill, children are born poets. We all know that. It's adults – we're the ones who force them into prose.'

'I don't get it.'

He shrugged. 'Poetry doesn't fear people who are different.'

I glanced away and didn't try to make a reply because it seemed pointless – our outlooks on life were really very different back then. And his way of talking ... it seemed like a kind of shorthand for which I hadn't learned the rules.

When I faced him again, he was staring down at his feet, his hands scrunched between his legs. His face was elongated, sad.

'What is it?' I asked.

He didn't look up. 'I'm remembering my mother,' he replied.

'How old were you when she died?' I asked.

'Eleven.'

'Had she been ill long?'

'I suppose. She had been in a camp during the war ... World War II. Things happened there. They gave her drugs, chemicals. She never fully recovered.'

I remembered Peter's book on Nazi doctors. Maybe he was searching for her history. I said, 'And after she died, you lived alone with your father?'

'No, no, he was gone somewhere. I never would have known him anyway. My mother only slept with him in order to have me.' Peter looked at me. His eyes shone and his voice gained strength. 'But she had been married once. Back in Europe. Long before I was born. To a beautiful Hungarian man – a Jewish man. She showed me pictures of him.' He smiled at me wistfully. 'But he was gassed in the camps. So after she died, I lived with ... with a couple that the welfare people found for me. It was awful. Then I was taken in, thank goodness, by a relative. You see, I had kept my mother's address books, hidden them. I was so unhappy with the first people who took me in that I wrote to several relatives. The letter to the man who eventually gave me a home must have travelled all the way around Hungary a few times. It was an entire year before the letter reached him. He came to Angola for me – my mother had moved there after the war. This man, he succeeded in getting me out of my foster home with money. He was a cousin of my mother's husband. Very different from most people. Very loving. Then, when he moved to Brazil, I moved with him, of course.'

We sat in silence again. The air between us seemed warmed by a fragility linking me to Peter and his mother. A gratefulness washed over me, one related to his being able to find a new family – related, too, to my thankfulness at the possibility of happy endings in this crumbling world. I felt myself about to cry, but fought successfully against the rising pressure.

Maybe the deep crack in my armour was closing for good. That frightened me; it was as if I were losing something important, were moving forward again, but into a future I no longer wanted.

'And where are your parents?' Peter suddenly asked.

'Oh, my mother lives near New York City,' I said. 'In the ancestral palace on Long Island, in Hicksville. In a big ugly house that looks more or less like all the others in the neighbourhood. My father died a while ago. At this very moment, my mom's watching television in the living-room and smoking. It's what she does. It's what they both used to do.'

'Always?'

'No, when I was little they had other occupations. My father worked as sales manager for a construction company and yelled a lot at everyone. He was Italian, like I said – had come from Naples to America around 1945 or something. My mother, she took care of the house and us kids as best she could. But she drank, and for a while she popped Valium like after-dinner mints. They were both very unhappy people, and they did their best to make things unhappy for Jay and me.'

'When did you leave?' he asked.

'Mentally or physically?'

'Either,' he shrugged.

'Mentally, I grew numb very early. I was a little boy with a head made of Novocaine. Physically, when I went to college.'

'You studied journalism?' he inquired.

'No, that's where I studied music. Journalism came later. I went back to school at Stanford for a year. Got my master's. That's when I moved to the Bay Area. Then I started working.' I shook my head; it seemed silly to be making a living by managing magazines for a multinational monster in downtown San Francisco.

Peter sat back and looked at me critically. The glare from a street lamp lit one side of his face and kept the other in shadow. He said, 'I had the impression you liked your work.'

'Oh, I've learned a lot. But enough is enough. At this point, I'd like to have more contact with people. I think that's why I went into journalism in the first place – to find out about different lives. But it didn't work out that way. I guess I'd prefer writing about something I was more interested in.'

'Like what?'

'I don't even know,' I emphasized. 'That's the silly thing.'

We talked some about American journalism, and when silence returned, I considered what I really wanted to write. I thought of how I used to walk home through the Tenderloin to watch the whores. 'Prostitutes,' I suddenly told Peter.

'What?' he asked.

'I'd write about prostitutes.'

'Anything in particular about them?'

'I don't know. What they think about. How they feel about sex, themselves. How they got started. What they think about what the rest of us are doing. I think it would be interesting to really talk with them.'

I turned and watched cars zooming up Columbus Avenue for a while.

'Have you ever been to one?' Peter asked.

'No, you?'

He shook his head.

Now it was my turn to remember my mother. I was standing on the upstairs landing, watching her as she modelled a gossamer nightgown in front of her three-way mirror. When she noticed my presence, she gave me a lunatic grin. She tugged the cloth from over her shoulder and lifted out one of her breasts to me like a present. It just hung there all fleshy and pink, with the nipple sticking out at me like an alien eye. She must have been drunk or high on Valium. It gave me the creeps even now to remember.

Peter interrupted my daydream to suggest we go somewhere else.

'Where?' I asked.

'An expedition – I've got someone for you to meet.'

'Who?'

'A surprise.' Peter combed his hands back through his hair and raised his eyebrows. He looked both evil and endearing, like Loki in the *Thor* comic books that I used to read as a kid. 'Come on, don't worry so much,' he said to stifle my forthcoming questions.

Chapter 7

PETER AND I walked south on Columbus to Broadway, then turned left toward the Bay. We passed two hawkers promising 'live nude girls' as if they were a novelty not to be missed, took another left down an alley, and ducked down a set of grungy steps covered with brown lettuce leaves. In between two Dumpsters was a brick wall and a single metallic door. It turned out to be the back entrance to a cavernous nightclub. Nasal Arabian music blared over loudspeakers as we entered. Drapes of brown jute hung from the ceiling. A hundred or so people were seated around ottomans covered with glass table-tops. A noisy crowd was standing at a long wooden bar at the back. 'You like it?' Peter asked. I nodded absently; the place didn't seem real, was more like some sort of tourist joke.

We sat down at an orange and red ottoman studded with tiny mirrors. I ordered a double whiskey, indulging my sense of being stuck in some 1940s adventure film. Peter got mineral water and asked the waiter if Mara was singing that night. When the young man shrugged, Peter described her. 'Oh yeah, she's here tonight,' he replied.

'It seems we're in luck,' Peter said.

'Is this the "Mara" from your story – the one about that belt that turned out to be a tapeworm?' I asked. 'The handsome little boy's daughter?'

He nodded.

'This place seems unreal,' I told him.

'Part of it is and part of it isn't,' he replied. 'Like most everything else, I've always found.'

'Everything? I'm not so sure. Some things seem too completely real. Like my life.'

'Yes, Bill, I'm sure everything has a very hard edge right now. I'm sorry.'

We talked some more about the nightclub, and after a few minutes, the whiskey began to make me heavy and tired. A fight broke out just behind us at the bar. I'd never seen anything like it before. Two men in business suits were tugging at each other. Maybe it was the alcohol, but to me, the fight looked as if it were staged. Until one of the men crashed into Peter and fell by our feet. He had short greying hair, thick lips, a wild look in his eyes. A cord of blood was coming from his nose. I absolutely couldn't believe it was happening.

Peter jumped up and glared down at the man with the look of a hawk hunting its prey. He was vibrating with anger. I reached for him. But before I could touch him, he shouted something in Portuguese that made me freeze. With impossibly quick reactions, he grasped the fallen man's wrists and twisted them back over his shoulders.

The man was on his knees and was crying out something desperate. I grabbed one of Peter's arms, but couldn't budge it. Maybe it was my weakness due to too much alcohol. Over and over I shouted his name, and as I pulled at his arm, an electric shock passed through my hands and thumped against my chest. I gasped out of surprise. My heart was racing. I let go of Peter, shouted his name again. He looked at me blankly. He let go. The man fell backward onto his behind.

I'm not sure what happened then; I was too stunned. At some point, I noticed a burly man in a tight-fitting pinstripe suit asking Peter if he was all right. Peter brushed at his trousers with a napkin and said he was fine. He smoothed his hair back over his ears, took a deep breath. He looked pretty much like his old self – calm, handsome.

'Are you okay?' I asked.

'I think so.' He spoke dryly and his eyes closed for a moment.

But he wasn't entirely the same; when he looked at me, I could see that he, too, had been shocked. His eyes were wide open, full of fear, like windows open on a pit inside him.

I wondered if a dwarf had assumed command for a time.

Yet I was so drunk that none of this frightened me. Nothing seemed real. When Peter sat down, I did, too. He watched the band setting up on-stage without moving, without even breathing it seemed. I thought about how astounding it was that when people needed extra force they could somehow find it. And control it; after all, he hadn't broken the man's wrists.

Given a little more anger, he, anyone, might even become a murderer, I thought.

The burly man who had asked Peter if he was all right escorted the businessmen involved in the fight up the stairs and out the door.

I leaned toward Peter. 'Are you *really* all right?' When he nodded, I said, 'Maybe it would be better if we just went home.'

He smoothed his hair once again. 'No, I'm okay. Really. I just scare myself sometimes, the way I react to this world. I must be careful.'

Peter said 'this world' as if there were another one in which he more truly belonged. I wondered if that was Angola or Brazil or somewhere more distant to which he travelled when alone in his room with Maria.

I watched Peter sipping his mineral water and returned for solace to the last drops of my whiskey.

∞

A tiny girl in a black camisole and prairie skirt then stepped out from the wings; Peter leaned toward me and whispered, 'That's Mara.'

She looked like an elf in women's clothing. She couldn't have been more than five feet tall and was fully as thin in relation to her height as Maria the hoopoe. Thick glasses framed her big black eyes, and she seemed to be no more than fifteen – to have just emerged from puberty. She had no womanly contours at all, and her crew cut made her look like a boy from certain angles.

Curiously, her physical awkwardness seemed to manifest something more deeply troubling inside her. She looked as if isolation had made her suffer terribly, as if she were one of a kind and – out of necessity – had learned to regard all other people as large, alien creatures. She could have even been a mutation, I thought.

Mara took a cordless microphone handed to her by the drummer and stood pointing up into the air with both hands. She appeared to be saying goodbye to someone already a long way off. The lights dimmed to red and green. I whispered to Peter, 'I didn't realize she was so young.'

'She isn't,' he replied. 'I'll tell you about her when she's finished the set.'

The bass began a deep, soft, endlessly falling bossa-nova pattern. She began to sing, had a full, throaty voice that contrasted with her size and which would have been more expected in some statuesque Amazon. She sang in Portuguese, mostly folk and bossa-nova melodies, but she also improvised from time to time. She liked to punctuate chords with breathy runs and wild, syncopated leaps that emphasized the difference between her dark lower register and crystalline head voice. Maybe because of her pixie quality, she had great stage presence. You wanted to follow her as she pranced, were curious about the way she forced her eyelids closed to reach for a note or twisted her mouth to capture a phrase. After my initial surprise and fear, I let myself swirl inside her voice. I ordered another double whiskey and allowed the music to lead me down into a misty, hypnotized landscape. Once in a while, I came out of the fog to catch phrases. All I really remember was her growling the words *assombrada do futuro* over and over. She sang this phrase as if she were summoning the strength to stand up to a continent of enemies.

When she finished her set, she smiled broadly. Her dark eyes shone with pleasure.

'She's quite a figure,' I told Peter.

'Oh yes, she is,' he said proudly.

'What's *assombrada do futuro* mean?' I asked.

'What?'

'From the song ... She kept singing it over and over.'

'Oh, it's a song she wrote. It means, "haunted from the future."'

'From the future?' I asked.

'Mara believes in hidden relations between events and people – occult explanations, I guess you could say. And she thinks we've got three choices when it comes to ghosts. They're either entities who haunt you because they're fixated on your house, stuck there, so to speak ... that's number one. Or they're repressed moments from your own past come back to get revenge. That's the one favoured by psychologists and nineteenth-century novelists. Or they're really from the future. You see? That's what nobody ever seems to consider.'

'No, I don't see,' I said. 'I don't get it at all.'

'Imagine you could go back into the past and help yourself at a difficult moment ... or someone else. Your brother, for instance, when confronting your father. At a moment ... a turning point. So that maybe he wouldn't take up so much of your father's personality. Wouldn't you do it? Wouldn't you go back and help you and your brother?'

'I suppose.'

'Well, a ghost is someone from your future come back to help you. A friend. Or maybe even yourself.'

'That's crazy,' I said.

Peter smiled broadly. 'That's more or less what I expected you to say.'

'Why's that?'

'Possibilities that you don't understand frighten you. You'd rather not feel that fear, so you call them crazy. It's your way of dismantling reality, of dismissing things from consideration.'

He spoke in a challenging voice, as if I were being unwisely stubborn about not accepting the possibility that visitors from my own future were the spirits who'd possessed my house.

On Peter's insistence, we got up and walked through a concrete hallway to Mara's dressing-room. I followed him sheepishly.

He knocked at a wooden door painted cerulean blue and called her name. She peered out as if she could barely see without her glasses, her made-up eyes looking like butterfly wings. When she realized who it was, she rushed into his arms.

Peter caressed Mara's cheek with his hand. 'This is my friend Bill,' he said with a wave toward me.

Mara took a step back to assess me. 'A pleasure to meet you,' she smiled.

She had a tinkly voice, delicate, and she spoke with no trace of a foreign first language – probably because she had such a good ear. Later, I would discover that when she was anxious, she'd sometimes slip into a Brazilian accent. I shook a hand no bigger than a child's. 'You were great,' I said.

'Thanks a lot.'

As we looked at each other, I saw that she was indeed older than I first had thought. I was judging by the wrinkles at her eyes, where a life of work seemed to show.

Mara turned back to Peter and slapped his shoulder. 'But why didn't you tell me you'd come tonight? I would have sung something special.' She frowned, put her hands on her hips, and leaned all her weight on her back leg in mock righteousness.

'I didn't know we were,' he answered.

She melted into a grin and took his arm. 'Look, if you'll

wait a little while, I'll go out with you.' She nodded at me. 'What do you think, is it okay?'

'Of course,' I said.

'I'll be ready in fifteen minutes. I'll meet you where ... at the bar?'

'Fine,' Peter said.

She popped back inside with a tiny, girlish wave at me. We walked into the nightclub. 'You gave me quite a scare when you nearly broke that man's wrists,' I told him.

Peter shrugged. 'I'm fine. I can control it when I need to.'

'What exactly do you mean by "it"?'

'I suppose it's a certain revulsion for the ugliness of this world,' he replied.

We stood at the corner of the bar. I wanted to make some philosophical reply, but couldn't think of anything. 'So how old is she, about forty?' I asked.

'A little older.'

'On stage, I thought she looked fifteen.'

'Mara was very ill when she was young.' Peter puffed out his lips as if giving in to fate. 'She had some sort of tumours that had to be removed. They were connected with her hormonal system, and so she never fully developed. She ages, but as a girl or boy might age – without ever fully becoming an adult.'

'She wouldn't mind me knowing that?'

'No, why should she?'

'It's very personal,' I observed.

'Yes. But she would trust you. And it doesn't matter. No one could hurt her with it any longer.'

'It must have been difficult,' I said.

'She's used to it now. And she can have a normal life ... sex. Just no kids. And you know, nobody gets away easy.'

'That sounds funny coming from you,' I remarked.

'Why do you say that?'

I smiled, embarrassed at revealing the edges of my jealousy.

But it didn't seem to matter. 'Come on,' I said. 'You must know that you're handsome. People must have told you all your life.'

'Some. You think I am?'

'Gimme a break. Of course.'

'And so, what does that make me?' he inquired.

'Oh, please ... it gives you an advantage over other people. Over people who look like me.'

'And so what do you look like?' he asked, as if he already knew and just wanted to hear me say it.

'No need to be patronizing,' I replied.

'I'm not being patronizing. I just think it's ridiculous. Don't you think I have my quirks ... my handicaps ... ? I can't even talk your language properly.'

'It's not the same. Your sense of smell ... your flowers ... your objects ... It's not the same. You've got odd things. But your face doesn't reveal them. *That's* the point.'

'So maybe it's all a beautiful lie. I'm not sure that's an advantage. It means that people I meet have expectations about a person I'm not. And who knows what will happen in the future? I could get ill. I could die in a year, for all we know.'

His mentioning his own death really upset me. I wanted to tell him not to talk so glibly about leaving me behind, but was afraid I'd sound dependent and weak. He bought me another whiskey. Looking at him through the amber distortions of my glass, I knew I'd be jealous of those born beautiful for my entire life. Possibly even after that, after my own time on earth was history. Though maybe angels can't feel jealousy, don't have emotions. Yet if they don't, then what *do* they have?

'How old are you?' I asked Peter.

'Me. Let's see, I'm forty this year. Yeah, I was born in forty-six.'

'You look a little older,' I said.

'My soul has been roaming around sniffing things for a long time,' he smiled.

I laughed. Mara arrived in jeans and what looked like a boy's lumberjack coat. Her make-up was gone. Maybe she really was an elf, because there was something spontaneously magical and sweet about her.

I guess I was staring, because she looked at me with a big smile. 'The transformation?' she asked.

'Yes,' I said.

'A snake has shed its skin.' She laughed, took my elbow, and stuck her tongue out at Peter as we left the bar.

'You think of yourself as a snake?' I asked.

'No, I'm ... I'm more of a ... what, Peter? Any ideas?'

Peter opened the door for us. He frowned for a moment, then exclaimed, 'A golden pheasant!'

'Ooh, that sounds nice,' Mara agreed. 'A bird ... like Maria! So I guess we could say I've just molted.'

'You know Maria?' I asked.

Mara nodded. 'Of course. Maria and I have been friends for years.'

She took Peter's arm as well. Their eyes shared amusing secrets. About the bird, perhaps. We walked together as a chain, Mara in the middle. While they talked in Portuguese, I thought about hoopoes and pheasants and hummingbirds given human form.

∞

We sat outside at Enrico's. Peter ordered a rum baba and cheesecake for himself. He sniffed with canine interest at both of them before gorging himself. I had yet another Jack Daniel's, figuring they could always attach wheels and pull me home. Mara ordered brandy, but she mostly swirled it around her snifter.

After about a half hour of talk about the various scents of flowers in Brazil's coastal rain forest, Peter said to Mara, 'Among other reasons, we came to see you tonight because Bill is curious about prostitutes. He's trained as a journalist, but is stuck writing things he doesn't want to. He may want to interview some prostitutes.'

Embarrassment made me shiver. I couldn't speak.

Mara was examining me with a critical look, as if trying to determine whether I was trustworthy.

Peter said, 'Mara used to be a prostitute, you see. Here in San Francisco, she counsels people, some of them prostitutes, at a . . . a what?' He looked to Mara for help.

'A social service agency funded by the city,' she answered. She resumed swirling the brandy around her glass and stared into it as if trying to divine a prophecy. When she looked up at me, her wide-open eyes expressed curiosity. 'So what exactly do you want to talk to them about?'

I was unable to find a clever way out of the trap. 'Nothing . . . I mean, I . . . I didn't know that Peter meant to discuss this with you.'

'Prostitutes would be really interesting to write about,' Mara said with a reassuring nod. 'No one ever says anything except romanticized things about them – or evil things, you know, punishing things.'

Peter strummed an imaginary lyre and added, 'The harlot with the big heart.' He gave me a questioning look and shrugged. 'People are afraid of whores, don't you think? They're like walking, talking genitalia.'

'And proof that torture produces results,' Mara interjected. 'That's what I find.' She leaned toward me. 'It's like what happened to me. After my father and mother died, my grandmother wasn't prepared to raise me as a kid. More like a tiny adult. It was okay until I had my medical problems. I had these . . .'

Peter rested his hand on hers. 'I told him,' he said gently.

'Oh, good. Then you can understand how disturbed I was. But my grandmother, after the operation, she thought me useless, a . . .' Mara looked at Peter . . . '*Sanguessuga*? What's the translation?'

'Leech,' Peter answered.

'She thought me a leech. She called me that once.' Mara shook her head, looked at me as if asking me to conceive of the impossible. 'So, when I got better, I ran – ran far away,' she continued. 'To São Paulo. And when I got started as a prostitute, it just seemed like the only thing to do.' She spoke in a whisper, 'You'd be surprised how many men liked making love with someone who looks like a teenager. I was very popular.' She laughed critically in a single exhale. 'I'd really like you to write something ... anything ... anything that's true. Writing the truth is what's important. It would be a very good thing to do. Peter's right, though. People are too afraid of them, of their sex. Don't you think you are?'

An image of a drunken banshee wearing a black lace slip came to me. It was the persona my mother had chosen in her desperation to try to attract my father's attention. I said, 'Don't know – maybe so.'

Mara said, 'I'll take you to meet some if you like.' She slapped the top of my hand playfully. 'You can just talk. And who knows, it might be fun. I'm working with someone now who's very nice. Maybe we could start with her.'

'Is it Rain?' Peter asked.

'That's right.'

'"Rain"?' I asked.

'A nickname,' Mara replied.

As I gulped down my whiskey, I thought: *please give me the strength to say 'no' to her.* For it was suddenly obvious that I wanted to hide for the rest of my life, to prevent the outside world from intruding into my home.

Mara wrote her address and phone number on a slip of paper, pushed it into my hand. 'If you don't find it interesting,' she said, 'you quit.'

I nodded.

She worked most nights, she explained, so we made a date

to meet the following Saturday afternoon at her house. She said that she'd try to get Rain to talk with me.

I decided that I'd back out at the last minute.

She and Peter got me home. I fell asleep right away.

Chapter 8

I WOKE UP with a crust sealing my eyelids together. My head throbbed and my back muscles felt as if they'd been hibernating for months inside a dank cave. My neck seemed to be moulded around a rusty chain.

As I warmed myself in a hot bath, I remembered another dream. I was with Peter in the woods, gathering acorns into a burlap sack. They were to feed Maria. Then the scene shifted; Peter was running again over the fences I'd envisioned the night before, only this time he had the triangular piece of wood he'd given me, was holding it up over his head as if carrying a sword. He stopped dead in front of a woman concealed by shadows. He handed her the wood. Around them was a city of crumbling walls and exposed foundations. All the way out at the horizon smoke was ribboning into a grey sky.

Sitting in the bath and remembering all this, I had the feeling that I had been carried back to Eastern Europe, just after the Second World War.

It seemed odd that my house was still standing, that I was alive, that the present world existed.

After work, while reading in the evening calm, I looked out the window of my room and even expected there to be snow on the ground. I was surprised the plants were green, that it was warm and sunny. It was then that I saw one of the images from my dream that had been hidden from me: Peter had been running over a ground blanketed with snow. The charred city and woman in shadow were dusted with flakes. And I realized that this storm was still happening somewhere inside me, that a reflection of me was living even now in the dream. That alarmed me. I didn't know why till the next night.

The dream continued. In it, I was in my house all alone, eating at the kitchen table, devouring the acorns that we'd gathered. They were terribly bitter, just the way they'd tasted when I'd tried them once as a kid. Even so, I kept munching away. I don't know where Peter and Maria were. But I could feel their watchful presence. When I looked out the window, I saw a San Francisco reduced to smoking rubble, as if after the 1906 earthquake. Smoke and snow. Ruined buildings. Bodies scattered across the ground. But I just kept eating.

Recalling these images made me realize for the first time that my dream world wasn't stagnant, wasn't a haphazard landscape of unconnected stories, but was rather more like a film. Time passed inside that inner world as surely as in my waking life, though not necessarily in sequential ways that could be easily ordered. A story was unfurling inside me, progressing toward some end. And yet I didn't even know who the writer was, Peter or me – or even what part I was playing.

∽

A keen unwillingness to disappoint Peter made me keep my appointment with Mara that Saturday. She lived in the Mission, on Eighteenth Street between Valencia and Guerrero, in an ornate Victorian house painted violet with a sky-blue and yellow trim. When I arrived, billowy white clouds were passing overhead. Their cottony exuberance was very unusual for San Francisco, and I took it as a good omen.

I approached Mara's door and the upcoming expedition as if it were a dive off a cliff into a cove below – with the promise that I would do it just once to prove my courage. She answered my knock wearing a black gaucho hat with a red plume arching a foot behind her into the air. To my expression of surprise, she said, 'I like to be a little extravagant when visiting prostitutes.'

The combination of the hat and her elfin face made me realize I liked her a lot. 'I guess so,' I smiled. 'Where are your glasses?'

She shook her head. 'Oh, those are just for the stage. My protection against the audience.' She gestured to her eyes. 'Contact lenses for everyday life.'

She was ready, so we got into my car. 'Where to?' I asked.

'The Tenderloin, or would you prefer Polk Street? You want women I assume?'

'What's my other choice?'

'Boys – hustlers. We could even find you a transsexual or two if you're interested.'

'You're kidding, I hope?'

'No, not at all,' she declared.

'Too weird, too subterranean,' I said. 'I don't want to descend all the way down into the underworld, just poke my head a little way inside.'

She grinned as if she knew something I didn't.

'What?' I asked.

'Your morality is showing,' she said.

'You think so?'

'Yup, I sure do.'

'I have gay friends at work – it doesn't bother me.'

She laughed, let her body go limp. 'Excuse me while I gag.'

'I really think you're jumping to conclusions.'

'Maybe so.' She let her hand drop to my thigh for a moment. I felt a contracting twinge in my groin, the first in weeks. It seemed that the ghosts and tears hadn't blocked those pathways permanently, after all.

We shared the smile of mysterious possibilities. It would be almost like sleeping with a kid. Or maybe an older woman.

'Let's get going,' Mara said.

I headed to the corner of Jones and O'Farrell; Mara said that Rain usually worked there on Saturday afternoons. We talked about Peter as we drove. 'We met in Brazil, through William,' she explained.

'Who's William?'

'He raised Peter. And he took me in after I ran away from my grandmother. He's an amazing man. He bought a house here when Peter was transferred to San Francisco.'

'The relative who came from Hungary to get him?' I asked.

'That's right.'

He must have been the *friend* Peter had argued with just before moving into my house. 'He followed Peter here?'

'They're very close,' Mara explained.

'Sounds strange to have moved here though.'

'You think so? Me, I think that moving so that you can be near someone you love ... I think it's quite reasonable behaviour.'

'Maybe, maybe not. I don't know. Peter's a strange guy anyway,' I said, using the opportunity to elicit some explanations.

Mara shook her head. 'Yes and no. Once you get to know him, what he does, you know, it makes sense.'

'It does?'

'I think so,' she said, as if someone else might not.

When she changed the subject to prostitutes, I was convinced that she wanted to conceal something. But I made no protest. We discussed pimps, prices, drugs. Mara wasn't sure of the going rates. 'I don't even ask any more. It's not what really concerns me. I'm interested in getting them to find out what they really want to do with their lives.'

I was parking as she said this. As I took out the ignition key, she squeezed my hands. 'We only get one life, after all,' she said. 'It's too important to waste on fucking strangers we don't really care about. Don't you think?'

I got the distinct feeling that Peter had told her more about my sexual past than I liked.

∞

We found Rain on Jones Street, near the corner of O'Farrell. She looked like Shelley Duvall with those sunken eyes and puffed lids, a thin, wan, sickly face. Decked out in red hot-pants, a matching yellow tube top and feather boa, and a pink fake-fur jacket, she looked like a kid experimenting with her image. When we approached her, she shifted her floppy leather bag over her shoulder, bent down and kissed Mara's cheek. 'You're back,' she said with an amused twist to her mouth.

'Yeah, with a friend. This is Bill Ticino.' Mara explained what I wanted. 'Is that okay?' she asked, scrunching up her nose as if to apologize beforehand.

'Sure,' Rain said dryly. She pointed a finger at me as if to keep me in my place and said, 'Normally, I'd charge even for a conversation. But not for a friend of Mara's.'

We walked to a deli at Polk and O'Farrell. I offered the girl anything she wanted from the menu, but all she asked for was coffee. 'Watching my weight,' she explained.

'You too?' I asked.

'You too who?'

'I have this theory that every woman in America is on a diet.'

She laughed, took off her jacket.

We sat at a table in the back. I distributed the coffees and took out my notepad. Rain folded her arms in front of her chest as if she were chilled. In an amused voice, she asked me, 'So, has our dear Mara convinced you with her theories about me?'

'No, I don't think so.' I looked at Mara questioningly.

'I just think that Rain is special,' Mara said.

The girl scoffed. 'Sure I am ... special ... real special.' She leaned over the table and slurped her coffee without unfolding her arms. 'Where you from?' she asked me.

'New York originally. But I live here now. For eight years. I have a little house near Fillmore Street. Where are you from?'

She tilted her head up and squinted. 'North Carolina.'

'Which part?'

'Look, man, it's all the same,' she sighed. 'Same people, same streets, same pets.'

'Why's the city important?' Mara asked me.

'I just thought it was worth knowing.'

Rain rolled her eyes. 'I'm telling ya, it's all the same.'

I wrote *a bit cantankerous* on my pad. 'Is North Carolina where you started as a prostitute?' I asked.

'No, unless you consider fucking my daddy so he wouldn't beat me up prostitution.'

I scribbled her answer. When I looked up, I saw in the girl's cunning eyes that she'd hoped to have shocked me. I wanted to show her that it hadn't worked. 'Did your dad fuck you often?' I asked.

'Mostly when there wasn't anything good on TV.'

Mara grinned.

I said, 'And do you think that that contributed to you be-coming a prostitute?'

The question sounded silly as soon as I asked it, and Rain laughed from the belly. 'You're too fuckin' much,' she said. After she'd lit a cigarette, she leaned away from the table and took out a hairbrush from her bag. Propping her cigarette in a foil ashtray, she ducked down and spread her tresses in a cur-tain in front of her face. In this position, like a giraffe bent to drink at a watering hole, she combed her hair. 'Go on, I can hear ya,' she said.

Her face was completely hidden behind the veil of her hair.

'So you started when you came to San Francisco?' I asked.

'Right.' She straightened up, tossed her hair back on her shoulders and continued brushing.

'How long ago was that?'

'Two years.'

'And why'd you start?'

She fluffed her hair with her brush as if she were whisking

eggs. 'Beats working in McDonald's,' she said. She stuffed her brush back in her bag.

'Does it really?'

'You wanta work for three and a half bucks an hour serving people those fuckin' McNuggets, have fun, mister.' She poked her tongue into her cheek, then licked it back and forth over her lips. 'That life ain't for me.'

I jotted down a note about her tongue, then took another question from my notes. 'How old were you when you started?'

She shifted in her seat and fluttered her eyelids. 'Don't you know you're not supposed to ask a lady that?' she said in the voice of a Southern belle, looking at Mara as if their solidarity went beyond the comprehension of a man.

'Well, why'd you come to San Francisco then?'

'Why San Francisco or why'd I leave home?' she asked. In her irritation, her voice had dropped a good part of an octave, and I suddenly realized how husky it was. She sounded as if she smoked and drank too much.

'Let's begin with why you left home,' I said.

'I guess I got tired of my dad's cock. And sick of my mom too – the bitch knew everything.'

'She knew about you and your dad?'

'Yeah.'

'And she didn't do anything?'

Rain laughed. 'She was scared shitless of the motherfucker. She said just to wait and when I'd be eighteen I could escape.'

'How old were you when it started?'

'Can't remember.'

'Eight, ten, fourteen?'

'Like ten, maybe.'

'So she wanted you to wait eight years?' I asked.

'I don't think she knew till I was maybe twelve.'

'Six years, then.'

Rain nodded, went on to explain she'd come to San Francisco because she'd liked the way the city looked in films. She bragged about her fees, said she didn't work with a pimp, and had only been beaten up once by a client – or *date* as she called them. 'Let's just say my nose ain't this crooked naturally,' she told me.

As for complaints, she despised vice cops and drug dealers. 'Attracts the same kind of asshole, people without souls – they get their kicks beating up kids.'

'You use drugs?' I asked.

'Just a little Valium,' she replied.

'Why Valium?'

She rubbed her fingers across her cheekbones. 'Makes my face relax, look more feminine.'

As I wrote down her words, it never occurred to me that they might be significant. I asked, 'How much do you take?'

'A pill every few hours.'

'How many milligrams?'

'Are you for real? I don't have any fuckin' idea.'

'Where do you get it?'

'On the street.'

'Did you take drugs when you were a kid – I mean when you were with your mom and dad?'

'No, but you can bet your ass I drank some.'

'What'd you drink?'

'What was around the house. Mostly beer. Mom and Dad drank a lot of beer.'

'Was your dad usually drunk when he raped you?'

She took a rushed drag on her cigarette, glaring at me as if I were her enemy. 'Would that have excused it or something? Fuck, man, is that what you're saying?'

'No, not at all,' I replied.

Mara covered my hand with hers for a moment and spoke gently with Rain. 'Bill only meant that some people lose their inhibitions when they drink. Maybe having a six-pack and abusing you were tied together. That's all.'

'He was drunk sometimes.' She fiddled with her tube top to regain her composure. 'He stank. You ever make love to anyone who stank like a garbage can?'

'No,' I replied.

'I didn't think so. Well, it ain't much fun. You end up smelling like shit yourself. Getting his stink off me was a full-time job.'

'Sorry.'

'Yeah, right. Sure ya are.'

'My wife was nuts for showers,' I said. 'She'd shower twice a day sometimes.'

'Christ – she must have been just perfect,' Rain said sarcastically, hiding a grin as if she could somehow tell that things had gone very wrong between us, but not wanting to offend me more than was necessary.

'We're separated now.'

'Everybody's separated these days.' She took a greedy inhale on her cigarette, shifted in her seat – she was getting impatient. She opened her bag and started rummaging for something. 'So what else you wanta know?'

'Tell me more about your dad,' I said.

Without looking up she said, 'Him? He wasn't very interesting. He was just a big fat slob.'

'All the same.'

She came up with an open pack of Wrigley's Spearmint gum. 'You want some?' She pulled out the tip of one of the sticks and held it out to me.

'No thanks.'

She turned to Mara. 'How 'bout you, honey?'

Mara took the offering and smiled mischievously at me. 'We didn't have gum in Brazil when I was growing up. It still seems a bit exotic and dangerous.'

Rain and Mara started chewing away. It was disconcerting.

'So, where were we?' the girl asked.

'Your dad – it would be good to know something more about him. Like what he did for a living.'

'He was assistant manager of a bank – Carolina Central Bank. In fuckin' Chapel Hill, as a matter of fact.' She tossed her head back and began doing what sounded like a bad imitation of Peter Lorre: 'You efil man – you beat that answer out uff me! I didn't want to tell you.' She laughed from her gut at that. Mara giggled.

I was pleased by the coincidence of Rain's being from Chapel Hill and my having gone to college just ten miles away in Durham. I said, 'Where was the bank? I mean, where in Chapel Hill?'

'Right on Rosemary Street – the main drag.'

'How far from the Carolina Coffee Shop?'

She started, pulling her head back like a hen. Squinting at me, she said, 'Hey, man, you know Chapel Hill?'

'I went to college at Duke, class of 1975.'

'That's kind of cool, Bill,' she said, nodding, chewing her gum. Then she winked at me. I wasn't sure what that meant. Maybe she thought she knew what I was like because I went to Duke, that I'd led a privileged life.

'I got a scholarship and some loans,' I rushed to add. 'We couldn't have afforded it otherwise.'

'Hey, man, good for you.' The offhand way she said it ... I could tell she really did think I'd had it easy. I knew I was an idiot for even caring, but for a moment, I couldn't think of what to ask. Mara said, 'What was your dad saying to you after he raped you?'

'You mean, *what did he used to say?*'

'That's right.'

Rain smiled at me. 'I like it when Mara makes a mistake in English. I like translating for her. It's like I've got an extra job or something.' She took a last drag on her cigarette. As she was stubbing it out, some smoke got in her eyes. Rubbing them carefully, so as not to smudge her mascara, she said, 'He used to say that I was real good. Not like he meant that I was a good girl. More like I was good in bed.' She leaned toward us and whispered. 'He said I had a nice tight pussy. He said I was a little bitch who wanted it. He said I needed it, too – like I was the one who asked him.'

She leaned back again, and her eyes opened wide with a kind of evil humour. 'And do you know what he told me the first time? Get this – the fucker said that all little girls lose their "cherry" to their daddy. And you know what – this is the great thing...' She laughed in an ironic exhale. 'I was such a fuckin' bimbo that I believed him!'

'You weren't a bimbo,' Mara said gently. 'You were only maybe ten years old. You wanted to believe your daddy. And you didn't want to think he was a bad man.'

'Hey, if I want a damn psychiatrist I'll pay for one!' Rain snapped. 'I make more money than you, you know. I can afford it.'

'We know you make more money than I do,' Mara said calmly. 'That's not the point. And I wasn't analysing you. I was only stating a fact.'

'Why don't you just state facts about yourself? I don't want to be no fuckin' fact for you. I don't want to be a fact, *period!*'

Rain lit another cigarette. She hugged her arms around her chest as if she were real cold again. The three of us were silent for a while. I lifted the girl's coffee cup and handed it to her. 'Drink, you'll be warmer.'

She took it from me and nodded her thanks. I realized she was fighting tears – angry tears. She took a big gulp.

'My father never raped me,' I said. 'But he did something else.' I don't know what came over me then, but I started to talk about my dad's Ethiopian keepsake. I guess it was partially Peter's influence. I mean, feeling comfortable telling a story to other people. And I wanted Rain and Mara to know that I was broken, too – not so different from them.

As I spoke, what my father had done half a century before – how he'd cut away the *niente* and saved it in his silver jug – came to represent, in some crazy inexplicable way, everything in my *own* life that could never be repaired or made good. Afterward, Mara caressed my arm and excused herself. 'I've got to go ... go outside for a moment,' she said. Tears were caught in her lashes.

'I'm sorry I upset you, Mara.'

'It's okay, I'm glad you told me,' she whispered. 'I just need fresh air.'

When we were alone, Rain said, 'Hey, man, your father was a real fuckin' asshole, wasn't he?' When I nodded, she added, 'And you still don't know if he was telling the truth?'

'No, and I never will either.'

She said in an encouraging voice, 'Hey, Bill, you want a Valium?'

'No thanks.'

'I've got some right here in my bag. It's no trouble.'

I shook my head. I was feeling distant from myself. Maybe because it was the first time I'd told that story to anyone. Even Alexandra didn't know. I guess I didn't want her or anyone else to think my dad was a bad man. Or *I* didn't want to have to think he was. Which is undoubtedly why I added now, 'Dad could be nice sometimes. He worked real hard, too. I mean, we never went without food or clothing or anything. It must have been hard for him coming to America. And I think maybe he did love us in his own strange way.'

'Valium is really super for stress,' the girl repeated. 'I couldn't get through a single fuckin' day without it.'

I thanked her again, but refused.

'My mom was the weird one in my family,' she volunteered. 'I mean, Dad was kinda predictable. I'll give that to the fat slob. I pretty much knew when he was going to come kiss me good-night and stay a little longer than he should.' She closed her eyes. 'I knew that if I just squeezed my eyelids tight and let him do what he wanted that I wouldn't get any more bruises. I knew if I tried hard enough I could make myself go really dead down there. And I knew that he couldn't stop me from leaving his fuckin' house forever when I decided it was time to go. I knew it.' Her eyes popped open. I noticed her jaw throbbing. 'But my mom – now there was a lady you couldn't predict. She used to volunteer at the Student Health Clinic, you know. And when I was little, she was always running around for the PTA – was on all sorts of committees. She once organized a whole fuckin' health fair at the school around the theme of drug abuse – all by herself. I mean, everything from lining up speakers to getting the place decorated. And she got really big people. You know the guy with the beard ... the Surgeon General? – Cooper or something.'

'C. Everett Koop,' I corrected.

'Yeah, him. Well, he came. He gave a whole speech. My mom picked him up at the airport and everything. I met him. He seemed like a nice man, but kinda stiff. Anyway, I'm sure he thought my mom was the greatest – a hard worker, intelligent, good cook ... Everybody thought she was just perfect. Like your wife, I guess – two showers and everything. But the thing was, I could never ever depend on her for a fuckin' thing. Other people could, but me ... her daughter, I couldn't. That's what was really weird.'

Mara came back inside and rested her hands on my shoulders. She squeezed the muscles there till the pain was so sharp that I yelped.

Rain began laughing, but good-naturedly.

'What was that?' I asked, jerking around to face Mara.

'A sudden physical intervention sometimes helps,' she answered.

I was about to ask what she was talking about, but Rain said, 'Don't worry, she's done it to me, too. Nothing ever gets broken or anything.'

Mara sat back down. When I repeated for her benefit all the good things I could think of about my father, she said, 'Bill, don't work so hard.'

I turned back to Rain. We both shrugged as if to suggest that life was way beyond our control. I took a deep breath. 'So where'd you get the name "Rain"?' I asked.

That seemed to bother her. She smiled nervously.

'God,' she whispered.

'God gave you your name?'

She nodded, jumped up. 'Hey, you guys are a lot of fun, but I gotta go.'

'So soon?' I said. 'I thought we were just...'

'Gotta get going.' She snapped her fingers. 'Time is money.'

'Just a few more questions, okay?'

'Gotta go – really.'

When she grabbed her bag, I pushed a few of my cards in front of her. 'What are these for?' she asked.

'In case you want to talk some more. Give a couple to your friends to call me. Maybe we can do a better interview after I've done this a few more times.'

'Right, sure. Nice to meet you.' She grinned at Mara as if I was being silly, then strode off.

∞

That was all the interviewing we did that day. On the way back to Mara's house, I imagined what it would be like to kiss her. Right away, I grew sad. I had no idea why. When I stopped the car in front of her house, I sensed my body suspended in time, locked inside unhappiness like one of those immobile figurines in glass paperweights.

She smiled sweetly at me. 'In some ways, I'd like to go to bed with you,' she said. 'But not now. Call me. Tell me how you're doing on the story.'

That was it. She patted my leg and hopped out of the car. In an instant, she was inside her house.

Part of me felt discarded, another part reprieved. And I was stunned that my thoughts had been so obvious. How strange sexuality was. Mine seemed really to have tilted off its axis. Maybe my body was now imbued with the knowledge that going to bed with Mara – whom I knew I'd never truly love – was as absurd as making love to all those other women. Though more likely it was just a momentary upset.

When I got home, I was relieved to be with Peter. For all his hermetic strangeness, I realized that I felt at ease in his presence. Leaning over the keyboard on Alex's piano, he was playing Mussorgsky's *Pictures at an Exhibition*, grumbling to himself in Portuguese as he coaxed thundering chords from the printed page. After his final cadence, I applauded. He stood up, swivelled his neck toward me like an owl, and looking over his nose, thanked me.

'It was beautiful,' I said.

He gave me a little bow. 'So did it go well with Mara?' he asked.

'Okay, I guess.'

'You saw Rain?'

'Uh-hum ... we spoke for a while,' I said.

Peter listened carefully as I told him about the interview, then lifted his sheet music and stood up. 'Sorry, I'd like to talk some more,' he smiled. 'But I've got to go out soon.'

He went to his room. I went to the kitchen and made myself tea.

A few minutes later, I heard him leave the house. I decided to water the plants in the back yard, was up to the gladiolus when I spotted an elderly man walking around the side of the house toward Peter's entrance. He was maybe seventy, tall, skinny, slightly hunchbacked, and he was wrapped inside an immense grey trench coat that was far too bulky for the balmy weather. He took cautious steps around the roots of the plum trees, as if he were in a treacherous marshland. His eyes were dark, deeply set, and his grey hair was scattered in mad tufts. His nose and cheekbones jutted out, giving his face a gaunt appearance. Behind him, catching up, was a tall young woman or man — it was hard to tell which. Her disproportionately long arms and broad shoulders gave her a distorted, ungainly walk. At first I thought she was a woman, because she wore a tight black dress, which emphasized her lean contours. But the closer she got, the more I saw that she had an angular masculine face — even stubble on her chin. She or he was maybe twenty-five, had straight brown hair cut in a crude line at the shoulders and an impossibly pale face. She looked as if she'd led a life of forced seclusion. Reaching the old man, she or he took his elbow and helped him across the roots.

I watched this quiet drama and made no effort to catch their attention. The man knocked at Peter's door. When no one answered, he glanced around and spotted me. His escort helped him forward.

'Hello, I was just looking for Peter,' he called. 'I thought he was home, but he doesn't seem to be here.' He spoke with a thick accent that was hard to place, had a voice that sounded too deep and resonant to be natural. I walked forward, and as we came together, he put out his left hand to shake. 'I'm afraid my right one doesn't work,' he explained. His hand was cold and hard. It surrounded mine. His escort stopped by his side. We nodded at each other, and she or he smiled coyly. It disturbed me.

'You must be Bill,' the man continued.

'That's right. Are you a friend of Peter's?' I asked.

'Yes, William Schreiber.'

So this was William, Peter's surrogate father. I was surprised at the sudden rush of warmth for him in my heart. I smiled and said, 'I'm really glad to meet you.'

'This is Lee,' he said, presenting his companion.

I said, 'Nice to meet you, too,' and shook his or her hand. It was delicate and feminine.

William gave me a concerned look. 'So Peter's all comfortably moved in, I hope.'

'I think so. He and Maria have adjusted well. I know it was difficult for him to come.'

'And how are you enjoying having him?'

'Oh, we seem to get along well. He's a nice person. Incredibly talented. I like him a lot.'

William twisted his lips into a contemptuous frown. 'Nice? I'd never describe Peter as nice.'

I was stunned to silence. I looked away to gather myself, and when I turned back, they were both staring at me with puzzled faces, as if I were a curiosity. I said, 'I'll tell him you stopped by,' then picked up my watering can.

'Good to meet you,' I added. 'If you'll excuse me, I've got plants to attend to.'

'Wait a moment,' William said, urgency in his voice. He turned to Lee. 'Something to write with, my dear. And some paper.'

Lee lifted a pen and card from her leather bag. She held the card in her hand while William wrote a message. He handed it to me. I made sure that I didn't touch any of his fingers, as if he were as bloated with danger as my father.

'It's for Peter ... please give it to him,' William said. When I agreed, he began staring at me as if assessing the nature of my particular inferiority.

'Anything more I can do for you?'

Without pause or reply, William turned and headed away. Lee took his elbow to offer assistance. By the plum trees, she glowered back in my direction as if I'd insulted them. Then William reached behind and seemed to take an invisible hand, to pull someone along with him.

As they disappeared from view, I realized that my own hands had formed defensive fists. It was as if I'd just confronted my father. I tucked William's card in my shirt pocket without looking at it and continued watering the plants.

I was unsuccessful in my attempt to forget that they had come.

Back in the house, I couldn't resist reading William's message. It was one sentence in a foreign language. Hungarian, I speculated. It occurred to me that that must have been the language on the wooden amulet, as well. And that this message for Peter was something I was supposed to see, but not understand.

In my living-room, I spun my globe and settled on Eastern Europe. I thought of Rain being raped by her father, taking megadoses of Valium to look more relaxed and feminine. She seemed to be poisoning herself into a premature grave. And I feared that the lessons of her parents had been learned only too well, that she was trying to drug herself into being a *real good girl* – for Daddy. Maybe it was my gloomy mood, but it seemed then as if the two of us were surprisingly alike – repeatedly welcoming the punishments of the past while looking each time for a different and happier ending that never comes.

Chapter 9

*A*s a little boy, I used to sneak into my parents' bedroom when they weren't home. Tingling with excitement, I'd search through their closets and drawers for the treasures of clothing and toiletries they contained. The smell and feel of their worlds filled me with a closeness to them that I could never achieve in person.

I was also searching, I think, for an entrance to their adult universe.

Of my mother, I particularly recall her nightgowns – translucent, salmon-coloured veils invested with the heady smell of her French perfume. I also remember a black lacquer jewellery box on her dresser in which I could see my nervous, ghostly reflection.

Of my father, I was most impressed with his suits – hanger upon hanger of dark masculine jackets smelling of tobacco, all impeccably pressed and impossibly large. Then there was his lounge chair, piled high with the dirty trousers and shirts that my mother would clean and put away. I'd caress his clothing, sniff at the pockets and necklines, bury my head inside his coats, emerge again and study shaving cream and razors, run my hands over the bed and pillows and furniture, douse myself with the scents of their surroundings – all without ever leaving a clue that I'd been there.

∽

Inside my mother's closet and my father's chest of drawers, I never discovered the key, passport, visa, secret entrance – whatever it was I was looking for – to reach their Eden. My failure in this respect became especially clear years later when my obsession for women emerged. Under the driving force of my absolute need, I believed that the only way to get the password to adulthood — to power — was from the women whom I chased.

As I slid William's message under Peter's door, I reined in my urge to repeat the past and search his room. I remembered Alexandra once telling me, 'It's like you're always looking for things you don't have. You just need to control yourself more — to get a real good grip on yourself and never let go.'

At the time, I bought what she was saying. But her words now sounded so trite that they infuriated me.

I went to the kitchen and boiled up some spaghetti, then opened a frozen container of pesto sauce I'd bought at Ferucci's on Fillmore Street and chipped pieces on top of the pasta. I sat on the brown couch in the living-room and vacuumed up the food as if maybe I'd be dragged off to the gallows the next morning (for cheating on Alex, of course), cleaning the last specks of basil off my plate with a slice of Levy's rye bread. With the waning of sunset, I began listening for telltale creaks and groans. The desire to invade Peter's private domain weighed on me. This time, however, it was Maria who dissuaded me from entering. I considered that — in some preternatural way — the bird would report back to him about my illicit presence. The very thought of having to suffer Peter's look of betrayal — his anger — was impossible for me to bear. So I stacked my plate on top of the colander in the kitchen sink, then eased back into the brown couch and turned on the television. Suddenly, my traitorous mind presented me with a revelation: I could search through Peter's bottom room by using my spare key to enter through his outside door. Maria's feathers would ruffle so to speak, but from her position upstairs, she would have no way of knowing that I was the person who was nosing around.

Creeping around the side of the house, I unlocked his door and stepped inside. The room was dark — the blinds had been drawn — and musty. I stood still, imagining a spirit with the head of a vulture standing invisible before me, about to reach out with a talon-like hand of leather and bone. I flipped the light switch. Nothing. Peter must have disconnected it. I shivered, then gathered my courage and opened the blinds. My invincible Excalibur – the last rays of evening light – streamed in. Upstairs, Maria squawked.

She knew, of course, that someone was there.

I took a look around.

Candles, thick and white, were everywhere – on the wooden floor, on Alex's desk, on shelves Peter had built. Against one wall, above his bed, he'd glued bird feathers in all shades of blue and red and green, spaced them out at different angles like comets in a random patch of sky. On the opposite side of the room, he had done the same with dried flowers – poppies, pansies, and oleander. The touch of their desiccated petals was disquieting, and I realized that I shouldn't have come. I was certain that this place was not meant for me to see. Nevertheless, I glanced quickly at the titles of the few books on his shelves and a pile of letters on the floor bearing postmarks from Brazil. I looked up. There, in one corner of the ceiling, was a Nazi flag – a black swastika inside a white circle against a red background, burnt at the edges. A pair of brown boots was sticking down from the centre of the flag. A tremor shook me; I had a vision of a booted cadaver trapped with his body above the ceiling and feet below – a human statue for Peter's pleasure.

I had the disquieting sensation that I was sneaking a view at a mind turned inside out. My heart was thumping against my ribs. I was dizzy.

Reaching out to the wall, I began picturing my parents asleep in bed. It was almost as if they were upstairs. And I was fifteen years old, was standing at the threshold of their room with a blanket over my sagging shoulders, my legs heavy from another night of insomnia. My mom was curled into a ball.

Her breathing was choppy, and her legs would jerk every few seconds as if she were being chased in a dream. My father had kicked off the sheets, was lying on his back, bare-chested. It must have been summer. His hands were pressed over his belly as if he'd been arranged inside a coffin. I dared to hope that he was dead – for the very first time. And that my mom would finally escape her pursuer. But mostly I was scared that their eyes would pop open, that they'd see me there and know what I was thinking. Then they would have to kill me for sure.

When I woke to myself, I closed the blinds and locked the door on my way out, ran through the yard to the front entrance. It was getting dark quickly. A watchful chill pervaded the house. I grabbed my book on the Inquisition for some measure of purpose and went out. I drove into the Mission, parked on Twenty-fourth Street near the Café La Mancha.

As I got out of the car, I realized with a start that Mara lived nearby. Maybe that had been my destination all along. I didn't think it was such a hot idea to bother her twice in one day, but I started off for her home anyway.

As if in answer to my incipient sexual fantasies, Mara came to the door wrapped in a yellow bathrobe – an elf in terry cloth. A black-and-white furry dog poked its muzzle between her legs and barked furiously at me. Mara grabbed its leather collar.

'Bet you didn't expect to see me again so soon.'

'Come on in.' She waved me inside with her free hand, then let go of the dog's collar. She stood up straight and tried to shoo it away. 'Back, Alba, back!' she ordered. But the mongrel's higher nature was unreachable. Growling, it stood its ground as if defending a fortress. Mara bent over and took its collar again in one hand and kept her bathrobe together with the other. I saw the faintest glimmer of her tiny breasts as she bent over.

She tilted her head up and gave me a hassled look. 'Dogs,'

she sighed, adding, 'I'll get rid of her. Just follow me.'

I walked to the back of the house behind her and her angry friend. She steered it into a room and slammed the door shut. 'Don't you dare sulk!' she called. With a deep breath, she rolled her neck around and pressed her hands into the small of her back. She tilted her head toward me and gave me an apologetic look. 'Alba – it's for Albatross,' she said. Holding her robe closed with one hand, she rubbed at her back again. 'Like the albatross around your neck. I love that expression of yours. The damn thing was wandering around the neighbourhood last year, barking at people, especially men. Not at me, though. No, at me she'd look sad and hungry. So I took her in. The theory is she was beaten by a former owner – a man – and barks incessantly at any male visitors I get.'

'Understandable but irritating,' I observed.

Mara sighed. 'A good watchdog though. And I couldn't refuse to take her in. My healing ... I do that sort of thing. I'm a natural healer – though that sounds terribly pretentious. Anyway, she needs to be touched. And to be fed. She eats like a rhinoceros.'

I smiled at her affection for the dog and asked, 'What's a natural healer?'

Mara tied her robe closed, raised her hands above her head, and pulled them down dramatically in front of her face, her fingers spread like a fan. She snarled like a kabuki lion, then laughed at her own seriousness. 'With my hands,' she said. 'I can help people. It's important for me. I do it with the prostitutes – and with some drug users. For everyone, it's important, I think. It's why we touch when we love. At least it's one of the reasons.'

'You think so?'

'You know why you eat and sleep. I know why I touch.' She came toward me and caressed my arm with her index finger, drawing a line across my wrist. 'There are points on the body which correspond to your organs, both material and spiritual.'

'Spiritual organs?' I asked.

'Of course.'

My perversity lifted its horned head into the room. I asked, 'Can you hurt people with just a touch, too?'

'I could, but I wouldn't.'

'What if you were forced to?' I asked.

'I couldn't be forced.'

'You'd be surprised what people can make you do,' I noted.

'You think?'

I nodded.

Mara shrugged. 'Not if you'd prefer to die rather than hurt another person. That's the secret, isn't it?' Mara looked at me defiantly.

'Most people wouldn't prefer to die,' I observed.

'But I would.'

She spoke with such certainty that I almost believed her. She led me to her kitchen table, and we sat looking at each other closely, inspecting. I don't know what she found. But I discovered a woman I could sleep with, given half a chance. She poured me a glass of red wine from a carafe. I looked around, thought of the contrast with Peter's rooms. No feathers or flowers here, just pots and skillets hanging from a metal grating affixed to the ceiling; a range dotted with tomato stains; a wooden shelf supporting cookbooks. It was cosy, the kitchen of someone who took pride in preparing food. 'It's nice in here,' I observed. 'You must love to cook.'

'Not really,' she said, grinning. 'Even the stains are mostly for show.'

I laughed; at the time, I thought she was teasing me.

She asked, 'Any particular reason you came over?'

'I was out for a drive. Just thought I'd stop by. You don't mind?'

'Of course not. Why would I?'

'It's just that as I get older, I find that people want less and less spontaneous visits. Everything's got to be planned.'

'It's true. At least here. And it's unfortunate.' She sighed. 'Not like Brazil. People walk in the streets there, talk to each other. Oh, maybe not in São Paulo. But in the smaller cities and towns.' She stared into her glass of red wine as if remembering.

She looked up expectantly. 'So how are you doing with Peter?'

'We get along most times,' I said.

'He's a good man, isn't he?'

I drew my fingertip across the lip of my glass, wondering if I'd talk again about my misgivings. 'I guess,' I said unconvincingly.

'That's right,' she smiled, 'you said he was strange. What makes you think that?' She folded her arms and peered at me.

I stared at my wine in order to avoid her probing eyes. 'Well, for one thing, his sense of smell. He can smell things nobody else can. He's like a rabbit.'

When I glanced up, I found that she was grinning.

'No, I'm not kidding,' I said. 'His nose twitches, and he claims he can smell these things nobody else can – azaleas, cacti...' I looked around the room. 'Cookbooks, light switches, the colour blue – everything smells to him.'

Mara laughed from her gut. Then, apologetically, she said, 'I believe you. It's just that I find it amusing and not particularly weird.'

'There's more,' I said, with the pleasure of a prosecutor being able to state his findings. I went on to tell her about Peter's communion with objects at pawnshops and the rose petals he ate.

'I occasionally take a bite out of an orchid myself,' she smiled.

'I'm serious!' I said. 'Stop playing with me.'

'Look, he's a talented man – eccentric,' she concluded. She

brought her hands together into a position of prayer. She looked like Peter when she did that, as if she shared his rigid strength. 'Of course he's not average,' she said. 'But who would want to live with someone average? Not me.'

She was clearly not getting the point. So I told her about how Peter had grabbed the wrists of the drunken businessman in the nightclub. Moving forward on her chair, she clutched tensely at the folds of her robe. When I was finished, she sat brooding. 'You mentioned you were drinking,' she said. 'Perhaps you didn't see it as it happened.'

'I thought of that. But I don't think so.'

'People get pushed too far. I've seen it before. With the prostitutes.'

I was growing frustrated; she didn't see Peter's rage as part of a pattern at all. Maybe she didn't want to – or wouldn't admit to me that she understood exactly what I was getting at.

Rather too aggressively, I said, 'It was his strength, Mara. That was the unusual thing. You know Peter. He doesn't look that strong. If anything, he looks . . .' I stopped, embarrassed.

'What were you going to say?' she asked.

I thought of his eyelashes, the way his face softened at different angles. 'Well, he's very handsome, I'll admit, but there's an almost effeminate quality to him sometimes.'

'And a man who reveals his feminine side without shame . . . He couldn't be that strong?'

'Evidently, he could. But I certainly didn't expect it.'

From her sneer, I realized that I'd said something wrong. She fanned her fingers and made her scowling lion face. 'Could anyone looking like me be expected to have the vocal range I have?!'

'No, I guess not.' I was intimidated, but I was still convinced that Peter was strange. For that matter, I now felt that she was, too. *There's a secret that unites them*, I thought.

'Some people can do extraordinary things at times,' Mara

continued in a voice of peacemaking.

'And have extraordinary inclinations,' I said, now feeling that his being gay might just explain everything. I knew even then it wasn't logical, but I was reaching for any explanation I could find.

'What do you mean?' she asked.

'Is he gay?'

'I'd say it's not that simple.'

'Simple?'

She took a sip of wine. 'Peter's situation is fairly unique. Maybe it's wrong to say that it's not as simple as being gay. It may be. But it's beyond that. It's...' She searched around the room for the word. '... More unusual.'

'What's that supposed to mean?'

'I'd rather that you ask him about it. He'll tell you. If he didn't trust you, he wouldn't live with you. He must like you a great deal.'

'But you *do* know what it is?' I inquired.

'Of course. When you spend a lot of time with someone, you learn things.'

'And the swastika?' I asked. I spoke aggressively again, wanting to clear all the curiosities out of the closet.

'Swastika?'

'Yeah, he's got one hanging from the ceiling of his bedroom, with boots coming out ... down toward the floor...'

Mara turned her lower lip inside out and shrugged. 'Must be from William – a present.'

'A Nazi flag for a present?!' I shouted.

She shrugged.

'Is William a Nazi?' I asked.

'Good grief! Of course not!'

'And Peter ... I don't understand. I know what happened to his mother. How she was in the camps. How could he put a swastika up in his room?'

'It's as a reminder, I think. Of what they represent.'

I recalled Peter's magic worm and the beads made of teeth, how he had told me that he liked to keep objects that aroused emotions in him.

'Look, Bill,' Mara continued, 'Peter likes those sorts of things – he always has. I remember when we were younger, he would even pick up tiles from crumbling houses, dead lizards, hair from people's combs, flowers ... He'd just stand there focusing at them, I mean, looking ... gazing at them, like he was reading a newspaper. I think Peter is one of those people who sees big stories – even in small things. I'm not sure people like us can sense ... can grasp just what he sees.' Mara shrugged, folded her lip out, and held her hands up to me as if to say there was nothing to be done about it. Her black eyes were sympathetic but resigned. I nodded my understanding.

In response, she stood up and downed her glass of wine. 'I'm sorry to kick you out so soon, but I've got to get dressed. I'm working tonight at my counselling centre.' On the way out of the room, she asked, 'How do you feel about the interviews now? Still ambivalent?'

'I suppose. But I'm glad we talked to Rain. I can't stop thinking about her taking Valium all the time.'

'People who get caught in the middle have problems,' she said.

'In what middle?' I asked.

'Between right and wrong, left and right, up and down.'

I didn't know what she was talking about, but it didn't seem important, so I said, 'You want to come with me next weekend if I go out on more interviews?'

'Maybe. Will you call me?'

'It'll be my pleasure,' I answered with a gentlemanly bow.

Mara smiled, the happy elf again, and pushed me gently ahead toward the door. My desire for her had disappeared, but it was nice to have her touch. I glanced back to ask her how exactly she'd met Rain. But as I turned, I spotted something that silenced me. A toucan with a long green bill and powder-blue chest was sitting on a door handle at the back of the apartment. It was a foot long, and was staring at me with garnet eyes. I made believe I'd seen nothing. Alba barked once as we passed her room.

At the front door, I faced Mara again. I'm not sure what either of us said. Shredded ribbons of thoughts trailed across my mind. I know that she took my hand. I think I asked if she was trying to heal me. I remember that she squeezed my fingers very tightly and thanked me for coming over.

I walked to the Café La Mancha remembering the bird's purposeful stare, convinced now that there was something sinister linking Peter and Mara. Maybe they were trying to scare me off, to discourage me from finding the reason for Peter's singularity. They didn't want me to discover why Peter was living with me, why he'd chosen me – or even why Mara had got me started with prostitutes, for that matter.

It seemed clear that either I was nuts or they were – there was no in-between.

I tried to calm myself with the likelihood that any secrets between Peter and Mara had absolutely nothing to do with me. But I now feared Peter in exactly the same way I had feared my father, and an image of him confronting me with a knife refused to dissipate. I held up this image and looked at it from different angles – just as one might turn a trick box around and around in the hopes of finding its hidden entrance. I began to consider that there might have been something else about him that scared me so much that I chose instead to imagine it as physical violence. His sexual power intrigued me – I couldn't deny that. And between us was always the electrically charged possibility of our making love. Though it seemed far more likely that I was hoping that he'd become enraged at me and punish me for ruining my marriage. Or maybe I really wanted to hurt *him*, to get revenge through him on all those people who had managed to keep their emotions intact.

∞

Over the next few days, I made no mention to Peter of Mara's bird or the decoration in his bottom room. Actually, we didn't talk much; after our initial burst of conversation, we withdrew into a more reserved relationship. I realized, too, that he was more awkward around people than I even first suspected, was far more comfortable with his objects. When he did speak, I began waiting for him to slip, for the secret or some clue to pop out like a ping-pong ball from his mouth, or maybe even some opportune moment to ask him straight out what he was concealing. But I didn't find such a moment. I listened to him play the piano on a couple of evenings, mostly fugues originally composed for harpsichord by Frescobaldi, Scarlatti, Poglietti, and other Italian composers. We read, listened to the radio. I disregarded my doubts as much as possible. No more dreams about the wooden amulet came to me. I didn't bring up the subject for fear that the story behind it would scare me or alienate me from him further.

I did finally get back to my book on the Inquisition and the story of the group of Chuetas from Majorca who'd secretly plotted to flee their island because of the Church's persecution of descendants of Jews who'd converted to Christianity. In March of 1688, eighty-seven hopeful escapees boarded an English sailing ship for a land where they'd be able to live in peace. Delayed by storms, however, their secret was betrayed, and between two and three on the morning of March 8, the entire group – save one man – was thrown into prison and accused of heresy. Their sentences were carried out over the following five months. Thirty-seven of them were burned alive, the rest garroted, then also set aflame. Everyone died, that is, except for the one man – unnamed – who had apparently managed to escape on another English sailing vessel.

At the time, I thought I'd reached the end of the story.

∞

The major headline that week was the return of my sexual obsession. Desire swelled against my trousers for hours at a time. It was like having a fucking divining rod in my underwear, one that was hell-bent on locating water anywhere it could, and it drew me to the Tenderloin every lunch hour to check out the whores. One particular Thursday, I began watching a tall brunette with an air of melancholy. She had long beautiful legs and hunched shoulders. She wore a denim jacket and black leather miniskirt. Her brown eyes were distant and sad. I approached her, all sincerity and professionalism, and told her that I was writing profiles of prostitutes. She showed me a good-natured smile and agreed to be interviewed. She let me buy her coffee. I traced the outline of her thighs with my gaze. As I talked with her, my cock stiffened, sniffing out her waters. I played with myself under the table, though I really didn't want to fuck her, because I was paranoid about contracting any of several diseases. I did want to make her itch for my cock, though. I wanted her to roll her tongue around her lips, open and close her legs in anticipation, look into my eyes with submission.

I wanted to get her vagina divining for a few good thrusts – to make her just like me.

It was undoubtedly part of her job to pick up on such idiocy quickly. After she'd told me a bit about growing up as a high school principal's daughter in Lincoln, Nebraska, she said, 'You know, I think you got more than a professional interest in me, don't ya?' She smiled, and her foot brushed against my ankle.

'What do you mean?' I asked coyly.

She leaned back in her seat and gave me the knowing expression of a woman who's just figured out who the killer is in a murder mystery. Her foot rubbed up and down my ankle. 'What ya want from me?' she asked.

I whispered, 'How much?'

'Much what?'

'Money.'

She leaned toward me and breathed into my ear, 'French, seventy-five bucks. You want to speak some other language, we can discuss it.'

I made an effort to live up to a cool image of restraint. 'No discount for journalists?' I asked.

She frowned, puffed out her lips. 'Discount?'

Her theatrical show of puzzlement enraged me beyond all reason. As I thought of my mother, I was gripped by a mad compulsion to shriek at her. I jumped up, knocking over my chair, then looked at her and saw ... And saw what ... ? Just a bedraggled woman playing a silly game with me, a little girl moving through a life she'd never really wanted, lost like myself.

'Man, you're scary!' she said. She reached for her bag.

'I'm sorry,' I replied.

She stood up, squinted at me, sneered as if I were hopeless. 'Yeah, right,' she said.

I left the deli with my tail tucked between my legs.

Back at work, I felt a failure at having to submit to the caprices of my cock. It was as if I'd got precisely nowhere after such an important event as the break-up of my marriage – not to mention the visits from all my spirits. Obviously this was not *A Christmas Carol*, and I was not nearly so blessed as Ebenezer Scrooge. I closed my office door to relieve my obsession, but got nowhere. I was in one of those moods where my fantasies about ice goddesses seemed hopelessly repetitive. It was as if I were being swallowed by the same images for ever and ever, as if I would live till my dying day inside the belly of my thoughts like some frustrated Jonah.

∞

When I got home, the phone began ringing just as I closed the door behind me. I panicked that it would be Alexandra.

But it was a policeman, of all things, calling to say that he'd tried to reach me at work and had found out that I'd just gone home. He introduced himself as Detective Hollis. 'We've got a dead boy on our hands,' he said dryly. 'We found him in the Presidio. He was stabbed – and he had your card on him.'

I fumbled the receiver and my response, so Hollis spoke slowly: 'A kid, dead, with one of your business cards in his back pocket. That's all he had on him.'

A sense of receding diffused through me. I asked, 'Who is he?'

'We're not sure. You know why some kid would have your card?'

'No.' But as I answered, an image of Rain suddenly startled me. She must have given out my cards to her friends as I'd asked. One of them, a boy prostitute maybe, had been killed.

'Like to come down and see if you can identify the body?' Hollis asked.

'I don't know if I can.'

'Try.'

I agreed, took the address of the city morgue. It was on Folsom. As I hung up the phone, I tried to picture what the face of the dead boy would look like.

Strangely, he had Peter's eyes.

The morgue was a two-storey brick building. I met Detective Hollis in the reception area. Everybody else had already gone home. He had thick red hair, a bushy moustache, and a veteran's gut. With a friendly smile, he ushered me into a frigid examination room. On an aluminium table in the corner was a body covered by a white sheet. It was facing away from me. Only the head was visible. It looked like a paraffin voodoo doll with long brown hair, was just an agglomeration of dark holes and pinkish sacks and waves of brown cilia. I remember that the chin was pointing up into its neck like some ridiculous tulip bulb.

I had only to walk around the body to return to the usual il-
lusion that our faces make some sort of sense, however.
Suddenly, I recognized it, coloured it in with memory. I knew
why the police had called me.

'Her name's Rain,' I said.

I looked away. I shivered.

Hollis grinned like a moron and ripped away the sheet.

Rain had a penis and balls. Wiped blood was smudged over
her stomach and legs, as if someone had tried finger painting.

I looked away again. I was dizzy, so I knelt.

'*Her?!*' Hollis said. 'Funniest *her* I've ever seen.'

Tears slipped into my eyes, and I held my body rigid in defence. I felt the tug of a need to free myself. When I looked up
at the cop, I wondered why I didn't kill him on the spot. I
stood up.

'You're a real asshole!'

Hollis dropped the sheet back over Rain. 'Fuck you, too!'
he replied, sneering.

'Can I go now?' I asked.

He took out a stick of gum from his shirt pocket. 'After a
few questions. What's his last name?'

'No idea.'

'How'd you know him?'

I watched in awe of his perfect repulsiveness as he un-
wrapped the gum and curled it into his mouth. 'My work,' I
said roughly. 'I interviewed him for an article. You know who
stabbed him?'

'We're working on it. What was the article on?'

'Runaways,' I lied, feeling the need to protect Rain. 'Any
suspects?' I asked.

The detective frowned. 'So he's a runaway?'

'Yeah. Couldn't stand his parents – his dad used to rape
him.'

Hollis licked his lips and tried to look bored. We stared at each other like two prizefighters, and he asked his next question, then another and another. In between meaningless responses I let myself wade into stark remembrances of Rain. Mostly I saw her as I'd first seen her, standing skinny and windblown against the wall of a brick building, the white glare of the sun cutting across her legs.

After a half hour, Hollis let me go. I re-examined my memories of Rain as I walked to my car, trying in vain to recall if she'd said anything to indicate that she was in danger. The Valium . . . It was to make her look more feminine, she'd said. Now I understood.

I tried to reach Mara from a phone booth, but no one answered. At home, I found Peter standing over my globe. I told him about Rain. He blanched, grew faint. I sat him down. 'It was really her?' he whispered. 'You're sure?'

'Absolutely positive.'

Peter started to cry soundlessly. I grew embarrassed because I could feel my own tears about to come again. He wiped his cheeks roughly, asked what she'd told me during our interview. I spoke gently. He was especially interested in my sense that her penis and balls didn't fit. 'Maybe they didn't,' he agreed.

I talked about Rain's difficult childhood, and his fists clenched. When I was done, he jumped up and reached for his coat. 'I've got to go to a friend's,' he said. He squinted at me over his nose as if he had trouble seeing, wiped his eyes roughly.

'Okay,' I said. 'But are you all right?'

He nodded.

As he reached the door, I asked if he'd be back for dinner.

'I'm not sure,' he replied. 'Don't wait. And if Mara calls, please tell her I went to William's. Is that okay?'

'Fine.'

Peter turned to leave, then looked back at me with his fleeting smile. 'Oh, I forgot to thank you for passing on the note from him – from William. Thanks.'

I nodded. He left. As if I'd just turned the most important page of a book, I suddenly thought, *William is involved somehow in Rain's death. That's why Peter is going to see him.*

I glanced around the living-room, distant from thought. Under the sudden need to examine the writing on the wood Peter had given me, I went upstairs and ran my finger over the Star of David. It was as if something from William – his scent, perhaps – was trapped in the grain of the wood. I sniffed it. I wasn't sensitive enough to detect anything.

Back downstairs, I paced for a while. Then I sat in the dark thinking of Rain, about why William or anyone else would want to kill her. Was I in danger, too, for getting too close to Peter? I tried Mara again and got her in. When I told her about the murder, she didn't say a thing. 'Mara, you there?' I prompted.

'She was special,' Mara said to herself.

'I'm sure,' I replied. We didn't speak for a time. 'Did you know about her . . . about her sex, I mean?'

'No. I suspected something, but she never told me. And I wasn't sure. I thought maybe I was just . . . just imagining it.'

'Peter said to tell you he's at William's.'

'Thanks.'

The silence between us lengthened until it was drawn taut. I grimaced and asked, 'He's not involved in Rain's death? William, I mean.'

'Of course not,' Mara answered.

But I didn't believe her. 'Okay, then,' I said. 'I'll talk to you. I'm sorry about Rain.'

'Me too.'

I hung up, scared and frustrated. As if that weren't enough, my cock was getting stiff again.

∞

I fought the urgings of sex as best I could, but decided in the end to head to the De Young museum in Golden Gate Park; it was open late on Thursday evenings, and I'd had luck there before hunting down ice goddesses.

But there was little action that evening. Mostly tourists – women with faces like withered turnips and men with stomachs ripening over their silver belt buckles. Absolutely sexless, they were. It was amazing that people could become so barren. I mean, try finding a penis on one of those men. You'd need a microscope. And even then you'd only locate some skinny microbe – half-dead and ready to be used as a vaccine on their children. Same with the women. They just plugged it up or plain forgot about it, went their whole lives without an orgasm – like what was open between their legs was nothing more than a shameful burden to carry through life. I truly despised these people for their loss of sexuality and joy. It seemed to be their goal, their speciality. And it seemed particularly American, too.

As I walked around in a state of angry disbelief, I sneaked caresses over marble busts to make up for the flatness of people, then headed to the museum café. At a corner table was a blonde woman with a deep tan, sipping her coffee pensively. I bought some tea and a piece of lemon pound cake. I sat across the room and stared at her. I wanted her to see how sexual I was. It was as if my body were screaming, *Hey, you frozen squid, I've got a penis and it's throbbing for you, and if you just take it inside you it'll make you live again!*

In fact, I'd been shouting just that my whole adult life. Pretty infantile, I'll admit. But since most people didn't even realize they were infants in drag, I felt one step ahead of the game.

By now, my mark knew that I'd sniffed her scent. But she refused to glance back at me.

So I waited. When she finally got up and left, I trailed her into the hallway. I told myself I'd give up if she didn't look back.

I lived up to my word, but I didn't abandon the hunt. On the contrary, I walked through the museum again, past the Impressionists, past Rodin, past Blake, past ... Not a damn thing.

I went back to my car, rushed across town to Union Street, pressing at my need the whole way. I had some luck there, however; a woman with wan skin, metallic eyes, and red, mandarin fingernails was sitting on the outdoor patio of the Café El Greco. Her blonde hair was pulled constrictingly back into French braids, and her lips shimmered like newly washed slices of a perfect red pepper. Her slender arms emerged out of a silver sleeveless dress. I walked over and sat at the table next to hers. The shadow of her cleavage, impressive but restrained, held my gaze.

She glanced at me for just an instant, then stared off into the street as if I were dangerous. I was pleased. I ordered a whiskey and gulped it down. Under the table, I began rubbing myself.

As I considered how to start a conversation, a woman walking down the street recognized her and sat down with a shriek of joy. She was the ageing débutante variety, wore a turquoise jumpsuit and athletic shoes. 'You're looking superb,' she said to Miss Ice Age. 'When did you get back?'

'Sunday. And it was great. *So* good to get away. I really love England.'

Miss Ice Age's whining belied her words; she spoke as if she had been hopelessly bored by all the gardens and ever-so-pleasant bobbies, as if everything in the world were infused with layer after layer of tedium.

I prayed for the débutante to leave. 'Dennis is driving me crazy,' she confessed with a flap of her wrist.

The conversation went on for several minutes. Apparently, my mark had been on vacation for two weeks. 'You know the theatre over there is just great,' she concluded.

'Well, I love London – the shopping, Harrods ... And the people are so charming, so civilized...'

The two of them whacked clichés back and forth like a dead tennis ball. Finally, the débutante said, 'Gotta get back though, Dennis'll be coming home soon. And you know Dennis when he wants dinner...!'

In a moment, she was gone. Miss Ice Age was putting her cigarettes and lighter back in her handbag. She covered the check with five singles. I dropped enough money on the table to cover my bill and got up so she could see in the contours of my crotch how much I wanted her; subtlety only leads to an empty bed, I've always found. I followed her out to the sidewalk, trailed her till she paused at the window of a boutique that carried only black clothing.

I stopped next to her, felt myself at a cliff's edge. 'They have some nice things,' I said.

'Yes.' She licked her lips, seemingly bored, then looked back into the shop window.

'Can I buy you a drink?' I asked.

'I just had one,' she replied.

'No harm in another.'

'No, I don't like to drink too much.'

'Wise.'

She held out her hand and smiled coyly.

'I'm Lisa,' she said. Her hand was cold and tiny. Tendons stood out on her wrist. Composed interest showed in her eyes.

'Bill Ticino.'

'Italian?' she asked.

'Uh-hum.'

'I like Italians,' she smiled.

It was flirting time. I did my best for the next few minutes. If she couldn't see the desperation down my trouser leg, then she was blind. When I couldn't take any more, I jumped over the edge. 'I'd like to go to bed with you,' I said.

She laughed. But it didn't resonate. It skated over her reflective smile. 'We don't know each other at all,' she noted.

'Does it matter?'

She licked her lips again and stared below my belt. 'No, I don't suppose it does,' she said.

'Would you like to come over to my place?' I asked.

'No, I live around here – right around the corner. I prefer familiar surroundings for this sort of thing.'

∞

Inside her apartment, my breaths came long and deep. My heart drummed against my chest. My cock felt as if it was going to explode. 'Ever been hit by penis shrapnel?' I asked her.

'What?' she replied.

'If I don't fuck you quick, there's going to be a mess.'

I grabbed her in the living-room, pulled the dress free from her shoulders, and cupped her breasts. I pressed my cock against her hip to end the pain. She pulled back. 'Wait a second!' she ordered.

She slipped into her bedroom, headed to the bathroom. 'Take off your clothes,' she called back. I followed her orders. The place looked like a hotel for Barbie dolls – all plush and fluffy and pink. She came out wearing only a white lace slip. 'Okay,' she said. 'Come over here.'

She spoke as if she were going to perform a medical exam on me ('turn your head and cough'). She sat on the bed. Reaching into her night table, she took out a condom and slipped it on me as if she were a teacher lacing up galoshes for a kid. No rush, no need. Just professional efficiency.

My stiff cock was poking right into her face and she wasn't even going to take a good look – let alone a nibble. She made Alexandra look like a Polynesian goddess of passion.

I stood at the foot of her bed, afraid to touch her, angry with myself. She slithered out of her slip and lay with her legs open. She held out her arms to me.

I sensed it was going to take a combination of Sherlock Holmes and Casanova to discover this woman's warmth.

'I'm ready,' she said.

Her spontaneity in this foreplay was indicative of the way she made love. I failed completely to find that ganglion of pleasure and pain I always hunted. Oh, I got off, exploded way up inside her, but I don't think she felt one blessed thing. Did she come? Hard to tell. Lord knows, I tried. I vaulted into manic efforts and still couldn't raise anything but phony television-sex noises from her. She winced once or twice, as if she'd got a paper cut, but it was all hopeless. By the time I climbed off, I was exhausted. She was circumcised but didn't know it, and I found myself in a rage again, not exactly at her, but at the people who cut those feelings out of you.

As I sat with my feet dangling over the side of the bed, the touch of her feet raised goose pimples on my back. I felt soiled, as if I were covered by silvery snail slime. My gut ached from an acid that had nothing to chew on. I wanted to be cleansed, and I knew that the only way I could do that was by fleeing. So I showered and dressed, forced myself to kiss her goodbye – she was almost asleep – and rushed outside.

Night had descended. It was as if I'd escaped from a Hieronymus Bosch painting, just popped right off the canvas into a real evening without a look back. I ran to my car, shivered in appreciation of its familiar cosiness, and headed north where the world seemed wilder, free of men and women. I had this vision of the Golden Gate Bridge, wanting to cross it, that somehow it would take me into another world.

Passing through the orange spans, looking at the electric grid of city to my right and the black horizonless ocean to my left, I did indeed sense that I was bursting into another future. I slipped through the hills of Marin County and crossed San Rafael, Novato, Napa, trying not to think, to simply watch the darkness, to ward off tears and anger with numbness, with flight. Memories of Alexandra, Rain, Peter – and the absurdity of this latest escapade – chased me north to Calistoga.

In any of my usual states of mind I would never *ever* have stopped at a roadside antique store, and definitely not at one with a cutesy name at eleven-fifteen in the evening, but just outside town there was an ancient wooden barn with the lights still on and a pink and green neon sign flashing over the doorway: 'The Midnight Snark – Antiques.' Like everybody else, I'd guess, I misread the name as Midnight *Snack* at first, only realized as I was going in that it was *Snark* – a reference to Lewis Carroll's fantasy creature.

A beat-up Ford pickup and an old silver Cadillac with an American flag flapping madly around the radio antenna were parked in the gravel lot, the Ford with its headlights on, flashing two big white-brown eyes on the side of the barn. I pulled in next to it, sat in the car with the bass on 'Addicted to Love' giving my dashboard fits, running my hands through my hair, wondering what the hell I was doing, not just here, but with my life. When I got out, the cold wind jostled me more than it should have, as if I were no more solid than one of those balsa wood planes Jay and I used to fly around our back yard. I tried to get into the Ford to turn off the lights, but the doors were locked. The idiot must have been drunk off his gourd not to have seen he'd left them on. I headed inside.

I hadn't a clue, of course, that I was about to buy something there that would turn out to be crazy proof of a right move on my part a few years later. If I *had* known what it would come to mean to me, I think I would have been scared shitless that I was going to pick the wrong thing – a good reason, I suppose, for not being able to predict the future.

The Midnight Snark was kind of a mess actually, brimming with objects that looked as if they'd been looted from the czar's winter palace and then hidden away for a few years in somebody's basement in Jersey City – Tiffany lamps, porcelain dolls, mother-of-pearl cigarette cases, gilded clocks – that sort of thing. All more than a bit dusty and smelly. Right above the entrance was a cascading chandelier of blue and red Venetian crystal with a spider-web stretched between two serpentine arms. Either it was one of the most beautiful things I'd ever seen or a candidate for the most hideous – it was shimmering right at that borderline between worlds. In fact, everything in the store seemed to be either hanging or standing right on that cusp.

There was a young woman behind the clunky cash register, her black hair pulled into a ponytail, wearing an overly large San Francisco Giants T-shirt. A black couple was down one of the side aisles, by a row of lopsided wardrobes, walking arm-in-arm, whispering to each other as if they were out for a secret promenade. Nearer to me, a short bearded guy in jeans and a denim jacket was kneeling, examining a wooden gaming table.

One thing I noticed right away was that the labels on everything were lettered in gold calligraphy and attached, oddly, with red and white bakery string.

I asked the young woman at the register if she knew who owned the pickup. She pointed to the bearded guy, and when I told him he had his lights on, he said, 'Shit, I'm always doing that. Thanks, pal.' When he smiled, I saw that one of his front teeth was gold. I'd never seen that before. And I hadn't been called *pal* in months.

I was still standing right at the entrance, was about to turn tail and slink off back to my car, when I noticed that there was a small section of vintage clothing at the back. A stack of old sweaters looked promising, but when I got there, a pair of blue shoes sitting atop a black lacquer night table caught my attention. They were the exact shade of those Italian frescoes I liked so much, and they were made of the softest leather I'd ever felt. Size forty-four was stamped on the soles, which must have meant they were from Europe. They had turquoise laces. They were beautiful. But I couldn't think of anyone wearing such colourful shoes except Peter, and I didn't know his size. Also, the label said they were forty bucks, which seemed pretty steep for used shoes. 'Can I try these on?' I called over to the cashier, excited about buying him a present, about doing someone a good turn for a change. I was hoping that they'd be a bit tight on me – I thought I remembered that Peter's feet were smaller than mine.

The guy with the Ford truck was back and was staring at me tying the laces. I was seated on a high-backed leather desk chair that smelled of mildew.

'Pretty goofy,' the guy said. This was years before *goofy* became a popular word. At least in the Bay Area. I thought that maybe he was on drugs or something because of the boyish grin he kept flashing me. His gold tooth was disconcerting, seemed out of place on him.

I discovered that the shoes fit me perfectly. 'Those look pretty good,' the Ford guy said.

'They're not for me,' I answered, wishing he'd go away.

'What size does he wear?' the cashier asked. She'd appeared out of nowhere.

'Don't know. I don't know what forty-four means anyway.'

'They're Italian. It's a ten-and-a-half or eleven in our sizes, I think. We got them in a few months back. Some guy who comes to San Francisco once every few weeks from Milan. A big stockbroker or something. He buys shoes like Imelda Marcos, then sells us his old pairs.'

'How much?' the Ford guy asked.

'Forty,' I said.

'Bargain.'

By now, the black couple was watching me, too, and I realized what should have been obvious earlier – people came here late at night to stave off loneliness. It was getting to seem as if everyone in America was driving further and further each night just to make human contact. The realization that I was part of some sort of sociological phenomenon spooked me, and I told the young lady I'd take the shoes because I couldn't think of what else to do.

I fled out to my car and tossed my purchase – which now seemed totally idiotic – into the back seat. By then it was nearing midnight, so I raced into Calistoga and rented a small suite at the Calabash Inn, a dingy spa at the end of town I'd been to once before with Alexandra. It had grey carpets stained with vague yellow splotches, bug spray on a windowsill, peeling linoleum on the kitchen floor. It smelled of dust and burnt toast. A bulky metallic television in the bedroom looked as if it had been built from spare 1959 Pontiac parts. I turned on the news, buried my head in my hands.

I hated myself for not being able to love.

When I ceased crying, I found the television still on. I took the blankets from the bed, stuffed them in the trunk of the car, and drove into the hills east of town. I passed vineyards and farmhouses and two big furry dogs barking at me from atop a tractor parked at the side of the road.

A strange thing happened for which I would get an explanation only several years later:

I felt magnetically impelled to stop for a time in front of a two-storey Victorian farmhouse topped by a weather-vane of a falcon pointing due north. *There is something inside the house that I'm meant to see*, I was thinking.

The lights for the porch and bottom floor were on. Smoke was ribboning out of the chimney.

I approached, figuring I'd say I was lost if anyone saw me.

Around the side of the house was a window partially blocked by a row of hydrangea bushes.

I could hear a man's voice as I got closer. He was shouting. I squeezed through two bushes and peered in.

It was a living-room cluttered with books. A man was sitting on a rug by the fireplace. He had long brown hair. His back was to me. He was naked and he appeared to be reading from a leather-bound book.

Now and then, he grunted monosyllables in a foreign language.

After perhaps half a minute, the edges of his body began to take on a red glow.

For a moment, I thought I saw two violet lights at the back of his head. I thought of hidden eyes, but figured that these glowing shapes must have been caused by light diffracting at odd angles through the window; at the time, I deeply distrusted my own senses and instincts.

A sentence began repeating inside me: *you've made love to a stranger for the last time.*

It was as if a period of my life had ended; as if now, making love would mean something different.

Suddenly, the man stood up. I sensed he was about to turn to face me.

I raced back to my car like a frightened kid.

∞

I drove until I found a wooded area, then parked on the side of the road. I walked into the trees, spread out the blankets, and sat among the leaves and mushrooms and ants. The half-moon had risen, glowing and watchful. Stars quilted the sky. Were there other worlds where people didn't feel awful after making love? I took off all my clothes and lay down. When I closed my eyes, I felt the wind blowing inside me, the nearest tree standing guard over me like a mother – the mother I never had.

I woke up with no idea what time it was. A light of grey and purple at the horizon drifted into my eyes. My body was cold, and I covered it with a blanket. I sat very still, looked through the woods to my car waiting for me. I pictured Peter sleeping in his room. I wanted to tell him a story – an adventure story. But I didn't know any. *Except my own*, I thought. *But it hasn't been much until now*. I wanted to learn about the wood that he had given me.

∞

I got home two hours later, tiptoed back into my room, and tossed the blue shoes, which I now thought were ridiculous, deep into the nether regions of my closet. I fell asleep for a few more hours with the moon still watching over me.

I dreamed about the wood. Peter and I were shivering in the living-room; the air was cold and hollow. He was looking at my globe, spinning it. His hand stopped on Poland. Our breath was escaping into the air as a frigid mist, and when I followed it I spotted a guard tower with a window that looked like an eye. It was staring at us. Peter was cutting his own hair under this invasive gaze. He used a knife, and blood oozed from the cut ends. William appeared as a skeletal figure. He handed Peter the wood. Peter tied some hairs around it and gave it to the shadow woman I'd seen before. She was holding it out to me, wanting me to pass it on to someone, asking me to take my place in a history that they were forming. It was a ritual I was to be made part of.

Now, Peter was standing at the centre of a maze made up of hedges with big blue flowers, and he was talking to me. But I couldn't understand what he was saying. I heard the words clearly enough, but they didn't make any sense. It was as if I'd forgotten language itself.

Chapter 10

IN THE MORNING, I took the wooden amulet from my night table so I could remove it from my dream life. Peter was already awake and was sitting on the white couch in the living-room. He looked to be in a trance of sorts, was staring out the window at the plum trees.

'Time for explanations,' I told him. I held up the wood. 'I need to know what this is all about.'

His concentration broke and he said in a concerned voice, 'You only got home early this morning.'

'I drove up to Calistoga,' I replied.

He nodded and whispered, 'Yes, Calistoga,' as if he understood something I didn't. 'What did you see there?' he asked.

I told him about the woods, the moon, and the house with the weather vane.

He nodded as if I'd given the correct response. 'And your dream?' he asked.

When I told him about Poland and the guard tower, he replied, 'You see how sensitive people can be?'

'Not really,' I replied. 'Why don't you tell me what you think it means.' I sat opposite him.

Peter leaned forward and pulled on his ear to free his sinuses. He picked up the wood and moved his index finger over the inscribed writing as if he were caressing a baby's tiny hand. 'It's a twin language,' he said. 'Sometimes identical twins speak a language when they are very little. Only they know it. And usually they lose the ability to speak it later.' He shrugged. 'Maybe they just forget it when they begin to converse with other people.' He pointed to the writing. 'This is such a language.'

'What's it say?' I asked.

'Something like, "I send you my strength for one day I will

watch you dance and dance beside you." Then, "I will live for that day." And finally, as you know, there's a Star of David. You see, it's a kind of correspondence. A friend gave it to me – William. The man I grew up with. He taught me the language.'

'And it's William who wrote it?'

'No, his twin, Victor. And a friend.'

I gave him a puzzled look and said, 'Go on.'

'You see, they were living in Hungary,' he began. 'You were right about that.' He smiled weakly, as if straining. 'Outside of Budapest lived William, Victor, and this friend, a woman named Sarah. She was really Victor's girlfriend.' Peter nodded at my globe. 'It's so strange how much geography means at times. Had they been living elsewhere...' He nodded and breathed deeply.

'So it was 1943. They were teenagers. I don't know exactly how old.'

'Seventeen,' I said. I don't know where that answer came from. I figured that I must have dreamt it.

'Very possibly,' Peter replied. 'Anyway, it was 1943, as I say. Victor and William had kept their twin language going. They never forgot it. They conversed in it when they didn't want others to understand, joked in it, made up puns and rhymes in it. William says it is his favourite language. And he knows many – he's very good at them. He feels most at home in it, in its ... its conjugations.' Peter looked at me questioningly and held the wood up to me. 'Well, why not, it had been created by him and his brother – he dreams in it to this day.

'Victor and Sarah, they met at high school and they fell in love. He felt compelled to teach her the rudiments of the language so that she might know ... know his most intimate thoughts. After a year of struggle, she knew enough to converse. They spoke in it after making love, while discussing death – always in their most private moments.

'In 1944, their lives were interrupted when they were taken

from their ghetto – with all the Hungarian Jews, I mean. They were marched right past the other villagers into cattle cars for the trip to Auschwitz. A hundred people – no place to pee or shit, hardly any air. Like a cage. And when they next emerged, they were there, in the camp.' He looked up at me and nodded. 'You saw that, too. Victor and Sarah were separated, but both were chosen for work, not the gas chambers. You were selected on the way in, you see. William, too, was chosen for slave labour. But Mengele, Dr Mengele, you know of him, of course? I'm reading that book now...'

'I know of him,' I said.

'Well, it was Mengele himself who did much of the selecting. One line for the sick, the old, the young – straight to the ovens. The other for slave labour. And he was always hunting for twins. When he came across William and Victor, he was ecstatic, of course. He adored experimenting on people – performing these pseudo-scientific experiments on identical twins, in particular. And others, of course. Like my mother. But twins, they were his pride and joy. To study heredity by measuring them – the length of eyebrows and fingers, ear lobes, everything.' Peter shook his head, then wiped his hand across his mouth as if gathering his courage.

'He would have killed them using ... using different methods. For instance, he would infect them with different diseases to see how they would spread through their organs. To him, William and Victor were ideal. They were kept in a separate block of the camp with other twins, little kids – Gypsies, Jews, some Poles. In abysmal shape, of course. But the ones who remained healthy, they were better off than the other prisoners to some extent. They ate a little better and could keep their hair. They even got presents from those very strange doctors. Imagine...'

Peter questioned me with his hollow stare. '...Just imagine, giving a child a present before you kill him, Bill. And killing him only because you want to dissect his liver or kidney.'

I nodded my understanding of the horror he was feeling.

'So, in return for this somewhat better treatment, the twins had to pay a price,' he continued. 'William and Victor were measured for hours on end. And while making the measurements, the doctors discovered that they both had ... I think you might call them undescended testicles. It happens sometimes. They stay in the body and don't descend.'

'Yes,' I nodded.

'This was great, you see, for Mengele. Another thing to study. He had them operated on, crude operations, with little anaesthesia, to have the testicles lowered, then removed. I don't know what he did with them. He must have dissected them or had them put in jars, so they could be sent to a museum for Jewish types or something. And after that, more bizarre experiments.'

I was suddenly ashamed that I'd had mean thoughts about William. Accompanying my guilt was a numbness protecting me from the fear I felt about having dreamt some of Peter's story. I considered that I might simply wake up soon and realize that he and William and the rest of my present life had all been parts of an intricate and ever-expanding hallucination, that I was actually still living with my wife.

Peter breathed in deeply. 'Then, one day, Victor found some wood in the camp, a few pieces saved from a cooking oven. And he managed to steal a scalpel from one of his examining doctors. So, he wrote messages to Sarah, carved them. He didn't really know if she were still alive. For all he knew, she could have been part of the odour of burnt flesh rising out of the chimneys. But he etched a few words of encouragement and love in the twin language. Then he wrote her name along with a message in Hungarian to pass it along. And he tossed it over the fence to another prisoner who picked it up and tossed it over yet another fence, all the way, you see, till it finally reached her. To Sarah, of course, it was a miracle. She hadn't known if he was alive either. With a nail she stole, she etched a message and sent it back the same way.

'It was lucky, in a sense, that Victor was in the special section for twins. If not, there's no way he would have been able to communicate even in this crude way with Sarah. Over the next few weeks, the two lovers wrote messages to each other. They reused the pieces of wood, found new ones when they could, burnt old ones so they wouldn't be found. They decided to write poems, each taking a turn at a line or a verse, till one was satisfied it was complete. It took weeks at a time. In this way, they could create something together. As a way of retaining purpose ... purpose and hope, of course. Anyway, Victor or Sarah would always etch the Star of David below the last line. When either one of them had decided that their poem had reached its end, I mean. They always wrote in the twin language. Partly to protect themselves, of course. But really, as I say, out of need to have intimacy.'

Peter held up the wood again. 'This, I believe, was their final poem. Sarah had been a student of the dance. She loved all kinds. But especially modern dance. She was very influenced by Ruth St Denis and oriental forms. Do you know her work?'

I shook my head.

Peter reached for one of the colourful Turkish pillows on the couch and put it on his lap, folded his hands on top. 'She introduced Indian and Japanese dance techniques to Europe and America. And forms developed by the Mevlevis. She was really quite popular, though by now her name has all but disappeared.'

'The Mevlevis?' I inquired.

'You call them Whirling Dervishes, I believe. They're a Sufi order. You've never studied Sufism, I take it?'

'No.'

'They're Islamic mystics. You'll find out about them sooner or later.'

'I will?'

'Of course.' He nodded without explaining. 'Anyway,' he began again, leaning toward me, 'Victor was a very serious mathematics student, very shy of dancing because of a dislike of his own body. He told her it was frivolous. He'd never dance with her, no matter how she pleaded. And it frustrated her so much, William said. Not to be able to share her passion with the man she loved.

'So in this last poem, Sarah said her strength was giving out, that if she did not survive that Victor should forgive her. Victor answered with all sorts of encouragements and pleadings, imploring her to hold on, that the Red Army couldn't be far away and that their revenge against the Nazis would be to survive ... to have a life together. Nothing worked, however. She was slipping away.

'Finally, he had an inspiration. He wrote: "I send you my strength, for one day I will watch you dance and dance beside you." You miss the poetry, of course, because it's in another language. But there is a rhyme, and a lively meter. I won't try to translate. I'm not very good at it. In any event, to give part of himself to her in the only way he could think of, he pulled out several of his hairs and tied them neatly around the wood.

'And it worked. "I will live for that day," Sarah responded.'

Victor then etched the Star of David below to finish the poem because nothing more needed to be said and returned it to her.'

Peter laid the wood on the table between us. He leaned his head back and scrunched his eyelids closed for a moment as if fighting physical pain. 'Then, Victor got very ill,' he continued. 'He had developed an infection. From the crude castration operation. It got worse and worse. The Jewish doctors tried to cover it, to heal it. They did everything to prevent Mengele or any of the other Nazis from discovering it. But they did, and to see how quickly it was spreading, Mengele had Victor given an injection of phenol directly into his heart and then dissected him.'

Peter spoke with a broken voice: 'Mengele dissected him ... dissected him still warm.' He stood up and turned his back to me. I could see him wiping tears from his cheeks. He apologized.

'Peter, you don't have to go on,' I said.

'No, you don't understand – I must. It's important that they be remembered.'

He sat down again. His eyes were so red I thought they were bleeding.

I said, 'Peter, you're hurt. You have to stop.'

I stood up and was about to go to him, but he waved me away. 'No, sit,' he pleaded. 'I must finish. I'm fine.'

He wiped beads of sweat from his forehead with his wrist. 'William found out about his brother's death only later,' he said. 'At the time, he knew just that Victor had disappeared, that he most likely had been murdered, his body turned to ash. German construction companies, they ... they used the ashes of murdered Jews for insulation between the walls in wooden houses. And as fertilizer. Did you know that?'

I shook my head.

Peter was angry now. He was almost shouting: 'The hair they took from Victor and the other prisoners, companies made a profit selling it for ... for stuffing mattresses. People slept on hair they stole from my mother! Can you understand what I'm saying? Those bastards made money selling fertilizer made from Jews, so they could get nice red radishes and...' He caught himself and breathed deeply to get his composure. 'William was healthy, you see. Although Mengele would have killed him, too, just to see if he had any even tiny infection. Or to check if there were differences in his organs, things that had prevented him from developing the same infection as his brother. But the Russian army was coming closer. Auschwitz was evacuated. It was chaos. William and many of the other twins hid. They were among the first liberated. The wood was found by another prisoner and given to William. Those few hairs were all he had left of his twin. He hunted for traces of Sarah. But he soon learned from another survivor that she had died on a forced march ... a march from Auschwitz to Bergen-Belsen. And do you know why they were marching?'

'No.'

'The SS didn't want any prisoners to be found by the Russians. They didn't want anyone to be able to tell them what ... what had been done to them. The Nazis were gazing into the future. They wanted a future of absolute silence, of disbelief. They were hoping that I'd never be able to tell you what I'm telling you now. And that if I told you, you wouldn't believe me.'

'But I do believe you. Everything you've told me.'

'Yes.' Peter tried in vain to smile. He closed his eyes, then glanced at me with a lost expression. 'I think that maybe Sarah knew that Victor had been killed and wished to go on no longer,' he whispered. 'No hope of dancing with him, you see. And William, he was left all alone. Though he still sees Victor from time to time.'

'Sees him?'

'As a presence.'

I remembered how William had reached out to take an invisible hand while walking in my yard. I said, 'That must be awful.'

'For a time. Because he thought Victor was furious at him for surviving. He thought that his brother wanted him to die, too. But that wasn't what he wanted at all. Victor returned not to take William away, but to push him back into our world. The dead are much more generous than we think.'

He took the wood again, sat with it on his knee. He talked with his head down. 'I'm the last person who can speak their twin language. When I die, a whole language will perish – a whole world.' He picked sadly at the hairs. It seemed that he was failing to find strength in himself for the first time since I'd known him.

'I'm sorry,' I said.

Peter nodded. He was crying.

I felt so close to him at that moment that I wanted to hug him. But I didn't move. I didn't want to risk melting into my own pool of tears.

We sat like that without talking, both of us watching the plum trees outside, swaying gently in the wind. After a few minutes, Peter wiped his eyes, stood up, and put the wood in front of me. 'So you see,' he said, 'your dream was not just a series of haphazard images. Strong objects can do that. At least, to some people.'

He noticed my sceptical look and said, 'I assure you it happens with me all the time. You see, if I touch an object, I can ... I can many times see the story behind it. I thought I was crazy when I was little, because I would touch ... let's say a chair, or a fence or a piece of clothing, and I'd see many things. William helped me get over those feelings of insanity. And if I touch a person, a hand, well, you can imagine ... It's sometimes overwhelming, which is why I don't touch people very often, why I may seem reserved ... why I am reserved. And if I do touch someone, it leaves something very strong with me. I have to choose people very carefully. So I'm sorry if I've seemed cold to you these past weeks.'

'You've nothing to be sorry for,' I said. 'Although I have to admit that I've wondered at times if you and me living here together was such a good idea.' He looked so despondent as I spoke that I added, 'I think you know that I like you, and that I've enjoyed your being here. It's been a godsend for me. But it's been hard, too. What with Alexandra leaving and all. And you *are* like a visitor from another planet sometimes.'

Peter laughed in a burst, then shook his head and faced

away, pleased but embarrassed. When he turned back to me, his eyes were filled with a soft light. 'I'm afraid I haven't been out in the world very much. Mostly with William and Mara. I've really just lived in the company of a few objects from my mother and my friends, mementos that are very dear to me.'

He smoothed his hair back over his ears with both hands. 'I know you were concerned when I got so angry in the club where Mara sings, when that man knocked into me. I don't know if I can explain, you're the first of ... You see, I don't like to be touched by people I don't want to be touched by. It's an invasion for me. It's like being violated, raped. And when someone is violent, it brings up other things. Things inherited from my mother and William, from the couple I lived with before William, about being attacked, taken away, about Nazis returning for me – things like that.'

I nodded my understanding; it suddenly didn't matter to me whether he was as sensitive to inanimate objects as he claimed. It only mattered that – like all of us – he was a fragile, vulnerable creature who needed love.

Peter smiled tensely. 'I have a theory that there are a lot of people like me. Not to the same extent, but somewhat. Even if only in dreams, visions. That's why I asked you to wait and see what the wood did ... what it produced in you.'

'An experiment?'

'No ... well, yes. A little. I hope you don't mind. It was the first time.'

'I probably should, but I don't. Though if I think about it, you know, it frightens me a little. I guess it's unnerving because there might be connections we can't see – that aren't under our control ... my control.'

'And you imagine they could hurt you?' he asked.

'I suppose.'

'They create themselves to help,' Peter said with calm assurance. 'If you do have spirits in this house...' he lifted his hands up toward the ceiling and looked with wonder around the room, 'then they are here to assist you.'

'You think so?'

'Bill, I promise that they are here to help. That is, in fact, precisely why they've come. And it's also why they've come at this particular time. I know it. It's just like Victor returning to help William stay in this world.'

His words were meant to comfort me, but in the hollow silence that followed, the swastika in Peter's bedroom appeared to me. I said, 'Peter, I have to tell you, I went down to look at your bedroom the other day. I'm sorry.'

He shrugged. 'It's okay ... I've nothing to hide from you.'

'It was wrong of me to go there ... to go there without your permission. I want you to feel comfortable here, that you have a right to your privacy. And I saw the swastika. It kind of scared me. So I spoke about it with Mara.'

He scoffed. 'No, it's fine. My secrets are in my head, not my room.'

'They seem to be there as well,' I smiled. 'But don't you feel that a Nazi flag is too ... I don't know, too morbid?'

Peter puffed out with his lips as he considered his answer. 'Sometimes, but that's what I want,' he said. 'I want it to be *too* morbid, to be bothered *too* much. That's why I asked William for the wood, in fact.'

I suddenly lacked the desire to press him about Mara's bird or the origin of his violence. Maybe I feared the answers he'd give me.

I went upstairs and got dressed for work. I wanted to give Peter something to show that I was moved that he had told me a story that meant so much to him. All I had were the blue shoes I'd bought.

When I handed them to him back in the living-room, I shrugged. 'Last night, when I was feeling lonely, I started thinking of you. Of how I liked being with you. I wanted to give you something in return. The leather is really wonderful, really soft, and I think they're beautiful.'

'They *are* beautiful,' he smiled. 'Thank you. But they're not really for me.' He offered them back.

'No, I bought them for you – really. I didn't know your size, but I thought that just maybe...'

'They're way too big,' he said.

'You're sure?'

He nodded. When I took them back, he said, 'But thank you for thinking of me. That means a lot to me.'

'You're sure you won't keep them? Maybe you know someone...'

'No, Bill, you hold on to them. I feel certain you'll find out who they're for. And then you give them to him – from both of us. That's it – give them to him from me, too.'

I got my briefcase and left Peter sitting on the couch, running his finger over the departed wishes embedded in his wooden talisman. With my last look back, I saw his fingers moving over his face as if to soothe an ache. I had never before noticed what strong, angular hands he had, how they seemed to have been created for a sketchbook. 'I'll see you later,' I said.

'Yes, yes,' he whispered.

∞

Work was uneventful, was no more than a Hollywood backdrop for the real life I had with Peter and my memories. I speculated for a time that maybe he only thought he saw all those stories behind objects – behind those Easter eggs and emeralds and amulets.

Then I frightened myself. I thought: *Maybe it's all a set-up. Maybe he made up the story about William and Victor and Sarah to fit my dream.*

Peter had the intelligence and creativity to fool me. I broke out into a cold sweat. I washed my face in the bathroom. I closed the door to my office and laid my head on my desk. I didn't want to go home.

I found myself thinking about Rain. It was about four-thirty in the afternoon. I sneaked outside and walked to the corner of Jones and O'Farrell, where I'd first seen her. There were two prostitutes out working. The one closest to me was a light-skinned black woman with varnished hair curled up off broad, powerful shoulders, eyelashes caked with liner, lips glistening with beet-red lipstick. When I told her about Rain, she kicked her heels on the pavement with a pained expression, waiting for me to get to the point.

'Hey, babycakes, nothing without money,' she told me.

'I just want to know if you knew her,' I pleaded.

'Only rain I know falls from the sky.'

A short blonde girl with Napoleonic curls twisted over her forehead posed across the street. She had a drowsy glance and a pixie nose. After I described Rain to her, she said, 'I think I'd seen her maybe once or twice.'

'Lately?'

She flapped her hand. 'Not in a month, at least.'

'Was she with anyone when you saw her?'

She shook her head.

'You're sure?'

'Not really. I don't pay all that much attention to the competition.'

I waited around for another half hour, but it must have been too early in the evening for more prostitutes. When I got back home, Peter's door was closed. There was a message on the answering machine from Alex, and the moment I heard her voice, I felt myself descending into a thick gloom.

Her voice was such a monotone that I was sure she was reading a prepared statement: 'Bill, I'd like very much to come over tomorrow after work with some movers to take some furniture I want. I've rented an apartment. Also, I've spoken to my lawyer to start divorce proceedings. I just wanted to let you know that. Bye. Oh, if it's okay for me to come over tomorrow, you don't have to call back. I'll just come. Early evening probably – around six. I've got work to do all day. Call back if that won't work. Though I hope it will, I'm very busy.'

I went upstairs to bury myself in my bed. I read for a time. It took me hours to fall asleep. I had no dreams that I could recall.

∞

Alex arrived that next evening encased in another of her mummy wraps; brown tweed this time. Her face was shimmering. No wrinkles, no pain, no anger. She had ascended from our world into her Mount Olympus, and she spoke like the recording, slow and measured. I found myself prepared to give her anything if she'd only leave. I didn't want any of the objects we'd shared. I said, 'Really, just take whatever you'll need – either couch, some chairs, of course, all the books you want.'

She frowned. 'Believe me, I will,' she said. 'And I won't need *your* permission!'

The movers walked in as I was sighing. Of all people, it was Steve and Renette, two ex-acid freaks who had painted the inside of the house three years earlier. Big smiles all around. Renette, who was the controlling member of the tandem, gave me a look of *California compassion*, the kind of nodding, knowing empathy that was so consciously sincere you could throw up. Framed by her scraggly blonde hair, she looked back and forth between me and Alex as if she were about to say something alchemical that would magically bring us back together. She wanted us to say: *All's forgiven, let's go bake bread!* I prayed that she wouldn't start counselling us. Steve was an emaciated, eager, forever-teenager with a simpleton's face. He looked with excitement at the furniture he'd be moving. You could almost see his tail wagging.

Renette was aching to say something soothing. She took my hands and stared ponderously into my eyes. 'I was very sorry to hear about you and Alexandra.'

'Thanks,' I said. I turned to Alex for support, found her feigning an interest in something she'd spotted on the upstairs landing.

'Hi, Bill,' Steve waved cheerily.

'Hi,' I waved back.

'You can start with the brown couch,' Alex suddenly said to Renette, for it was a rule that no one ever spoke voluntarily to Steve when Renette was in the room.

Alex glared up at me, daring me to disagree. When I didn't, she said, 'Well, you told me it was okay.'

'And it is,' I said. 'Be my guest.'

While Renette and Steve manoeuvred the couch outside, Alex surveyed the room.

'So where's your apartment?' I asked her.

'Noe Valley.'

'Oh, that should be nice.'

'It is, Bill ... *very* nice.'

I tiptoed around the room, wondering where to put my body. Alex started taking paintings and prints from the walls. I resolved not to argue even if she took something I wanted.

'Is it a big flat?' I asked.

'Big enough.'

Alex was biting at her nails the way she used to when writing a difficult legal brief. I waited in silence. Steve and Renette popped back inside. 'What's next on our shopping list?' Renette chirped.

'These,' Alex said, handing her several framed paintings. 'And a couple of the chairs at the dining-table.'

Renette's face gave me another blast of California compassion. I managed to look away before receiving its full surge.

Alex began lifting netsukes of lizards and snakes from the

mantelpiece. She grabbed two wooden spoons brought by a friend from Uruguay, a squatting demon from Indonesia. When Steve and Renette were outside again, I continued talking. 'I guess it's completely unfurnished,' I said.

Alex glared at me with shark eyes. 'Why else would I be here?!' She shook her head at my stupidity.

'Well, you might want these things anyway,' I proposed.

'Bill, do you really think I'd want that ratty couch if I already had one of my own? You can't really think that. Not even you...' Her voice trailed off into silent disbelief.

I felt embarrassment for both of us and plopped myself down on the white couch. I looked at pictures of genetically modified fruits in an issue of *Americas*. Apparently, you could get just about any two fruits to marry and produce a cross if you worked hard enough. Steve, Renette, and Alex made a few more trips in and out, took some things from upstairs, too. I didn't even look to see what they were. As long as it wasn't the bed, I would be fine.

'I suppose you want to keep the globe?' Alex suddenly asked. She was glaring at me.

I was so shocked that I couldn't talk at first. I stammered, 'Of course, well ... I'm the one who ... who cares about that sort of stuff.'

'Just checking,' she said with a cruel smile.

'Pretty obnoxious,' I observed.

'You think so, do you?' She stared at me superciliously, eager to give the impression that she didn't care that she was behaving badly.

'Fuck off!' I said.

She smiled at having provoked my anger, shrugged as if I were the one being silly. 'Okay then,' she added with a sigh. 'That's it, except for the desk downstairs.'

'Fine,' I said. Then I realized that she'd be sure to see the swastika on Peter's ceiling. My stomach sank. Maybe I could explain away the flowers and feathers, but the swastika ... I started making these awkward hand gestures that I inherited from my father and which I tend to resort to when I panic. 'No, no ... you can't. Peter ... he's not in and I don't feel I have the right to disturb his room.'

'Bill, it's my desk. My ... desk!' She separated her words for emphasis.

I tried kowtowing to get her to relent. 'I know, but look, I'll bring it over when he's home,' I said. 'I promise.'

'No thanks.'

'You're not being fair,' I protested.

'Fair?! *I'm* not being fair!' Renette and Steve walked in. Alex recapitulated the argument for their benefit: 'It's my desk and you tell me I can't have it because your tenant isn't in, and you say *I'm* being unfair! Who the fuck do you think you are?!' She glowered at me with predatory eyes.

In the past, I would have tried to diffuse the argument at this point with a joke. But that was all over.

'Alex, fuck it!' I said. 'Just fuck it! You know he's more than a tenant. He lives here. He has his right to privacy. Or don't you think that's a right?'

'Funny coming from you,' she said. 'You sleep around all over town and talk about privacy ... you ... you fucking asshole!'

It was Renette of all people who saved us from more melodrama. 'Steve and I will come and get the desk when Bill calls and says it's ready,' she said. 'There's no problem.' Renette looked between me and Alex. 'There's no problem. It's all settled.'

She sounded like someone who'd been through this before. I guess because Alex had freaked out, I regained my calm. I knew her pride would prevent her from speaking first, so I volunteered: 'That's okay with me.'

Alex breathed in deeply and closed her eyes. She turned to Renette. 'Thanks for offering. That'll be fine.'

'I'll call tonight or tomorrow – no later,' I told Renette. 'And I really appreciate all your help.' I wanted to speak graciously because Alex had thanked her and I wasn't about to be one-upped at this point.

Alex surveyed the place once more, grabbed an ancient shard of Mexican tile from a bookshelf. She nodded to herself. 'Bye,' she said to me, adding a quick glare of challenge. 'And expect a call from my lawyer. We have to get the papers going and work things out with the house.'

'What *things* with the house?' I asked.

'If we want to sell it.' She saw I hadn't expected this, and her voice grew confident. 'Or if you want to buy me out. If you've got enough money in your account. I've no way of knowing.'

Again I was too stunned to utter a sound. We had agreed that the house would be a home for me and a long-term investment for her. Now, aware for the first time what an idiot I'd been to believe her, my brain refused to link coherent thoughts together.

'See you,' Steve added with a big smile. Renette gave me a card with her telephone number. 'I understand how you're feeling,' she said. 'Just call when the desk's ready. We can talk, too, if you like. Really, just talk.'

I smiled weakly. She grabbed Steve with a look that said, *don't say anything more to the poor man*, then left.

I was alone, imprisoned in a pillaged house, one that was no longer mine for ever and ever. It was as if Alex had destroyed my last good feelings about my life. I almost laughed at the absurdity of it, then that little game wheel spun inside of me and pointed toward hopelessness.

I dragged myself upstairs to assess the damage. A turquoise-blue ceramic vase purchased on our trip to Santa Fe was gone. And a sweet drawing of a sleeping elephant we'd both liked and bought from a gallery on Sullivan Street in

New York. There was a dust-free rectangle on the wall where it used to be. I turned. My soul soared. The bed – my bed, the one I'd had even before I met her – was still there. I collapsed face down, buried my head in the foam scent of a pillow. And yet, despite my comfort, or maybe because of it, I suddenly felt a deadly hate for Alexandra stronger than any I'd ever experienced. She was surely the cruelest person I ever met. I felt justified in every mean thing I'd ever done to her, said to her. I only wished I had done more.

When Peter came home, I was lost in daydreams of how I could make the divorce difficult – lie and mislead and grin maniacally through it all. I heard his footsteps in the living-room and rushed to the stairs. He looked up at me with a puzzled face. 'What the hell happened?' he asked.

'Alexandra came through with the Huns. I escaped with my life but I'm afraid they got the best part of the furniture.' Peter didn't smile, but I couldn't stop the flow: 'You'll be happy to know I defended your rooms with great valour. No, don't thank me. Not yet, at least. I think it's okay for now. But they might be back. So guard your furniture well. Guard Maria and that worm and the necklace and your bed.'

Peter stood there stunned. He said, 'I hope you'll let me replace some of it.'

'Peter, you can replace anything you like. You can even replace me!' I looked around at the ruins. 'At least she left the piano. And the globe.' I went to it and gave it a spin. 'You know, I even had to fight for it. What a bitch. What a fucking bitch! But I suppose it's okay. You can still play. And I...' I spun the globe again. '...I can still daydream of escaping on seven different continents.'

Peter took me seriously and said, 'I really don't want to play the piano right now. I had an awful day at the consulate. I'm really going to have to get out of this line of work soon.'

'You don't have to play,' I said. 'I was really just kidding.'

We shared the silence of an ineptly staged play, of actors who'd forgotten their lines. 'Peter, I need to know something,' I said. 'What you said before, about William's wooden amulet. You didn't make that up to fit my dream, did you?'

'Of course not,' he said. He looked confused.

'You would tell me if you did?'

He nodded. 'I'm not here to hurt you,' he said. 'You have to believe that. Even if ... even if you don't believe everything I say.'

'I guess it's just my mistrust of people,' I confessed.

He began sniffing around the room. 'Did you just eat?' he asked.

'No.'

He puffed out with his lips. 'Doesn't matter.' He looked behind him and reached out for a chair as if about to collapse, then dropped down. My remaining couch was directly opposite. We faced each other like two chess players without a board between us. His eyes closed suddenly, and he smiled as if entering a dream.

'How long ago did you join the diplomatic corps?' I asked.

Peter's eyelids quivered. 'Six years ago.'

'Did you always want to?'

'No. But I wanted to travel. And William thought it would be good for me to get out of Brazil.' Peter's expression became pensive as he looked for the right words. 'He's got this theory that Brazil is doomed. He didn't want to stay there. After he made some money, we could have left at any time, I suppose. But he wanted me to have a job in the new country and wanted to come with me. Mara was here already. Family is important to him. So we tried hard for San Francisco and made it here. But now, I've just grown so tired of it all.'

An image of Rain's body came to me. She was blanched and stiff. 'I interviewed more prostitutes,' I said. 'But no one knew Rain.'

Peter sat up. 'It's really a tragedy, you know. She was great. She was very bright, was doing really well. You could sense something about her. Something different.' He saw my knowing look. 'And I don't mean her sex. Or not only that.'

'Who do you think killed her?' I asked.

'I don't know.'

'A date?'

'A *what?*' he asked.

'One of her customers.'

Peter shrugged and ran his hands back through his hair. 'Maybe. Maybe someone who didn't like it that she felt most comfortable as a sphinx.'

∞

For the next few evenings, I picked up take-out Chinese food after work, ate in bed, and read until I was too tired to keep my eyes open. No friends, no family. I called no one, not even my mother or Jay, both of whom left messages on my machine.

Peter came home promptly every evening after work. When I told him that he didn't have to, he said, 'Too much darkness faced alone isn't healthy.'

He rearranged the remaining furniture and placed flowers all over the living-room and kitchen. We were emblazoned with daisies and mums, carnations and dahlias. The place began to look like an English cottage furnished by cheerful gardeners. 'Blue and white are particularly good for you when you're feeling isolated,' he told me once as he was putting cornflowers together with ivory carnations. Adding three long pear tree branches to the arrangement, he said, 'This *pereira* bark contains the skeleton of a powerful hamadryad I once glimpsed in Brazil.'

I nodded absently. When he left for his room, I looked up hamadryad in the dictionary. It meant wood nymph.

So Peter saw wood nymphs in tree bark ... It didn't seem to matter from within the safety of a living-room in full bloom.

I cloistered myself inside that landscape, and when I finished my book on the Inquisition, I started Doris Lessing's *The Good Terrorist*. I enjoyed it, but couldn't help thinking that in her treatment of my life, she'd have made Alexandra the heroine and me the villain. And when I read that the narrator, a lost young woman, had 'felt some instinctive warning or shrinking' at first meeting her future boyfriend, I remembered how Alexandra had once told me that she knew I was going to be 'big trouble' the very first time she saw me.

There was really only one interruption of my newly patterned life. I called Steve and Renette the day after Alex's raid, and they came for the desk. Peter and I had carried it outside where Renette would feel less inclined to share her feelings with me.

∞

Then came Thursday, July 31, and things started to speed up toward the end of our time together. Peter was closing his outside door just as I got home.

'Going to dinner?' I asked.

He looked up, disturbed from thought. 'To find Maria,' he said.

'She's escaped?'

Peter bit his lip and squeezed his fists, made a grunting noise. 'Stolen! *Puta de merda...*' He let out a string of curses in Portuguese.

'Stolen? Who could have stolen her?'

Peter frowned and marched past me. I stood behind the oleander bush in the front yard and watched him disappearing down the street. I grew deathly afraid that he was leaving my life forever.

Chapter 11

PETER MARCHED WEST down Clay Street, cut left on Arguello, then continued west on Clement. I did my best to hide behind other people as I followed in case he should turn around. He didn't look back, however. Either he knew where Maria was or he was being drawn in this direction.

After about three quarters of an hour, we reached Lincoln Park. At the entrance, he paused and sniffed at the air. I was maybe fifty yards away from him at this point, thankful for stopping. Too soon for me, he took off again. He marched up the road past the golf course into the wild fringe of park bordering the sea cliffs. It was a path hedged by cypress trees contorted into bonsai shapes by swirling gusts lifting off the ocean two hundred feet below. A cold, salty wind blew hard against us even now. I turned up my collar and buttoned my jacket. Through the heavy branches of trees, I could see the Golden Gate Bridge spanning the white caps of the channel and giving access to the bare brown hills of Marin County to the north. Now and again, we cut dangerously close to the jagged cliff faces. Sea water buffeted the lonely beach below. The sky had darkened and lowered. Cormorants rested on a gigantic boulder close to shore.

I followed Peter across a valley overgrown with fennel bushes, then climbed up a hill and switchbacked down toward the cliffs again. Suddenly, he stopped. He turned slowly around, as if he'd heard something. He sniffed at the salt air, then ducked into some thick underbrush.

In a moment, he was back on the path. He held Maria's empty birdcage.

Peter rested his discovery on the ground, looked out at the

sea as if caught between decisions. I called his name.

When I reached him, I explained that I'd followed him.

He was crying. 'I think he's killed her,' he whispered.

'He who?'

'William. Or...' His voice trailed away.

'William?' I glanced at the empty cage. 'Why him? I thought he loved you.'

Peter wiped his eyes and looked at me from what seemed a great distance. 'To make a point,' he said.

'What point?'

'That I should stick to my own kind.'

'Your own kind?'

He picked up the cage. 'Let's go home. I don't want to talk ... talking's useless.'

We walked to the edge of the park as if punished by fate. I dared to ask, 'What is the special connection you have with Maria?'

'Isn't that obvious?' he replied in a whisper.

'It's more than friendship,' I said. 'It's like there's some connection. There's something...'

'Bill, what would you say if I told you that birds are beings so holy that ... that their souls can't be chained to earth? And that that's why they have wings.'

'I'd say that it was a nice idea.'

'It's not an idea,' he snapped.

'But Maria?' I insisted. 'What about her specifically?'

'Hoopoes are frequently used by angels as servants, as couriers. You should take a look at some Middle Eastern literature. Read Attar and Rumi. They write about the nature of birds.'

'*Angels?*' I inquired.

'What about them?'

'They use hoopoes as couriers?'

He nodded. 'Maria's crown is a sign of her calling. It's a

sort of manifestation of her regal nature. She ... I guess you could say, she helps me.'

'Peter, are you saying ... look, are you saying that you think you're an angel?'

He turned away from me as if it were a forbidden subject.

'Peter, what is it you're telling me? I mean, what could you ... what is it ... ?' He kept refusing to face me, so I gave up on my questions.

I called a cab from a phone booth. Peter stood on the sidewalk holding Maria's cage, his hair blowing wildly. His shirt rippled in the wind like a flag. He looked tiny against the stormy sky and stately Victorian homes. I realized that the power he gleaned from his beauty was useless against pain. He'd told me that once, and he had been right.

We rode back home inside a hollow silence linked by the presence of Maria's empty cage. I recalled William's words to me, his hostility, wondered why he would kill Maria. Inside the house, I made Peter some jasmine tea, sat with him in the living-room. He didn't move. His eyes glistened. Stalks of feathery pampas grass arched over his head from a black vase on the mantelpiece. Tears ran down his cheeks. I said, 'Explain to me what point was William trying to make.'

He wouldn't reply.

'What did you mean by "my own kind"?'

Peter's lips were sealed to silence.

It was then that he started to shiver, his teeth to chatter.

'Are you okay?' I asked.

He sat holding his teacup, staring straight ahead with unfocused eyes. I got a woollen blanket from the closet and put it around his shoulders, took the cup from him, and felt his forehead. It was hot, and my hand retained his touch as I took it away, as if this contact with him had once again imprinted a pattern on my nerves – much as looking at a strong light leaves an after-image. I rubbed at my hand while listening to the silence. I tried to take his temperature. He wouldn't open his mouth. That made me angry. I demanded that he speak to me.

He said nothing.

I considered calling a doctor. But I didn't know one I trusted. And I knew somehow that he wouldn't want that. I went upstairs so he wouldn't hear and called Mara.

'Maria's been stolen and Peter's sick,' I told her. 'I'm not sure what to do.'

'I'll be right over.' She hung up without another word.

While I hovered over Peter, part of me also marvelled at him, as I might at some exotic animal. He had descended into my life from out of nowhere, by pure accident it seemed to me at the time. And here he was, making himself sick because the pet he loved was stolen. I was wondering what I could do for him. Though maybe he would just shake himself free of the fever in a moment, pop up and exclaim that he had controlled the infection and was now as healthy as ever.

The doorbell rang. It was too soon for Mara. The possibility of Alexandra invading my life just now terrorized me. I felt too unsettled to see her, that I'd have to move fully into my new life before I'd be ready to allow her the slightest entry. The visitor turned out to be Jay, however. In his jeans, brown corduroy shirt, and blood-red braces, he looked like a boyish model for an outdoorsmen catalogue.

'Long time no see,' he said cheerfully.

I didn't want to talk to him, but I waved him inside. 'Peter's sick.'

Jay walked over to the couch and said to him, 'What is it? Have you got a fever?'

Peter didn't answer. He shivered.

'He's not talking,' I said.

'You call the doctor?' my brother asked.

'No.'

'Why not?'

''Cause I don't want to!' I whisper-screamed.

Jay took my arm and spoke like an elder: 'I really think you should.'

I did all I could to prevent a shriek from ripping the air. I squinted angrily at him. 'Look, a friend of his is coming over who'll know what to do,' I said, warning him to shut up with those whirling hand gestures I'd inherited from my father. 'Until then, let's just wait.'

Jay sat down on the couch and licked his lips bitterly. I walked to my globe and spun it to escape his stare. He talked with Peter to no avail, then said to me, 'I guess Alexandra took some furniture.'

'You got that right.'

As I looked at Jay, I wondered again why we had grown apart. While we sat in the silence of Peter's illness, I turned the problem over and over searching for its keyhole. Of course, I knew it had a great deal to do with his having unexpectedly taken on the judgmental posturings and voice of our father. But it wasn't just that. That was more like a road sign that pointed to the reasons: 20 MILES STRAIGHT AHEAD TO THE TRUTH.

Those twenty miles were always the hardest.

'I'm sorry I yelled before,' I told him. 'Just give me time.'

He nodded, and as if to answer my unspoken inquiries, replied, 'Maybe if you grow up with enemies, you always need to keep at least one around.'

'Maybe so,' I agreed.

Peter was still shivering. I added another blanket to his shoulders. Jay paced. When Mara knocked at the door, he let her in. She marched past him to Peter. She was wearing baggy red sweatpants, a black T-shirt, and a pink vest, looking for all the world like an elfin bullfighter. No introduction to Jay. No pleasantries. It might have been comical in some other situation. But Mara was in some sort of trance. Her black eyes were glowing. She knelt next to Peter and squeezed his hands. They were limp. His teeth were chattering again. She looked up at me. 'How long ago did this start?'

'A half hour maybe,' I replied.

'He hasn't vomited?' she asked.

'No.'

'Good. Help me put him to bed.'

Jay and I stood Peter up and walked him toward his rooms. He took heavy, laboured steps. His clothes were damp from sweat. His face was beet red. I introduced Mara to Jay as we walked. 'You know what it is?' I asked her.

'Maria's disappearance,' she replied.

Jay asked, 'The bird?'

I nodded.

At Peter's door, I realized his bedroom was down the spiral staircase. 'Shit, we'll never get him down there,' I moaned.

Jay said, 'Let's bring him to your room.'

We trudged upstairs. Jay and I laid him on the bed. On Mara's instructions, we tucked him under the blankets. He was trembling.

'Shouldn't we take off his clothes?' I asked.

'No!' Mara said forcefully, too forcefully. But I wasn't about to press the issue. She opened the buttons on his shirt and pressed both her hands to his chest. She leaned over him. Motionless, she stared at him. It was the strangest thing comparing their faces. Peter's, masculine and adult, but strangely soft; Mara's feminine but boyish. Yet there was a link. Maybe it was the eyes – windows on a dark interior world that they both inhabited. I thought of what she'd told me about her healing powers and added my own prayers to whatever was happening.

Suddenly, as if hypnotized, Peter's eyelids closed. Mara passed into our world again and stood up. She turned to me and unfurled her impossibly pink tongue with a sigh. She folded her arms in front of her chest. 'He'll sleep now,' she said.

'What did you do?' I asked.

'Helped him rest.'

'How?'

'Never mind that for now.'

'Why all the secrecy?'

Mara walked past me toward the door without an answer.

'So should we try to get a doctor?' Jay called after her.

She turned back. 'No, there's no need now.'

We followed her downstairs. When she reached the front door, she said, 'Keep Peter still and call me if he's worse when he wakes up.'

'You're not going to tell me what this is all about, are you?' I asked.

'It's about Maria ... about Maria being stolen, I told you!' she replied impatiently, a Brazilian accent noticeable in her voice for the first time since I'd met her. Anxiety began to create fissures in her grammar as well: 'He's had her since many years. Look, you can talk of it with Peter at any length you like when he will awaken. But you let him sleep now.' She reached out for the handle to the front door, then twisted back with a critical frown. She folded her hands into a position of prayer. 'Listen, Bill, he'll need you to help him when he wakes up,' she said. Her voice had changed back. 'So don't be angry with me.'

'Okay,' I said. 'Anything else we should do?'

'No, just let him sleep. Call me if he seems worse.' She gazed down for a moment to gather her strength, then waved to Jay and me.

The moment the door had closed, my brother asked, 'How old do you think she is?'

'About forty I guess.'

'She's got this look of...'

'Yeah, she does. A childhood illness screwed up her hormonal system, so she retains some of her girlish qualities as she ages,' I explained.

Jay pushed his questioning face toward me. 'So you and Mara think Peter got so upset at the bird being gone that he made himself sick?'

'Me? I don't know anything any more.' I told him about the walk to the park, the empty cage, William.

'Well, it seems to me, it's William you've got to check out,' Jay said, jumping up with determination. He grabbed the phone book and looked up William's name – all the spellings of *Schreiber* he could think of. 'Nothing,' he concluded. 'It's probably unlisted. You were a reporter once upon a time, how do we get those?'

It riled me that I didn't know. 'We don't,' I said.

'Peter must have the number. Where's his address book?'

'I've no idea.'

Jay snapped his braces. I was sure that he was trying to drive me crazy. 'Let's start the treasure hunt,' he said, and he lifted his eyebrows as if preparing for mischief.

I looked to heaven for support. 'Jay, you can't just do that.'

'Why not?'

'Because it's an invasion of privacy. How'd you like some-one looking for your address book while you were sick?'

'There's nothing in it I'm ashamed of! Do you think there is?!'

Here we go again, I thought. 'That's not what I meant,' I said.

'Then what did you mean? It seems to me finding this creep who stole the bird is important.'

'It is, but what are we going to do even if we find his phone number? Call him and ask for the bird back? I suspect it won't work.'

'We'll go pay him a visit. Or we'll call the police.'

I moaned theatrically. 'Forget the police. The SFPD's not so big on missing birds. Besides, we shouldn't leave Peter.'

'Then I'll visit him,' he said with naïve bravado.

'Look, if he stole Maria, he's probably insane. Forget it. We'll go with Peter to get her later.'

We sat without speaking. Jay turned on an old Dana Andrews movie. He glanced back at me from time to time trying to elicit the apology I wasn't going to give. I checked on Peter. He was still asleep. I was struck by how gentle he looked, reminded again of how anyone slumbering looked innocent to me. You could probably put the devil himself in a bed, rest his little horns on a down pillow, slip his cloven hoofs under a wool comforter, and presto ... he'd look like a choirboy.

As Peter slept, I allowed myself to imagine him as a close friend of mine, someone in whom I could confide everything. There had been no one like that for many years now. A long time before Alexandra had left, she had ceased being that for me, and I had stopped being that for her. Or maybe we'd never even risked going that far, had only been willing to reveal the more colourful blooms of our deeply rooted secrets. I watched him breathe, sensing myself close enough to share the rise and fall of his chest. Sweat had beaded on his forehead, and I imagined it moistening my own brow. I lowered myself next to him to wipe it away with my fingertips. I believe that this was only the fourth or fifth time I'd touched him. Again, I retained our contact for long afterward. It comforted me, and I felt the power inside me of fighting for someone else, of not disappointing, of having the courage to destroy impossible obstacles for others, for yourself.

I sat by Peter, pervaded by the fierce loneliness that was always coiled inside my numbing armour. I returned downstairs, watched the end of the movie with Jay. He jumped up as the credits were rolling. As he stood at the door ready to leave, I said, 'Sorry about being so touchy.'

He nodded his easy acceptance of the apology and yawned. We looked at each other, both of us wondering how far apart our paths would take us in the future. 'Bye,' I said.

'See ya.'

Our voices were hollow. The front door snapped shut. I realized we'd never be friends.

∞

I took one of Peter's flower arrangements from the mantelpiece — an elegant pink and white day-lily surrounded by a bright circle of orange poppies — and walked upstairs to check on him. He was still asleep, wrapped inside his sarcophagus of blanket. I put the vase on my night table, tiptoed around the bed, strangely calm, confident he would recover soon. I picked up two pillows and, with a last look back at him, returned downstairs. I made up the couch, turned off the lights, and stretched out in the dark, capturing the pleasant feelings that come with helping, releasing those mysterious fluids of goodness. It seemed as if it had been a long time since I had been certain of my own virtue. Struggling with Alex, watching the white flame of our craziness burning away our marriage, it was impossible to think of myself as anything but a monster.

I slept, comforted by this realization, but was woken into darkness some time later by a stirring upstairs. I lay still, listening to a ruffling of sheets. I heard footsteps, imagined Peter standing up. Curious about his condition, I got to my feet, slipped on my robe, and tiptoed upstairs.

I pushed the door open gently. Silhouetted against the moonlight shining through the window, Peter stood grey and naked in the middle of the room like some magnificent shadow creature come to life — silent, mysterious, an inhabitant of another world. I looked down across his chest to his legs, and his behind twisted toward me into the light, soft and gently curving from his chest into his legs. He did not have the buttocks of a man at all, but the gently enclosing behind of a woman. My cock swelled. It raised itself against my robe, and I felt myself swaying with my heartbeat. A wave of anxiety descended over me like a netting of death. I felt faint, a cold sweat seeping out of me, dampening my skin. I could not move. Yet my penis kept pulling me toward the dark figure.

This creature turned to me, noticed my excitement, glided up to me, stood against me. A shadow hand reached for my sex, stroked it, teased it. I felt a strength building up from my gut, a power trying to move my hands around his sloping behind, pulling my penis into his legs. I stood still, sensing an archway I could walk through or turn away from. It was high and foreboding and the landscape beyond was menacing, deserted, held rigid by a dusky sky. Insect creatures from the distant past were buzzing around me, seeming to search for an entrance. A great wind was blowing in from the west, from the sea, as if bellowed from the lungs of an invisible god.

I was on the edge of crying, of exploding, too, of grabbing this creature in an unbreakable lock and taking it. Its lips touched against my own, gently but electrically, and I felt myself moving under a shadow of death through the hot night into the archway, the insect creatures slowly dissipating behind me, my body emerging on the other side, alone, hopeless, desperately wanting the touch of another person. A hard and warm wetness flicked against my lips, hunting for an opening. I fought this probe from inside my mouth, felt the shadow pass over me again, begin circling above me. I pulled back, whimpered. A moist exploration sought entry once again, and my soul opened a crack. On the edge of tenderness, I whimpered again, fought back, closed the wall. The stiff wetness left without entry, crept across my neck, searching, exploring the inside walls of my body, testing the hidden corners of my caves, making room for itself in me. Then it was gone. I was in my penis again, pushing against him to ease the teasing pain, inhaling the luscious woven scent of warm hair rubbing against my gut. My robe dropped to the floor and lips kissed across my chest. Warmth licked at my hairs, my nipples, moved down across my stomach. An impossible clenching squeezed around my cock, a crying, caressing wetness was circling all around me, swallowing me, moving back and forth over me, curling me, bathing me, pushing me forward. Lips moaning, moving up across my pubic hair, my stomach, back over my cheeks to my ears, exploring me, twisting around me, enveloping, coiling, bursting, gripping my behind. Hard jagged breathing of desperate desire. My fingers trembling, caressing across the silk of his hair, holding his wide, smooth hips, squeezing them, creeping through his pubic hair, searching out his crevices, reaching for his penis, waiting for it to swell powerfully inside my hand, waiting for its weight and desire. A warm strange wetness welcoming my fingers. Death. The shadow of death chilling me. A swaying heartbeat. The scent of oceans rising over me, a mouth biting across my ear and chin, breathing hot inside me. A whisper lost to silence. A hand guiding my penis inside the warmth. Wet warmth. Surrounding me. My penis searching. A panting rising into a wail, a sharp scream, like pain twisting into desire. Another hand pulling me down into hands slapping against me, kicking, biting, tearing against me, holding me, pushing, moaning, ripping, exploding...

I came inside Peter. He lay under me crying. I had returned from beyond the archway and could feel my penis still swollen inside ... inside what? Not his behind, for I was balanced on top of him. He held my buttocks firmly in his powerful hands. I felt as if leeches were seeking entry to me through the tip of my penis and drew back out of him. I stood up. I covered myself with my robe. I was dizzy, felt a sharp, blood-soaked tension in my stomach, as if I had swallowed glass. I stared at the dark creature on the bed who had seduced me, repeating to myself over and over that it would never happen again.

'I ... I don't understand,' I said.

Peter lay still, then rolled his feet over the side of the bed, stood up and turned on the lights. I backed away from him. When I dared to look at his face, I saw the old Peter, unbelievably handsome, confident. But below, there was a desolate triangle of pubic hair where his penis should have been. Silver eyes stared at me. Breaths raised and lowered his chest. My emotions seemed to recede. I listened to my inadequate words from far away: 'I don't understand.'

'I'm an androgyne,' he whispered.

He continued speaking, but I didn't hear. Ineffable sentences framed his face. His eyes closed as if from behind a pane of glass. Symmetrical breaths were exchanged between us. A tissue was taken from a night table and wiped around his sex. There was the desire to watch the world passing forever and never participate.

I don't know how long I just stood there staring, concealed deep under layers of silence. Peter spoke for a time, but I didn't hear what he was saying.

'What ... what are you?' I finally asked.

He bit his lip and shrugged. 'I have some attributes you would consider male and some you would consider female.'

There was a sickness building in my chest. 'How ... how's that possible?' I asked.

He smiled as if about to cry, then laughed in a lonely exhale. 'People are born this way. Oh yes. Not often, but it happens. And I ... I am one.'

He opened his legs so I could see his sex. 'I was born this way. There are many ways it can happen. An extra X chromosome, for instance. Have you never heard of that condition?'

'Vaguely. But I don't see...'

Peter raised his hands as if seeking to make peace and explained in a patient voice that when he was little, he was raised as a girl. His mother didn't know that he had male characteristics buried inside him.

It seemed preposterous. 'Why are you trying to fool me?'

'I'm not fooling anyone,' he said. 'At puberty, when male characteristics began to emerge in my body, I became a boy.'

'And now?'

'And now, what?'

'What do you tell people?'

He looked up at me, puzzled. 'Nothing. It's not any of their business.'

'Does Mara know?'

'Yes.'

'Why her?'

'How could she not know? She joined William and me when she was still a kid. She knows it all. I consider her my sister. And she's like me.'

'Like you how?' I asked.

'It doesn't matter,' he sighed.

'Peter, she can't have a penis,' I insisted.

He shook his head.

'Then how?!' I demanded.

'Don't you see? She's in-between, too. In-between sexes. We're closer to the middle than most, than you for instance. But we're hybrids, all of us, even...'

He cut his words short, gave me a cold, challenging look. I understood that he was ready to accuse me of being an anomaly as well. Rage swelled inside me. He had waited until I was most vulnerable, then attacked. Maybe it had been his plan all along. My depression had left me open to someone like him. In an insane voice, I shrieked, 'Mara has a fucking bird, too, you know! Just like you!'

'Oh yes?'

'Yeah, a toucan. A fucking toucan!'

Peter nodded absently. He glanced outside at the plum trees, then turned with a melancholy smile at the floral arrangement I'd brought up. How out of place his lily was now. He gazed back at me, probing.

'It's what you're attracted to, Bill. Alexandra's hard masculinity, for instance. It frightened you because you wanted it. And then there's your own sensitivity. It makes you terrified. After all, what would your father think if he could see it? And what would Jay think? But it's a big part of what you are. And it's the part you actually like the most. That's the irony. Those women you trail ... Those dead women with frozen emotions ... You don't need me to tell you that you're really just trying to revive yourself when you sleep with them. That little boy who grew up numb ... that's still you. You've never really thawed, have you? It's still the Ice Age wherever you are. Look, Bill, if you're going to learn how to love ... If you're going to learn how to give and receive love, you've got to look at yourself in the mirror. You've got to look a lot closer than you ever have before and you've got to accept what you see.'

Sweat beaded on my forehead. A great chill descended through me in waves. There was a whirling sense of falling. My hand reached out for the door handle. I was about to flee.

'Let me tell you a story,' Peter called in a conciliatory voice. 'A myth about how I came to be ... about how androgyny came into the world. About me. Sit ... don't be afraid. I'm here to help. I promise. Just like your spirits.'

I stood by the door, afraid to move.

'Sit,' he said. 'I won't touch you if you don't want me to. I promise. But just sit with me.'

I fought the urge to turn and run, was swaying with my heartbeat, looking into the night through the open window. Pulsating music from Paul Simon's *Graceland* album was entering the room from far away. Someone was having a party at this moment; people were conversing, laughing.

'Do me one last favour,' Peter said. 'Sit with me for five minutes.'

I must not have been able to think clearly, because I remember wanting to leave, but the next thing I knew I was sitting on the edge of the bed. Peter gathered up a blanket and placed it gently over my shoulders without brushing against me. He brought his knees to his chest and snuggled back against the wall. He was drawing away from me, wanting to make me feel safe. And yet, I wished I could ask him to comfort me. Though I knew I never could.

∞

'This story takes place thousands of years ago,' he began. 'And it concerns a journey. Of a young man named Amarta. If it helps you to picture him, Bill, you can think of him as me. That would probably be good for you to do. Though later, there's a secret I'll tell you about him, about his identity.'

My back was to Peter. I sensed he wanted me to nod. Maybe I did. I'm not sure; I don't believe I'd ever felt so distant from my own movements. My breathing, my vision, my touch . . . it was as if they weren't fully under my control. Thoughts were coming from outside me, and I was at the centre of a very deep silence. And yet I was worried that a shout would suddenly fly up out of my chest. Or that I'd stand and race out of the house. I wanted my body to stay very still.

I guess that absenting myself was the only way I could remain in the room with him after what we'd done.

'So this young man, Amarta, he lived in a city called Anthus. Tradition holds that it was somewhere in Anatolia, in Turkey. But that may be wrong. The girls born there — it is said that they had the most beautiful round faces and knowing eyes. And because of that they'd always been prized as concubines and slaves by the aristocrats of another city not far away, of Ereka. Now, in the war between the two city-states, Anthus fell to the Erekan army. And slave traders began making regular visits there, to that unfortunate city, in order to take back with them to their capital all the girls of child-bearing age.

'Amarta was the orphaned son of an Anthen blacksmith and seamstress. And when he was nineteen, he watched this sad departure of the city's girls for the last time. Because the adventure that would change all our lives, Bill, began the very next afternoon.'

Peter spoke these last words as if they should have been followed by a fanfare. He shifted his legs over the sheets. I took a deep breath and faced him. He was sitting erect, his feet pinned back under his behind. His arms rested lightly on his thighs, and I had the feeling he might simply rise into the air or disappear.

I'll never know anyone else like him. That's the thought that was unfurling down to me. When our eyes met, I turned away. The hope that it would be possible to travel back to a time before he'd come into my life began to ache in my gut. *I'll sit here five minutes*, I reasoned. *Then I'll just get up and leave, even if he hasn't finished talking. And I won't look back.*

'Amarta was sitting alone in the city's central square. On the edge of the ruined fountain of a withered rose garden. A woman in yellow robes, sitting atop a camel, approached him. The amber light in her eyes transfixed him as she spoke: "Long ago, I heard of wonderful linen cloth from this region. Do you know of a seller?"

'"You can no longer buy linen here," Amarta replied. "All our flax fields were destroyed by the Erekans many years ago and never replanted. Our young women live as concubines, our men as breeders and farmers."

'The woman nodded sadly, reached down to caress the boy's shoulder. Pulling on the reins of her camel, she started away. Amarta followed her covertly as she crossed the town. He imagined that her touch had placed a yoke over his head, binding him to her. He looked out across Anthus, and it seemed to be a city already left behind, a land long-abandoned to strangers. He decided to make his presence known to the woman as she reached the Eastern Gate.

'"I followed you," he told her. "I want to go away with you."

'"I go to the east, to Telure," she replied. "It's a long journey."

'"All the better," he smiled.

'"Is there not a rule against your leaving – as a breeding male?" she asked Amarta.

'"If the Erekans find me outside the city, they will kill me – and you."

'The woman laughed. "They couldn't kill me. I would never allow it."

'The young man was stunned by her words, amused as well; she spoke like the crazy hierophant, Sidli. *Perhaps she is a priest of the religion of Telure*, he thought. *Or a sorceress*.'

When Peter spoke the word *sorceress* I could feel my anxiety rising into my chest. I was worried it would leak out as tears. 'Peter, you're not telling me this story to scare me, are you?' I asked in a hesitant, child's voice. 'I mean, you didn't do anything terrible to anyone? You've never killed anyone, cut anything off anyone?'

He gazed at me gently. I knew he wanted to hold me, but was afraid he'd scare me off. 'No, it's not about anything like that. Mara told me what your father said to you years ago. About the Ethiopian baby. But this story, all my stories ... If you'll just wait, I think you'll see. Wait and see, Bill.'

He smiled awkwardly, seeming to apologize for not being able to say more. Then he made fists and shook them, as if to ask me to have some courage. And faith. It was the hardest thing he could have asked me for at the time. I didn't give it. *Four minutes and counting*, I said to myself. *Then we can go our separate ways forever*.

'So there he was about to leave the city of his birth,' Peter started again, 'and the disquieting feeling arose in him that their trip together, Amarta's trip with this woman visitor, that it had been woven long ago into the pattern of his life. "May I come then?" he begged her.

'The woman nodded her assent, and she began to tug on

the reins of her camel so that the animal would kneel and let the young man mount.

'"No, I must return home first, to tell my aunt and sister," he said.

'"Very well. I will wait outside the gate."

'Amarta raced home, pushed by a wave of enthusiasm he'd never felt before. When he told his aunt of his plans, she asked, "But why would you leave us?"

'The young man found no answer in his heart. He saw only the welcoming blue sky beyond the city's walls. "Just to leave," he said.

'"I do not give my approval," she scowled. "We need you to work here."

'"Your approval is not needed. I must go. I have no choice. If I stay, I'll die."

'When Amarta faced his younger sister, Sentar, she covered her eyes with her hands and began to tremble. He kissed her cheek and said, "I promise to return for you before you are taken away by the Erekans."

'And so he left. At the Eastern Gate, he rejoined his amber-eyed visitor. She told him her name was Palor. Amarta mounted her camel and rode behind her, holding on tightly to her back. In a rushed, confessional voice, he spoke for a time about the terrible fate of his homeland. Palor listened without comment. Then the boy went silent, stricken by the sadness of his departure.'

Only three minutes, I thought.

'By the time sunset had spread across the horizon, Anthus had disappeared behind them. Amarta looked up at the risen pole-star and remembered the words of Sidli, the priest, who often spoke to him of the goddess Fresta: "This twinkling light is the centre of Fresta's mill wheel. It is the axis around which Her universe turns. When you can feel your own life moving around a similar focal point, you will then know that there are many tinier mill wheels turning inside each of us as well."

'The two travellers spoke little over the next several days; Amarta discovered that Palor, though an easy travel companion, preferred silence.

'Once, late at night, while he was resting, Amarta thought he saw her unfurl long, dark wings at her back. He crept around the fire and approached her on heron's feet. He saw that he had been mistaken. Palor turned to him with a modest smile. "There are many things to learn," she said. "But first, there is the dance."

'That night, Palor instructed the young man in the dance around the fire. Under her guidance, he continued whirling until sunrise, when, looking around into the blazing world, Amarta knew not who was turning, he or the landscape. For a moment, the sky and earth, the trees and flowers and fields, all disappeared. He felt himself both deep inside his body and spilled out into the world as water off a spinning top.

'Now, to trace their journey to the east, Amarta studied the hide map given to him by Palor. He was fascinated by the bands designating the mountain range beyond Telure where the Medli were said to live in their cave below the cold white powder that melted to water in one's hands. He saw that some day he would visit these peaks, search for the Medli in order to save his people, his sister, himself.

'Bill, have you heard of the Medli?'

I started when Peter spoke directly to me. I realized my eyes had closed and that I had been watching Peter spread a vellum map in his hands. I've often wondered if there wasn't some hypnotic quality to his voice, though the only thing special about his storytelling technique that I can recall was a sort of endless rhythm of rising and falling, as if he were speaking to the accompaniment of one of those droning Arabic melodies he preferred, as if his voice were part of a ritual long forgotten in the modern world.

'No,' I said. 'Are they gods?'

'No, not gods. Watchers of a sort. Watchers and weavers. Beyond the temporal gods. Creators. Like the difference between Brahma and Indra.'

I shook my head to indicate I didn't get it.

'Indra is a god caught in time. His era is limited in scope. Brahma is beyond time. Or he is time itself. *That's* the Medli. There are two of them. Because we think in twos. I mean, our brains are kind of fixed into thinking of things in terms of hot and cold, soft and hard, love and hate, right and left ... That's one reason why being neither one thing nor another creates problems for people. Like those Chuetas you discovered. The Medli ... anyway, there are two of them. But they are essentially one, because they're twins – identical twins. Like Victor and William. That's the paradox – two into one. Amarta had never seen them, of course. But he'd heard that it was possible. He didn't know if Palor had heard of them, so he asked her. It was about a week into their journey.

"I know *of* the Medli," she told him.

"Do they really know the answers to all questions?"'

I turned back around away from Peter, closed my eyes again. As Peter spoke his dialogue, he began now to change his voice to fit his characters – inquisitive and youthful for Amarta, calm and slightly amused for Palor. I was with them in the darkness, centred inside Peter's voice...

"It is said that the Medli do indeed know the answers to all our questions."

"But what do you say?"

'Palor's eyes glimmered, and she said, "When they join hands, the Medli form Fresta's loom and give birth to all our woven patterns. But do they know the designs themselves? Does the loom record its own movements? I have no way of knowing."

"And have you ever seen them?"

'"Not with my own eyes. One can only see the loom in the reflective pattern of one of Fresta's creations. Remember that, should you make the journey."

'The next day, Amarta mounted the camel behind Palor once more. They rode in silence under the isolating canopy of a great forest, Palor stopping now and again to pick up jewels from the ground – onyx, topaz, tourmaline, garnet, and rose quartz. "The different colours of light filtered through the leaves enter the stones and bestow upon them their brilliance," she explained to Amarta.

'When he searched the same ground for gemstones, he found only pebbles. "Apparently, I can recognize them and you cannot," Palor said with a smile. "Perhaps it takes more vision than you have at present."

'"Are you a sorceress?" Amarta suddenly asked her, his worry about Atserf, the god of evil, propelling his words.

'Palor grinned. "I don't think so. But then, I wouldn't know a sorceress if I met one. Do they have horns like goats? Roots like palms?" Palor laughed, brushed her hand gently over Amarta's shoulder.

'Despite her humour, Amarta rode to Telure in doubt as to Palor's allegiance. He had heard tales of men and women who had gained mysterious powers while in the service of Atserf, Fresta's nemesis. It was said that that was how the Erekans had developed their prowess at killing.

'Now, when the two travellers reached the gates of Telure two days later, the splendour of that city erased the boy's doubts. Palor was hailed as they entered. She pointed up a hill toward a palace topped by conical towers. "We go there," she told Amarta.

'The palace was embellished, inside and out, with blue, green, yellow, and white tiles that formed shimmering patterns – circles, diamonds, and eight-pointed stars. Palor told Amarta that the patterns were actually stories about the kings of

Telure recorded in Fresta's heavenly language.

'Inside the palace gates, she was welcomed by a man with long black hair and a thin, twitching face. She kissed him on the cheek and spoke in a dialect unknown to Amarta. When the man had departed, she led the boy to a bathhouse centred by a great flame whose tendrils rose from a blue tile fountain. Amarta and Palor undressed and cleansed themselves in the steaming water. The young man saw his host's eyes twinkling as they bathed. He smiled at her beauty, and for a time, lost himself in her eyes, just as he disappeared while dancing.

'Later that day, Palor led Amarta to the palace gates and told him to explore Telure. "Come back here when the Earth has turned to meet the sun at the horizon," she said.

'Amarta was drawn down to the centre of the city by the droning music of ouds and the mesmerizing voice of a storyteller.'

Peter shifted his legs again, and his foot brushed against my hip momentarily. I wasn't sure if I wanted him to touch me. It was as if he'd left a tingling brush stroke of himself behind. He may have sensed that, because he said, 'There will be a time when you'll want nothing so much as to be touched, when nothing will be quite as wonderful as that. But not now. I understand. I just didn't want you to disappear too deeply into my words. Or to grow frightened and vanish from the room. A nudge now and then helps.'

Before I could think of what to reply, he'd started up again. And I was closing my eyes.

'Amarta passed spice and dried fruit stalls, plazas with fountains spraying rose water high into the air, ornamental orange groves. Everywhere there was colour, odour, the different textures of life. He drank the wine mixed with fermented honey for which Telure was renowned and ate a meal of overcooked hare stew. The boy felt the bonds of Anthus loosening from around his chest, bonds of whose existence he was only now aware. *So this is what it feels like to be among the living*, he thought, now realizing how infused with death Anthus had been, as if everyone in the town harboured a stillborn infant inside him. It seemed as if he were standing upright for the first time, as if he were discovering himself.

'And yet, even as Amarta opened his arms to Telure, he felt an inexplicable loneliness surrounding him, as if he couldn't enjoy the beauty because it was merely an oasis surrounded by endless desert landscape.

'Charged by the sensations of the city, he raced to the palace at sundown. Palor greeted him and took him to a garden courtyard. Servants brought them dinner. They ate in silence, retired to a stone bedroom furnished with a straw mat. "I bring you a gift tonight," Palor told him, and she caressed the back of her hand across Amarta's cheek.

'That night, the young man lost his distrust of her and slept inside her arms. He awoke once and kissed himself thinking it was her. At sunrise, however, he learned that Palor had gone. The only trace of her was a rose quartz stone bearing her scent, which Amarta discovered in his hand. A servant doing his best to speak the language of Anthus told him that she had left the city on her camel. "When will she return?" Amarta asked.

'"No one ever knows," the servant replied. "She often departs without telling us."

'"What shall I do in Telure without her?"

'"You may study, learn a trade. Since Palor brought you, you are welcome to stay here as long as you like."

'Amarta decided to wait for his friend to return and was permitted to make his home in her room at the palace. He took a tutor in the local language and apprenticed to a tilemaker.

'For the next months, he studied grammar each morning, assisted the tilemaker in the afternoon, and wandered about the city and countryside during the evening. He practised his speech in night-time conversations with townsfolk. In them, he learned that Palor was the daughter of the city's ruler and was considered a saint, touched with a divinity that gave her unusual powers and an unquenchable wanderlust. "She is very strange but very good," said a storyteller. He told Amarta that on one occasion a palace guard had seen her flying like a bird.

'Apparently, there was no way of knowing when she'd return. "She is like a solar eclipse," was the familiar expression, for her presence was felt by all and would certainly come again, but there was no way of predicting when.

'The last evening with Palor had stirred Amarta's sexual appetite, and much of his time was spent in admiration of the handsome men and women of Telure, in searching out other amber eyes. Often, he locked in embrace with one or another during the night, and these encounters made him feel a part of the city. He began to accept himself as a Telurite, as one among many. Even so, the barrier always remained – the desert around the oasis. Sometimes in his happiest moments, he would feel the most distress, the most alone.

'Then, one morning, nearly a year later, as the young man sat with his language tutor, the Erekans came atop their camels, hungry for new territory. They were led by their king, Magrai, a muscular giant with a foot-long beard twisted into thick black braids. He called up to the Telurites, "Surrender your city and form a spoke in the Erekan wheel. Or else that same wheel will ride right over you."

'Palor's father, King Vesarta, the twitching man whom Amarta had met on his first day in the palace, stood in a turret of the castle and called down to Magrai, "We have no quarrel with Ereka. We wish to remain the hub of our own wheel."

'Magrai shouted a command and a volley of spears flew toward Vesarta. Pierced, he collapsed to his death calling Palor's name.

'Amarta sensed that he had been followed by death from Anthus to Telure. He understood in a single instant that the threatening desert would isolate him for the rest of his life unless he reached the Medli.

'A hand caressed across his cheek. The boy turned with a start. It was Palor. Her eyes glowed. "It is time you left," she said.

'A hoopoe suddenly took wing from the city wall and alighted on Amarta's shoulder. An ancestor of Maria's perhaps. "The bird is a present," Palor said. "Her name is Leren."'

Peter pronounced the bird's name with a click at the beginning, his tongue rapping against the bottom of his mouth. Maybe it was meant to demarcate her as a bird, as a creature with a beak. I never found out for sure. Though a few years later I learned that there are languages in southern Africa that make use of clicks. So maybe he originally heard this story in Angola or South Africa.

'When Amarta turned from the tiny eyes of this living gift toward Palor, she had already disappeared. He tucked the docile Leren under his shirt, retrieved Palor's map from his palace room, and left the city on camel through the Eastern Gate behind a group of Telurites dispatched to a nearby town for help. They fought their way clear to the desert, and a day and night later, at the road to the Medli's mountain, Amarta took his leave.

'Four barriers to his goal were represented by circular symbols of thresholds etched on his map.

'Yet Amarta saw neither gate nor obstacle at the first marking. A desert valley opened before him, turning to savannah as it descended through dry, cragged hills. Amarta rode through this grassland. And as he did, he took notice of a fog gradually sweeping over the slopes directly ahead, greying the landscape. He slowed his pace, watched with amazement as this cold mist swallowed first the hills, then the tops of trees, and finally his camel. The poor animal had neither head nor legs. And when his own hands grew numb, when his chest disappeared, the young man felt that he no longer possessed a body. He was only thought. And from where did these words inside him come? Without a vessel, what held him?

'Amarta remembered the same weightlessness from his dancing and floated ahead, to where he could not say, kept from fear by the memory of his whirling. When, the next day, the fog lifted, he gazed at his body as if from the top of a great mountain. He ran his hands over the landscape of his chest and thighs, took out Leren. The bird opened her black eyes.

'Suddenly, Amarta was looking at himself from inside the bird. *How nice to have wings*, he thought, flexing and folding them back in place. *And feathers, too*, he added, primping his chest.

'Amarta took wing as the hoopoe. He flew through the trees, searching out the sun, riding the wind. Down below, his human body sat atop his camel.

'Then, at the second indicated barrier, the young man came to a great river that rose and fell in cycles, swelling over its banks every few seconds, sluicing tongues of water over muddy ground. It breathed, its waters tossing with every exhale. Amarta dared not cross it as himself. So, as a bird once again, he took wing and flew over it. On the far bank, he looked back at his rigid body atop the camel. He sensed that he might need it later on the journey — that alone it might die. But how would he get it across? Amarta the hoopoe flew back and descended inside his body, stretched out to feel the limits of his fingertips and toes as stone walls to his avian freedom. He came once again to see the outlines of Leren as separate from his own.

'Amarta decided to rush along the banks downstream to the sea, hoping that the water there would be calm enough to allow a crossing. But the river continued to rise and fall mile after mile. He rode through outcroppings of forests, across sand dunes, under great natural bridges cut by water in centuries past. Once, in horror, he turned and saw ram's horns – the symbol of Atserf – carved into a granite cliff.

'That same night, while dreaming, Palor came to him and possessed him again.

'When the young man awoke, he felt caressed by the trees waving in the wind behind him. He did not travel that day or the next, but watched instead the breathing of the river. And when he resumed his journey, it was at the pace of one returned to the landscape of his childhood.

'Soon the river began to widen, its waters to repose. Amarta constructed a raft and set out on the crossing with Leren. Two days and nights later, he stepped onto the sands of another shore.

'Making his way through a forest of palms, he journeyed toward the Medli's mountain, a distant pyramid of grey rising into the eastern sky. He ascended and descended rolling hills, enjoying the warm humidity that seemed to protect him. He cut orchids and flame-tree flowers and wove them together into a necklace. He gripped the rose quartz from Palor tightly in his hand. And when the forest thinned and air grew arid, Amarta found himself emerging into the sun of a barren plain. Ahead was an abandoned village of decaying adobe huts arranged in a circle. This was the site of the third barrier.

'Standing at the very centre of this village, letting the sunlight warm his face, the memory of a melody began to entwine around him. When it twisted off with a sharp cadence, it left him spinning like a top. Leren flapped above his head. As the world whirled, tile patterns appeared to the young man as if signs from Fresta. Palor, too, appeared for a moment, pressing her chest to his. When her face disappeared into a darkening amber light that held him fixed at its centre, Amarta ceased dancing. He became Amarta the hoopoe once more and flew up to the thin blanket of clouds and down again toward the baking earth.

'A howling brought him into the eyes and ears of his human body. As he realized that this terrible noise had come from inside him, a violent ache clenched his gut. He took off his clothes and squatted. Sickness came from inside him and tainted the ground, then began to rise and grow, to expand into legs and arms and a face. Amarta jumped back. Before him stood Magrai, the Erekan ruler, his sword raised. He swooped toward Amarta. Leren took wing. Amarta twisted away.

"'You can never escape!" shouted the fierce Erekan.

"'I do not wish to fight,'" the young man replied. "Let me continue my journey.'"

'Magrai lowered his sword and grinned. "You want to reach the Medli, don't you?'"

"'Yes.'"

"'You'll never make it," he shouted, then charged. His blade pierced Amarta's shoulder. The boy's blood dripped to the ground, and at each meeting of blood and soil a musical note issued forth as if from a taut drum. The notes linked around Amarta into a melodic rosary. When the Erekan lunged again, his blade grazed Amarta's chest. Blood trickled to the ground, adding a deeper, more resonant counterpoint to the original melody.

"'And now you die!" Magrai shouted with a great lunge.'

Peter, too, had shouted, and I turned to look at him. He was sitting on his haunches now, his right arm out and fisted, balanced on his knee, like a warrior holding an invisible spear. His mien was threatening.

I understood somehow that I shouldn't ask him anything or talk. He wasn't entirely with me now.

'Amarta twisted past the blade,' he said, 'and he kept on turning to the music, gathering speed, spinning as fast as he could, as anyone can. Blood flew from him like a thousand red butterflies, adding tinkling melodies to the two principals. He whirled into a fluid cylinder. The Erekan stood back, then lunged. His arm and sword entered, disappeared, and flew out into the distance. Amarta ceased spinning and regarded the spot where the Erekan had fallen.'

Peter let silence gather around us. We were staring at each other. I caught a sudden glimpse of light and darkness sweeping over me like falling leaves.

'There, at the spot where Magrai had fallen, Amarta found that his own faeces had dried,' he continued. 'Leren flew to his shoulder. In his weakness, the young man knelt and listened to the bird's sighs of happiness. As he caressed her head, he looked up to see the clouds creating and undoing themselves, sensed the sunlight reaching out to them, to him, to the plants and trees and ground. He felt the vibration of the Earth in his feet, countless seedlings pressing against his sandals. He smelled the passing of a lizard, watched the heat of a mouse merging into the stone upon which it was sitting.

'The boy was clothed in a thousand different fibres of feeling, and carried aloft by their myriad patterns, he was able to recognize the weavings of the world in many more than their usual aspects. How to say that the breath of plants appeared to him or that the wobble of the Earth's rotation began to make him dizzy? He only knew that he could now see the wind and hear the chirpings coming from the sands around him, that Leren and other animals lost their boundaries and extended in coloured mists so far into the landscape that it was difficult to say where one being ended and another had begun. And now, the boy was able to see the great mountain to the east where the Medli lived. He listened to the groan of our planet under its weight. *Beneath the powdered water of its peak, I will find my goal*, he thought.

'He set off along toward the mountain and came to the sword of the Erekan. A rose, the emblem of Anthus, was clasped to the handle. Gently cupping the flower in his hand, he pulled it free and buried it in his shirt pocket with the quartz given to him by Palor.

'The next day, Amarta began his ascent of the Medli's mountain. High above him, the peak's rim shimmered gold, its caverns black. Three hours into his climb, already far above the wide plain, when night had replaced the day, he slept.

'In the morning, the young man awoke to a strange and powerful scent. He looked around and saw that he had been drawn to a field of violets, all shades of purple, pink, and white, popping up out of the mountainside like so many sentinels. They clustered into a fuchsia ribbon leading to the white at the top of the mountain. Within their perfumed embrace, Amarta walked, listening all the time to their leaves bending to receive the sun and their roots stretching toward the mist infused in the earth.'

I must have been watching Peter, rapt, because he said, 'Now it's time for you to close your eyes again, Bill. You will hear me better.'

I did as he said. I could feel the tips of my fingers flexing, my toes curling into the rug at the foot of the bed. I had the feeling I'd been flying. I was grateful to be alive. I was grateful that Peter was talking to me.

'Give me your hand,' Peter said.

Touching him made me shiver. It was as if I were reaching down into the centre of my life, the point around which my past and future were turning.

'Are you cold?' he asked.

'No. I ... I ... it's just that touching you ...'

'Yes, I understand,' he whispered. He squeezed my hand once. 'All day and night Amarta climbed, and as morning broke, he reached the summit, the site of the fourth barrier. All around him was snow, the first he had ever seen. *So this is the powdered water*, Amarta thought, cupping the snow in his hand and watching it melt. The shade of the air had changed overnight, and he breathed this thin lavender vapour only to discover his lungs were still dissatisfied. They needed the more resonant hues of the lowlands. He looked around, let the landscape speak to his fingers, eyes, feet, and heart – to all his organs and senses and thoughts. Yet nowhere could he detect the presence of the Medli. He waited all that day and another and another again, shivering in the cold, growing feverish, huddling over Leren to give her his warmth. But not a single sign of the Medli appeared to him.

'Amarta felt his strength leaving him and saw that he would not be returning to Anthus as he'd promised, that on this mountain-top he would join Fresta. Yet in his weakness and abandonment, Palor appeared to him. She bedded next to him, held him fast. He lost himself in her eyes as she pulled him deep inside her warmth. Then, suddenly, out of this vision, he awoke with a start into bright sunlight. He saw that he was staring both into and out of the eyes of the hoopoe, and that inside Leren's ebony irises was an ethereal mother-of-pearl ribbon leading across the mountain-top. He remembered the words of Palor about seeing the Medli in one of their creations and followed the apparition in the hoopoe's eyes to a stone outcropping in the snow. It was a door. Amarta turned the bronze handle without feeling it in his hand and descended steps he could not detect. Trusting the vision in Leren's eyes, he saw he was inside a cave, a dot of radiance growing into a ball of black and violet light.

'"Welcome," two voices said in unison.

'"I have come to save my people, my sister, myself," Amarta said.

'"And what present do you offer us for our help?" the Medli asked.'

Peter paused. I sensed him staring at me. I kept my eyelids scrunched closed. I knew he expected me to answer. So I said the only thing I could think of, 'I offer everything I have.'

'"And what would that be?"' Peter replied, speaking as the Medli.

'All that I am.'

'Yes, that's right,' Peter said, his voice trembling, as if he'd been worried for me. He came up behind me, took off my blanket. He gripped my shoulders and leaned his warmth into me. If I could have melded with him, I would have; I'd have overcome my fear by becoming a part of him.

'So Amarta first took out his rose blossom,' Peter went on, his voice deeper than before. I sensed that we were coming close to the end. 'And then he took out his necklace of flame-tree and orchid flowers. He felt for the quartz gifted him by Palor and was taken by a sudden desire to hold it back from the Medli. But he offered it as well.

'The violet glow now became an image of Anthus — its withered gardens, dusty streets, and hill-top castle. All these images were seen by Amarta in Leren's eyes.'

I could feel another presence now, something hovering. But I kept my vision in darkness. I figured it was just the effect of Peter's voice.

'"We accept your offering," the Medli told him. "Now, when you return to your city, have all the men eat a petal from the rose you carry. As for the women, they must eat instead from your flame-tree and orchid necklace. Everyone should eat gratings from the quartz as well. And for two generations, have the Anthen women mate only with their brothers."

'"And what of the fate of Telure?" Amarta asked.

'"Palor and the daughter of yours she carries in her womb will soon free that city. Then she will join you in Anthus. Now return home."'

At that, I heard the presence in front of me of flapping wings. When I opened my eyes, Maria landed on my thigh from out of nowhere. She looked up at me. She blinked. Somehow, she'd found her way home. She was safe.

I lifted her up, overwhelmed by her beauty. And by her generosity, too, by her letting me hold her. I realized suddenly how much she and Peter trusted me. I hugged her against me. A little too hard. She squawked. I told her I was sorry.

Peter laughed, then leaned over my shoulder and caressed a finger down Maria's back. She curled around it and flexed her wings.

'Instantly, Amarta found himself looking out of his human eyes at the Eastern Gate of Anthus,' Peter continued.

Maria had closed her eyes, so I did, too.

'He ran into the city, letting his joyful tears fall, listening to the tinkling music of their cascade through the warm air. At home, as his aunt and sister sobbed, they told him that he'd been gone for three of their years.

'The young man gathered the people of his city together and told them what the Medli had instructed. He administered portions of the rose to the men and petals from the flame-tree and orchid blossoms to the women. Gratings from the quartz were offered to everyone.

'Their effect was gradual, but the two sexes steadily grew nearer to each other in form. The men's hips widened and their skin softened, their eyelashes curved and lengthened. The women's shoulders broadened, their breasts diminished in size, and their voices deepened.

'In the children of the sibling marriages, the change was even more noticeable; many of the babies had both male and female sexual organs.

'Upon their return to Anthus, the Erekan slave traders were horrified to see these metamorphosed men and women and children, and they believed that a curse had been put upon the city and its people. They regarded the Anthens as monsters and took no more concubines from the city lest the curse follow them to Ereka.

'Although freed from their slavery, many Anthens were

disquieted by the solution wrought by Amarta and the Medli. They, too, regarded it as a curse. And they were frightened by the new senses that the children of Amarta and Sentar and a few of the others had inherited along with their new forms. These unhappy people ceased intermarrying after the first generation. Their legacy of shame prompted many to leave Anthus for faraway cities on all the different continents.

'In this way, the seeds for new androgynous forms were spread throughout the world, where they sprout and sometimes even blossom...'

Peter pressed his hands to the top of my head and kissed me.

'...In you and me, Bill. And in all of us.'

∞

I don't think I can explain the effect this story of Peter's had on me. Maybe I was indeed hypnotized. Or healed. All I know is that I lay in bed with him, encircled by his arms, and sobbed for the longest time. Till I was so dry that I seemed composed of sand.

It was as if a baby that I'd given birth to had died long ago, and I was only now aware of it.

He asked me to spend the night with him – he pleaded – but I refused. I couldn't take such a leap. He smiled wistfully and said, 'I thought that autumn could precede spring. But you're right – we must have winter first. It's the way things are in this world.'

I didn't know what he was talking about. He pressed his lips to my forehead and whispered that I was beautiful. 'You're going to be well and happy,' he said. 'At your darkest moments, remember that I told you that.'

Peter left me then, and I got under the covers. I built a fortress out of my pillows. I was glad to be alone. I slept.

Chapter 12

IN THE MORNING, I awoke as if yanked free of desperate dreams. I went downstairs right away and knocked at Peter's door. I was thinking that he was the only person who could assure me that I was still the man I'd been, that no spirits were going to hurt me. I needed the encouragement of his voice, to feel the grace of his eyes focused on me.

But there was no answer. It was only 8 a.m. I entered. Maria was sitting in her cage. I knelt next to her. She stared at me and fanned her crest. I stared back and fanned my fingers. She hopped onto the ground and put her head to the bars. I pressed my forehead against the cold brass as well, caressed her gorget and belly. I asked if she was hungry. She blinked as if to say, *no*.

I stood, turned, and saw myself in Peter's mirror. My face seemed older. But my body ... it seemed to belong to someone else.

As I walked through the house, I felt as if I was there by mistake. My true home ... ? I had no idea where it was.

I went out to my garden. I felt more comfortable there. I sat in the sunlight by the honeysuckle and breathed its perfume.

Sometime later, a hummingbird came to watch me as if I needed guarding. Hovering just out of reach, his gleaming black eyes keenly aware of my every movement, he seemed to be telling me that I needed protection.

I called the office and told my boss I'd be late. Around noon, I walked to work. I closed my door and stared out the window at San Francisco, hundreds of feet below, spreading out toward a horizon that seemed linked to forbidden adventures. I wondered where Peter and I would go from here. And if I was in love with him.

When I got home, all of Peter's things had been removed from the house: his clothes and books, his Nazi flag, his tapeworm belt, his necklace, Maria and her cage. Everything was gone except his flowers; he'd left bouquets everywhere.

There was also a handwritten copy of the myth that he'd told me the night before. It was sitting on the kitchen table with a note clipped to it:

Dear Bill,

Need I say that this journey is your own? You are Amarta. And you will reach home and free yourself. I know of nothing more certain.

So remember this story and remember that you have no reason to fear what is about to bloom inside you. It will have a sweeter scent than anything you have ever smelled before!

> *Love,*
> > *Peter*

∞

Frantic, I called the Brazilian consulate. They'd already closed for the evening. I drove to Mara's house. I was sure she'd give me a sensible explanation. When I rang the bell, Alba didn't bark. A blonde woman with an English accent answered the door.

'Is Mara home?' I asked.

'Who?'

'Mara.'

'You must have the wrong address.' She squinted at me suspiciously.

'No, she was living here,' I said. 'A little woman with big eyes.'

'A woman was living here?'

'Yeah. I'm sure of it. A really tiny woman. Like an elf.'

'Look, I've been in Thailand for six weeks. No one's been

living here. At least no one I know of. And no elves.' She laughed. 'I never sublet to elves.'

'When did you get home?'

'That's none of your business,' she snapped.

'But when you came home, weren't there any signs that any-one had been here?'

'Look, you must have the wrong address.'

She closed the door.

∞

I sat in the dark of the living-room that night, trying to think what could have happened. I remembered Mara saying that she didn't like cooking and that the stains in her kitchen were just for show. Maybe they were someone else's.

Unable to shake myself free of a spiralling anxiety, I failed to get any sleep.

∞

The next morning, right at nine, I called the Brazilian consu-late. A receptionist said there'd been a *Pedro* who'd worked there several years earlier. He'd been short and fat, with eyes like a frog. No, he couldn't speak English very well.

I described Peter. She'd never seen him.

I headed to the brick building on Folsom where I'd seen Rain's body. It was a meat supply house called Jackson Foods. When I asked whether the city used any of their spare refrig-erators to house bodies, the assistant manager laughed.

At the San Francisco library, I searched through copies of the *San Francisco Chronicle* for the last month for news of a young man or woman who had been found murdered in the Presidio.

Nothing.

I called the police just to be sure. It took a while to get a de-finitive answer, but it turned out that no one had been killed in the Presidio for over four months. And no one had heard of a detective named Hollis.

I began to think that maybe I was crazy. I searched Peter's empty rooms for any trace of him I could find. There were marks in the ceiling where he'd tacked in his Nazi flag and glue on the walls where he'd hung his feathers and flowers. Nothing more.

I drove to the pawnshop that he and I had visited. It was early evening, but Mr Thalburg was still there. 'Do you remember me?' I asked.

'No,' he answered.

I described Peter. 'Oh yeah,' he said. 'The *dybbuk*.'

'The what?'

'*Dybbuk*. A spirit who's taken over the body of someone else.'

'What are you talking about?' I demanded.

'We had a long talk once,' he said, 'and your friend told me he loved the body he had inherited because it had such a distinctive sense of smell. He said that the nose is more intimately connected to memory than any other part of our physical structure. Having a sensitive one made his life that much more rich.'

'The body he'd inherited?' I asked.

'Yeah, that's why I started calling him the *dybbuk*. Funny guy.'

∞

When I got home, I called Jay and asked if he remembered Peter.

'Of course,' he replied.

'So you remember seeing him ... lifting him with me into my bedroom when he was sick?'

'Yeah, what is this all...'

'And Mara?' I interrupted.

'Her too. Why? What's going on?'

I recounted what had happened. He said, 'You know, I had the feeling they were really weird people.' He told me that he would come right over.

'No!' I rushed to answer. 'I just need to be alone for a while.'

As I sat in the dark that evening, I began considering that I had been stranded in some universe akin to dream that existed just below our normal reality. I held myself. I was here, real. I couldn't understand why this was happening.

∞

Over the next few weeks, I made a hundred phone calls to try to track Peter down, but the search proved fruitless.

I even visited the nightclub near Broadway where we'd heard Mara sing. An assistant manager remembered her. 'She auditioned for us,' he said, 'and worked out some songs with the house band. Must have been the night you were here. But we didn't think she was quite right. Band didn't like her either. They said that she improvised too much.'

∞

I ended up waiting for a letter or phone call, at least something. There didn't seem anything else for me to do.

At first, I was sure I'd get some communication, a sign of some sort. Maybe Mara or Peter would just show up on my doorstep and explain what had happened. Or Maria would fly in with a message banded around her leg.

∞

I never did locate Peter.

In the wake of his disappearance, I had what the doctors called a nervous breakdown.

I didn't think I was capable of feeling so much. I realized that the emotions that I'd experienced before were nothing.

It was as if I'd been cut open at my belly.

I groped through hollow days and nights weighed down by a thick hopelessness. I never slept that I remember. Fluid dripped from my eyes and mouth till I was empty.

It was as if I were a kid again. Alternately frightened, alone, enraged.

When I took notice of myself, I realized that I smelled like death.

Then, one morning, I passed out in the bathroom; I'd stopped eating and drinking, was dangerously dehydrated, the doctors later told me. By some lucky chance, Alexandra had come over to pick up the last of her things. She discovered me sprawled out on the tile floor and had me rushed to Pacific Medical Centre. 'When they finally got you conscious,' she told me, 'you started going on and on about falling through spirals. It was scary. You were totally delirious.'

In the hospital, they attached an IV bottle to my arm, gave me yellow pills, forced tasteless peas and broccoli into me. A psychiatrist with a far-too-neatly trimmed beard came around and asked me a zillion questions. I don't remember what I told him. I remember lying on my side for hours, just looking out at the empty Victorian houses climbing up and down the hills of Pacific Heights without any seeming purpose. People visited – Jay, Alex, some friends I hadn't seen in a while. Jessica, my old work buddy, even showed up once. I couldn't help crying in front of her. She felt really awkward and escaped as soon as she could. But I didn't blame her; nobody can bear the stagnant scent of death on another person for more than a few minutes at a time. And the sad leaden weight of not knowing what to say to someone who's sick gets to be too much after a while. I could see everybody wanting to shout at me, *why can't you just pick up the pieces and go on? Everybody does, after all*. I couldn't think of what to say to them either; I didn't know the reasons for my anguish. None of my emotions came with labels. I just wanted to lie by myself in my own bed. I wanted to crawl into a ball and disappear.

∞

Winter ...

Peter said winter preceded spring, not autumn. It was he who froze my life when he left.

Maybe that's why his wooden amulet had made me dream of a frigid, bombed-out city covered with snow. It was a vision of myself.

∞

I remember Peter saying that only a thin veil separated him from his dreams, that he occasionally disappeared into them.

Our making love lifted the veil, I think.

Why did he leave me?

∞

At times, everything that had happened to me seemed totally unbelievable. The most disturbing thing was that I knew that I would never be completely sure of reality again. Ever.

After being released from the hospital, I found myself living at home as if I had to verify that each footstep of mine would hit secure ground and not pass right through the earth, as if each morning I might very well wake up to find I was someone else.

∞

I was furious at him. And desperate for a glimpse of him.

I regretted not taking any photographs.

∞

Alex came back into my life for a short time. She fed me multi-vitamins and herbal extracts – a new combination she'd heard about – and gave me tranquillizers when I needed extra help. She sat with me, watched television while I paged through magazines, left only at bedtime. She heated can after can of Campbell's soup for me. I grew to rely on the simplest broth for comfort.

She'd changed, too. She'd cut her hair very short and told me that she was wearing only black and white.

She explained that a limited colour scheme helped her re-strain her exaggerated thoughts. Too many colours provoked outbursts, she said.

As for outbursts, they were unpleasant and unproductive.

We tried having sex a few times, but it didn't work for either of us. Her fingers seemed very hard, and I was very fragile. She didn't feel right. And she smelled dry and out of reach – like the past.

Her distance after coupling only made me disconsolate.

She ended up angry at me for crying all the time. She said that having a nervous breakdown was understandable in view of my having shared a house with what she called a *psychotic maniac*, but couldn't I just *snap out of it*. Finally, frustrated to the point of rage, she told me that I was a *spineless jellyfish* posing as a man.

'You're wrong,' I told her. 'I'm a mixture of things, a hybrid – part man, part woman.'

I wanted to add, *Just like you and everyone else*, but I was afraid she'd go berserk. Instead, I said, 'Before Peter came, you and I were twin zombies sleepwalking our way through life.'

She didn't know what I meant. I tried to explain, but she interrupted.

'Never mind,' she said dismissively. She sat me down as if I were a troubled kid and said that I needed a therapist *at least twice a week*. She wrote down the name of one *with an outstanding reputation* for me to call, someone with a long waiting list but who had promised her he would make time if necessary.

Despite her anger and resentment, she really did make an effort with me to be conscientious and kind. And she really came through for me that day in the bathroom. I owe her a lot.

When I was able to cook dinners for myself again, she left my life for good. She was greatly relieved. So was I.

∞

With a little help from anti-depressants, I started training as a bicycle repairman of all things, at Wheels on Fire on Fillmore Street. It was exacting, repetitive work. I needed that.

I was hired off the books at first, but even so I stopped

taking my unemployment cheques. I never went back to my old job. I couldn't even set foot in San Francisco's Financial District without getting nauseous.

Manual labour grew more interesting the more I worked, and the long bike rides I began taking in Golden Gate Park did me a world of good. The rhododendrons and tree ferns and dahlias reminded me of Peter. It made me sad to stop and touch them, but it was comforting, too.

I began to realize that I was thinking that Peter had died. I was in mourning.

A little while later, for no reason except maybe the passage of time, I was able to quit taking medications.

∞

Celibacy helped, too, I think. For one thing, it provoked the last-ever argument I had with Jay. He thought I was crazy for not wanting to go out with women again. We were standing in my living-room. We were about to go out to buy me a Walkman for my bike rides. It was going to be a gift from him. 'A good blow job is all you really need,' he told me with a pat on the back.

I was stunned that he or anyone else could really think that that was all I needed, all any of us needed.

I told him that I couldn't yet think of what I had to give to anyone else. And that an erect penis just wasn't enough of an offering.

He frowned and said, 'You've become really weird, you know that? It's like you're not all here.'

I looked out the window at the exuberant pompon flowers of a hydrangea bush I'd just planted, trying to stay calm. With the force of needing to be understood, I turned to him and said, 'I spent my childhood trying to shelter you from the worst of Dad's anger. Are you aware of that?'

'I never asked you to,' he replied.

'No, but I did.'

'Well, maybe you shouldn't have. Maybe you should have asked me what I wanted.'

'So what did you want?'

'I didn't want the pressure of you being so damn good to me all the time. Of you helping. I wanted to be on my own sometimes. I wanted to grow up! You get it, now?'

I looked back outside and thought about how everything I'd ever done in this life had backfired. I wanted to say, *I'm sorry if I hurt you. I thought I was doing the right thing*. I might very well have said just that, but he added: 'You always thought you knew best, and now look where it's got you.'

I faced him. 'Where's that?'

'Look at you – you lost your fucking mind over a man. A man!' He laughed as if to make me feel puny. 'How could you do that?' he sneered. 'Don't you see what everyone thinks? What I think?'

He was speaking to me with our father's voice.

'That's it!' I said. 'Get out of my house. I don't ever want to see you again. I mean it.'

I was angry, but I wasn't shouting. I was just tired of resisting the urge to give up on him, on the life we'd once had. I needed to toss up my hands and cede to what had always looked like a failure, but which now seemed like a giant step in the right direction. Jay wouldn't move though, just kept looking at me contemptuously. I walked up to him, pushed him, and said, 'Get out!'

He shoved me back. Hard.

So I bulled up into him and knocked him against the wall. He fell to the ground. I'm not proud of what I did, but I'd do it again. I was trembling. So was he.

'Shit – you're fucking crazy!' he shouted.

'Get out. I don't want to ever see you again.'

He left without a word. I locked the door. Even slipped the chain in place. It was like closing the lid on Pandora's box.

And ordering Dad out of my life forever ...

∞

Slowly, relying only on myself and my work at the bike shop, I regained my health. I still didn't know who I was, but there was a solidity in my stance that I'd never had before.

It was as if I'd stopped apologizing to my parents or anyone else for being alive.

Then I met Paul. He came in one day needing to have the front derailleur for his Fuji Finest racing bike adjusted. His dirty blond hair was pulled back into a ponytail and tied with a blue silk ribbon. His profile was strong and intelligent. He had a shy but generous smile. He smelled good, like wet moss – he'd just been for a long ride out by Buena Vista Park and was sweating buckets. He looked like someone who could be my friend.

On my lunch break, we went for a ride together down to Ocean Beach. We ate salami and cheese sandwiches he brought along. The next day, after work, we biked to Chinatown, then held hands while listening to an organ concert at Grace Cathedral.

Spending that time with him was good for me. Though it was awkward at first, of course – being with a man in that way. I felt as if I might have to start learning things all over again.

The next evening, he came over to my house for dinner. After making small talk about the Australian wine he'd brought with him, he said, 'You don't feel comfortable with me here, do you?'

'No.' I shrugged by way of apology.

He laughed. I didn't know why. 'You didn't try to deny it,' he explained. 'Most people would.' He came up next to me. I thought he was very handsome. He said, 'We'll take things slowly.'

He pressed his lips to mine. I let him slip inside. It was the first time I'd kissed a man in that way. I was expecting sirens to go off, was sweating like a safe-cracker at the moment that big leaden door creaks open. After we'd separated, I took his hand because I was feeling vulnerable and needed a word of encouragement.

He said, 'I won't ever hurt you on purpose. And you don't have to do anything you're not comfortable with.'

Maybe because this was something that Peter might have said, I began wondering what it would have been like to have kissed him instead. That spoiled things for a while. I could hardly talk. I was feeling that it was useless to try to find love with anyone else. Paul stopped wolfing down his apple crisp, put his fork on his plate, and sat up straight. 'Okay, why don't you tell me what you're thinking,' he said.

We had a long talk about Peter. Because I wasn't going to lie to anyone any more. Afterward, he got his coat, kissed me on the cheek, and walked to the door. 'You call me if you want to see me. If not, I enjoyed dinner and getting to know you an awful lot.'

Paul's got a voice that's strong and even, though a bit cautious when he's tired, as if he's gained the confidence of having gone up and over a lot of obstacles in his life but remembers clearly that some of them were really thorny and did their damage. He occasionally reveals the edges of a Midwest accent that's hard to place, too, but which conjures up images to me of isolated country roads and sparrow hawks keeping vigil from telephone wires – though a lot of that might be the hard knowing look he gets in his eyes when he's pissed off. I mention this because it was the way he talked to me that night at dinner and during those first couple of days together, more than what he said exactly, that kept on reassuring me that I was doing the right thing. It was as if a gentle curiosity infused his voice at all times – lit his clear brown eyes, too. No dwarf. No sorcerer. No magic. Just a man who wanted to find out more about me and everything else. That seemed good.

I let a few days pass while figuring out what to do. It was our strong and unexpected physical connection I couldn't get out of my mind – holding his firm chest against me while we shared that single kiss, feeling the scratch of his stubble against my cheeks.

And now I was glad I hadn't kissed Peter. I wanted us – Paul and I – to have something new right from the start.

I found I was most attracted to the presence of him, to his hands and eyes, certainly, but also to what I sensed below his surface – to his *Paulness* is the only way I can say it. Rather than any specific aspect of his personality, I mean. Maybe that completeness in another person is what we always feel ourselves drawn to anyway. Though it was also the contradictions I sensed in him – his softness and hardness, light and dark, naïveté and sophistication – that made me eager to hurtle into unknown territory and find out more.

I called him up and we went out to a Turkish restaurant on Sacramento Street. It was dimly lit and musty-smelling. I couldn't stop looking at him, at the butterflies of candle-lit shadow around his eyes, the smooth darkness descending down his neck. Neither could one of the waiters, a grizzled old guy with a thick Cossack moustache. I could see him sneaking covetous glances at Paul every time he cleared a table.

Even the way Paul drank his water that evening seemed sexy. Maybe wanting me inside him made him so very attractive. He told me later that that's all that he was thinking about.

We slept together in my bed that night. I learned the rise and fall of his ribs under my fingertips, the curve of his hips against my belly. I traced the shape of his calves and lines of his hands into my memory. I began to know his sounds.

I learned to be gentle, too. And to get pleasure from the darkness of my body, from refuges no one had ever touched before.

After our first time making love, Paul descended into waves of uncontrollable breathing. It was as if he couldn't get enough air. I got scared, thought I'd hurt him badly. But he reached for my cheek and said, 'No, no, I'm okay. It just happens sometimes when all of me goes away.'

At that moment, holding him, I wanted to give him something more of me. But I couldn't think what. It took me a few more days to realize it wasn't some*thing*, at all, and that I had no choice about giving it to him or not; I was already in love. Maybe we always come to that conclusion after the fact.

About the same time, according to what he told me afterward, Paul fell in love with me, too.

Almost immediately, the long slow winter in which I'd been dormant began to warm.

Objects took on textures again. Food sent me into ecstasies of pleasure. I remember eating a sunset-coloured mango one day and being convinced that all I really wanted from life was to be able to appreciate its beauty. And to contribute – to give back to Paul and the world until I was empty.

To live so that I could face death with nothing left in my pockets. That seemed an important goal.

Maybe in consequence, for the first time, people – even perfect strangers – seemed good and compassionate.

We began to go for weekend bike rides together. Sometimes, waking up in the middle of the night in our tent, we'd hold hands and talk till morning.

Touching became the most important thing – the best way to express my feelings, as Mara had said. It didn't even have to be Paul. A pebble in my hand seemed worthy of my love as well.

∞

Paul spoke to me a lot about books those first few weeks together. He told me about the novels that had marked his early life and that he used to read under the covers with a flashlight because his mom thought it was unhealthy for him to stare at a printed page for hours on end – *Huckleberry Finn*, *Light in August*, *The Foundation Trilogy* ...

Paul said, 'I couldn't sleep if I didn't have a book in bed with me. And I carried one with me everywhere I went – even to gym class. People laughed. They probably thought I was pretentious. But I always felt that if I could read, I'd be safe. I mean, even life in a dungeon would be bearable if you had books.'

∞

About a month after meeting Paul, I had to speak to Alex over the phone about house matters, and when I explained about him, she told me that she knew all along that I was gay, that that was what the problem between us had been. Maybe yes, maybe no. I don't know how to define myself any more. Or anyone else, for that matter.

∞

One morning over bran muffins and coffee, Paul told me that he never thought another man would ever fall in love with him because he was too *soft*. I thought it was a strange thing for a guy to say who's got lithe muscles just about everywhere. But he meant that he wasn't *manly enough* – something far too many people had been only too happy to tell him while he was growing up.

In my kitchen, smearing a healthy tablespoon of honey on a slice of muffin, he explained that he'd hidden the fragile edges of his personality all through his childhood in Michigan, but that he could no longer keep up the effort. 'I just got tired of it all. I mean, people back home in Escanaba thought that me not wanting to know the scores of the fucking hockey games meant I was a dippy queer. Hell,' he added, holding up his spoon and giving me a comic groan, 'they even thought I used more honey than any red-blooded American male should use.'

He told me it felt sometimes as if he'd spent his youth trudging across mountainous sand dunes, each step a heavy effort. That's why he'd taken up bicycling at college. So he could fly. *So he could feel as light and free as a bird*, he told me.

That brought back many memories of Peter, of course.

Paul had quit law school at the University of Michigan the year before and moved to San Francisco. He was twenty-seven years old.

From certain angles, he looks like a young woman.

Maybe it *is* strange being attracted to androgyny. Maybe not. I don't care any more.

∞

About four months after we met, I began to see how entangled we were going to get in each other's life. I wasn't sure I liked that idea all that much at the time, but I think that accepting that we were going to grow together like vines was the precise moment I stopped being a kid and became an adult.

This was also the beginning of my understanding that everything in my life was tied together in some way – Peter, Paul, Mara, Jay, my parents, Rain … My understanding, too, that love can become a point of contact between past and future – between worlds. *All roads leading toward love cross at some point*, Peter might have said.

As it happens, I had no idea that I might catch a fleeting glimpse of Peter himself – or at least a reminiscence of him – along one of those roads a little less than two years later.

I was home alone one evening, reading an abominable novel by Tristan Williams, when the phone rang. 'Is Paul there?' a woman asked in a fragile voice.

I said *no*, that he was working late that night. He had just started a job as a graphic designer at the *San Francisco Chronicle* and was doing his best to impress his boss. The woman on the phone introduced herself as a neighbour of Paul's grandmother, Lucie. In a hesitant voice, she told me that Lucie had died the day before in her sleep. She insisted that I tell Paul as soon as possible because, she said, *Lucie loved that boy out of this world*. She asked if I was Paul's *friend*, landing with both feet on the coded significance of that word. I said I was.

'It's good that Lucie knew about you,' the woman said. 'It gave her more comfort than you might think to find out that Paul had met someone.'

When I hung up, I found that I resented Paul for not having told me that he'd spoken to his grandmother about me. A selfish reaction, I know, especially since she'd just died.

I snapped my Tristan Williams novel closed and actually tossed it in the garbage (I'd later rescue it, however, though only God knows why). I thought it was really weird that a neighbour was calling instead of Paul's parents. I figured the only answer was that they must have disliked him a whole lot more than he had intimated in the few scattered bits of information he'd let slip about them; his voice tended to fade to nothing when having to talk about his family. I didn't know much about Lucie herself, only that she was Paul's maternal grandmother and had lived a few blocks from where he had grown up. And I knew that her husband, Wolfie, had died a few years earlier. Paul had spoken affectionately of them both.

When he came home, I sat him down on the white couch in my living-room. We didn't yet have our own place and were still staying most nights in the house I'd shared with Alexandra. I told him about his grandmother. His face went dead. I'd never seen anyone that pale. Then he kind of stared at me, searching like a little kid for an explanation for the impossible. I realized I was powerless to help him, but that I wanted to take his pain from him and make it mine. It wasn't as if Paul's desperate need for me had burned up all my resentment – though I guess we all wish love could do that – but it *had* reduced it to the point of insignificance, at least at that moment. Then he burst into tears. It was frightening. I held him like a baby.

Between crying on and off for the next hour, he told me a bit about why Lucie, and Wolfie, too, meant so much to him. I was holding his hand, and we were still sitting on the couch. 'They grew up on the very same street in a small town outside Berlin, had been sweethearts since they were twelve. You never saw two people so in love. They kissed all the time. And they used to sing to each other – instead of talk.'

'Sing – what do you mean?'

'Well, they'd kind of fit what they were saying into a song. Like Lucie would call down to Wolfie, using some old German melody, "Is the dinner done yet?" – Wolfie, he was the one who cooked. And he'd answer using some other tune. Like "Hey Jude" or something, and he'd go, "Hey, Lucie, I'm just waiting" – Paul was singing himself at this point – '"for the chicken, to cook all the way through-oo-oo-oo."' He burst out laughing at the absurdity. So did I. 'They did most of this in German, not with Beatles songs, of course. With these ragged old tunes they'd learned as kids, melodies from Kurt Weill, that sort of thing. So it sounded even weirder. It was like they were from another planet. Not that they always got along. I don't want to make it sound like a fairy tale. Lucie could be a real fucking bitch. Like if she had to wait on line for anything. And Wolfie, he was the most stubborn man I ever knew. And he was addicted to routines. If he didn't get to go to the Escanaba Central Library every Friday afternoon to read magazines and get a novel for the weekend, forget it. He made your life misery.'

Paul's angry eyes moistened with gratefulness. 'They had a hard time of it at the beginning,' he continued. 'They got married over their parents' objections, since they were only eighteen at the time. And then they fled Germany a few years later. This is about 1933, when Hitler came to power. They were only twenty-one. Can you imagine? Wolfie had been a Young Communist and would have ended up in the death camps for sure.' Paul sighed and stared out the window at the plum trees for a long time.

I began thinking of Victor, who *was* taken to the camps and whose dissected body ended up as smoke drifting over the wilfully blind and deaf countryside of Poland. And Sarah, his lover, who'd collapsed and died while marching from one barbed-wire hell to another, only a few days short of reaching the war's end. And Peter's mom, who'd been experimented on with chemicals that probably should have killed her, but who survived to give birth to a beautiful child.

'When I came out to them, I was twenty,' Paul continued. 'I was scared shitless. They were the first people I told. Though everybody knew, I guess. And you know what Wolfie said when I finally got it out that I was gay?'

I shook my head, praying it was something good.

'He kissed me on the forehead and said, "So vat's ze big deal? You find a boy you love, zat's vat counts." That's *exactly* what that beautiful man told me.' Paul's tears started flowing again.

Looking at him, I had my first inkling that if he and I dared to build a life together, then Lucie and Wolfie would become *my* grandparents, too, that his whole world would overlap with mine.

Getting his breath, Paul said, 'When my parents were first thinking of disowning me, Lucie frowned like she was going to have to wait on a long line and told me, "I always said your mother was an idiot." With a total straight face. I mean, she meant it.'

Paul's voice grew grave. 'When Wolfie died, he left me seven thousand dollars in his will. That's how I was able to move out to San Francisco. Otherwise, I'd still be walking across those gigantic sand dunes and thinking I could fake my life as a tax lawyer...'

This was the first I'd heard of his being disowned. When I

asked if his parents had really done it, he nodded and replied, 'They're never going to speak to me again. And my brother and sister won't either. That's why a neighbour had to call.'

'You told Lucie about us, didn't you?'

'We spoke a few times about ... about my falling in love with you. I'd never fallen in love before. I wanted to talk to her about what to do.'

'Why didn't you tell me you'd spoken to her?'

'I guess I should have. Are you mad about me not having told you?'

'I was. Maybe I still am a little.'

'I'm sorry. I should have mentioned it. I guess I just don't believe that this is all for real. I mean, you could leave tomorrow. You could discover you like women more than men and then...'

'I'm not going anywhere,' I said.

'You don't know that.'

'I didn't have a nervous breakdown so that I could throw away the first decent relationship I've ever had. I may be scared sometimes ... I mean, I *am* scared sometimes. But maybe that's the way it's supposed to be.'

'So you don't think I'm too fragile or weak? You don't ... you don't despise me?'

Paul let my hand slip from his and stood up. He walked to the window and faced away from me, looking out into the evening. Dusk was coming on fast. I realized that this was the moment when I either dove head-first into my life with him, no looking back, or walked away. It wasn't enough to just say I loved him again; that word means vastly different things to different people, anyway. So I said, 'I've never been with anyone before with wings. I'm very grateful to have met you. I just hope I can keep up. If I can't, look back for me from time to time. Look back for me as you fly.'

He was surprised by my words – by my asking for his

help. Maybe nobody had before. Or maybe he'd never heard any spontaneous attempts at verse. We just stood there looking at each other till he burst into tears again. I fixed us both some tea and got us under the covers.

I made reservations that night for a flight the next afternoon to Detroit, then Escanaba. It was while packing in the morning that I found those blue shoes with turquoise laces that I'd bought in Calistoga. They'd been hidden at the back of my closet.

I called Paul upstairs and told him the whole story about fleeing my latest sexual escapade and wandering into The Midnight Snark. I told him that Peter had said that I'd one day find out whom the shoes were really for. Figuring that he'd known I'd one day find someone like Paul, I handed them over proudly.

'Pretty spiffy,' he said. But he was looking at them sceptically.

'They're yours if you like them,' I said. 'And they're from Peter, too. He said that it should be a gift partially from him.'

'They're more your style.'

'My style! I never wear loud shoes.'

'But you'd like to.' He slipped into his grandfather's German accent: 'You bought zem for yourself. Zat's vat Peter vas saying.'

I stood there as if spun free of time; I realized that Paul understood things about my past – about Peter's way of thinking and what had happened between us – that I hadn't, that I couldn't. And his insight seemed to be the proof I'd been wanting, without knowing it, that he was the person whom Peter had meant for me to find.

∞

At the funeral up in Escanaba, I wore my blue shoes, of course. Everyone snubbed us except Lucie's neighbour, Clara, and her husband, Joe. We hadn't yet heard anything about Lucie's will, so we didn't realize that all the grudge-filled whispers and stares of metallic hate were partially because of the old lady's final reckoning. Clara was a small African-American woman with short grey hair and darting eyes. She just marched right on up to Paul and said, 'Dearest God, it's good to see you, honey-cakes.' She held his face in her hands and gave him lots of popping kisses. Then she gave me a hug and whispered in my ear, 'Lucie would have said, "Take good care of my baby." So that's what I'll say.'

It was meeting Clara and liking her so much that made me understand that we were going to get to know even the peripheral characters in each of our lives – that our histories were coming together.

In her will, Lucie left Paul her clapboard house at the end of Earlham Street, which we've subsequently sold for a tidy little sum, and twenty-three thousand dollars at Peninsula Savings & Loan. His brother and sister got nearly four thousand dollars each, and his parents – 'in light of their having had the uncommon stupidity to disown their son Paul' – got exactly one penny, which Lucie had the ferocity and foresight to actually include inside the envelope containing the will, so it could be handed to them right at the reading. We weren't there, but we got the details in a letter from Clara, who had heard about it directly from Paul's outraged older brother.

The next and weirdest part of the story – the part that has to do with Peter – comes about ten months later. As an homage to Wolfie and Lucie, Paul and I decided to visit their home town in the eastern part of Germany, a little town called Neuenhagen-Süd. This was in January of 1990, and we got the idea of going then because the Berlin Wall had just come down a couple of months before. We used some of Paul's inheritance to make the trip, reserved a little yellow Opel through Europe-by-Car.

On arrival in Berlin, we bought some winter clothes at the KDW department store. Then, the next morning, we picked up our car and headed off.

Paul just had Wolfie's address, 17, Preusstrasse, but for Lucie, he had an old black-and-white photo of a tiny Tudorish-looking house with a willow tree out front. He'd found it in a beaded change purse that was in her safe deposit box. On the back of the photo, she'd scribbled the address in jagged Gothic lettering, 84, Preusstrasse.

We headed out of East Berlin on a wide avenue lined with mammoth five-storey apartment houses, thirty-foot sculptures of muscular young supermen and -women out front – steroid enhanced, no doubt. It was straight out of some Fritz Lang nightmare. Then, without warning, the utilitarian monster buildings receded behind us and ... presto, wc were in the middle of the countryside, nothing but barren fields all around. The zoning in East Germany must have been pretty damn bizarre. Along the side of the pot-holed two-lane road we found ourselves on were broken-down gas stations and an occasional restaurant advertising the best *currywurst* around. We followed the signs along the country lanes and in about another half hour were driving down the main street of a sleepy little town with bare trees everywhere – Neuenhagen-Süd.

We stopped first to ask an old lady where Preusstrasse was, but she didn't know and steered us toward city hall. I remember the building as being of dark brick, with turrets of sorts – like an armoury, though that may only be my impression. Inside a dimly lit room with manual typewriters on hulking metal desks, to our great dismay, we were informed that Preusstrasse wasn't on any of the maps. It simply didn't exist. Which was impossible, of course. So this nice young girl in a bare-midriff halter top, with really red lipstick, a belly as pale as bone, looking as if she'd watched one too many pirated Madonna videos, slipped down to the basement archive. After an hour, she came back up holding a file card over her head. 'Victory!' she announced in English.

It turned out that the street had changed its name three

times since Paul's grandparents had lived there. It had gone from Preusstrasse to Kirchestrasse back in the twenties (something which Wolfie and Lucie forgot to tell Paul or which nobody in the neighbourhood ever accepted), then became Pushkinstrasse under the East German administration, and was now back to Kirchestrasse. Armed with that information, we followed the girl's directions and ended up on a wooded lane that circled around a plain brick church with a small bell-tower. Nobody was home at Wolfie's house, Number 17, but at Lucie's place, which looked exactly like the photograph except for different trees out front, an old couple noticed us staring from the fence and waddled out through the front door to greet us. They didn't speak a word of English. I hadn't a clue that Paul spoke so much German, but after a few moments, he'd explained it all and they were nodding and laughing, 'Ja, ja, ja,' and everybody was friends.

Now the first odd thing was that as we were taking a tour of the house, amazed at how tiny the rooms were and how neat they kept everything, the wife of the couple started calling Paul *Peter*, as if that was his name. At first, I figured that she hadn't heard him correctly when he'd introduced us.

When Paul corrected her gently, she rested her hand on his arm, laughed, and said, '*Ja, ich verstehe.*'

Then she made another slip as we said goodbye and called him *Peter* again. Maybe it was the name of a family friend or relative. Or maybe there was more between Peter and Paul than I might have first guessed.

The second weird thing happened when we went back to Wolfie's place to see if anyone had come home in the mean time. There was no answer again, so I walked around the side of the house a ways to see if there was someone in the back yard. It was empty. But there was a cylindrical glass vase sitting on a wooden picnic table, and a dozen dried cornflowers were standing inside it. The heads of eleven of the flowers were bent; they looked like tiny straw beings whose faces had desiccated out of sadness. The last cornflower, furthest from me, was charred, as if it had been set on fire.

Maybe the owner had carried the vase outside to throw them out, then got called away by the phone or an errand. One of the cornflowers might have brushed against a candle inside the house and started burning.

Of course, there must have been a logical explanation for why they were still sitting there, but to me, what was important was that it looked exactly like a creation which *only* Peter would have made.

The next day, we decided to drive out to Potsdam, just west of Berlin, because we'd read in a guidebook at the San Francisco library that the Jewish cemetery there had miraculously escaped the Nazi bulldozers. It was easy to find, was built on a sloping hillside – a couple of hundred neglected headstones in a grove of linden and pine. While nosing around, I came upon the grave of a man named William Schreiber – the same name as Peter's friend. This one had died on June 7, 1932. It didn't seem at all strange, though – I mean, it was a common enough name.

There was a crown sculpted on the headstone, however; and inside it was a feather pen – a reference to *Schreiber* meaning *scribe* in German, Paul would tell me later.

At the time, the feather got me remembering Maria the hoopoe. And Leren, the bird from Peter's story about Amarta.

Names ... gravestones ... Nazis ... winged messengers ... I had the feeling that I was living inside a myth created by someone – maybe William – using the dark ink of an ancient quill. Maybe it was jet lag, but I began to feel faint. I remember hearing the flapping of wings behind me. I jerked around and saw a magpie peering at me from the stone wall of the cemetery, about fifty feet away.

I was certain it was watching me. I had the feeling that it had been sent by Peter.

In the bird's eyes, even at this distance, I could see two brilliant violet lights, like the lights I'd seen up in Calistoga. Trusting my eyes this time, I began to walk slowly toward the glow. Or at least, I thought I did. But I couldn't get there. My legs were so tired. They seemed to be filled with warm sand. And the hot wind ... I hadn't noticed it before. I turned to face it and saw a cornflower on fire. It scared me. I wanted to shout, but I couldn't summon my voice.

Maybe I had already started to lose consciousness when I saw the magpie and the burning flower. It's hard to know for sure. Because the next thing I remember was Paul standing over me. There was a steady throbbing at the back of my neck and I was very cold.

'You okay?' he asked. His face was panicked.

'I think so. What happened?'

'You passed out.'

'Jesus.'

'Just take it easy. I'll call somebody.'

'No, I'm fine. I'm fine.' He helped me sit up. I was still at the cemetery. Which was a surprise. I expected to be back in San Francisco.

'There was a bird,' I told Paul. 'And lights. Maybe Peter sent a messenger to follow us to Germany. Or maybe he's come here himself.'

Paul said it was time to leave. He helped me to my feet and we trudged together to our car.

That night, lying in bed, unable to sleep, I said to Paul, 'I wish I could see Peter just once more – could talk to him. Ask him some questions.'

He rolled on his side and moved away from me.

I provoked a huge fight just to get him to talk. After some shouting, he said to me, 'If you prefer Peter, then you'd better just leave me.'

I tried to explain that it was not having a definitive end to my life with Peter that was so difficult to accept. Paul shook his head and said, 'But it did end. *That's* what Peter was telling you. He'd done all he could. Bill, don't you see? – *I'm* the continuation. *Me!* This relationship – you and me – this is what Peter would have done if he could have. But he couldn't. He couldn't! And I can.'

I thought he was going to run away from me – I was sure of it. But he came to me then and hugged me harder than he ever had before.

I realized that he was doing just as I'd asked, that he was looking back for me.

∞

I still didn't understand, however, just how intimately connected Peter and Paul were till one night, almost a year later, when I dreamt of the time I drove up to Calistoga to escape my sexual obsession. In my dream, I was peering through the window of the farmhouse I'd seen that evening. Only this time, the man in the house was a sphinx with Peter's androgynous body and Maria's crowned head.

You've made love to a stranger for the last time. Those words circled through my head, just as they had on that fateful night.

Then Peter turned to me, opened his beak, and said, 'Welcome home.'

When I awoke, it occurred to me that I'd only made love with Paul *after* getting to know him. I couldn't get that understanding out of my head. It was as if it possessed some occult meaning.

It seemed as if Paul and Peter were interchangeable. Because I loved them both.

Maybe Paul was simply Peter given different form – a form that could stay with me this time, just as Paul had said.

Strange and disquieting thoughts began occurring to me.

And yet, lying next to Paul, thinking about my dream, I

felt gloriously liberated knowing that I'd never have to make love to anyone else ever again. I was free. I had come home. I'd never have to worry about other people's assessments of my worth.

Then I realized why it seemed so important to me and burst into tears; by enabling me to fall in love for good, Peter had saved my life. Both our lives, mine and Paul's. Why?

This was November of 1990, and death had wrapped its cruel darkness around sex, was keeping it, in fact, in an unbreakable hold. Several friends of ours had already died of AIDS. By some miracle, Paul and I had found each other before being exposed to the virus. Though enduring love hadn't been nearly enough to save everyone, of course. Maybe not even most people. I knew that, and it constituted a real tragedy. But the love I'd learned from Peter *had* protected us, and I was grateful.

Postscript

ALMOST NINE YEARS have passed since then. It's September of 1999, and Paul and I are still together. If we hadn't found each other, if Peter hadn't taught me how to love, I'm sure that my ashes would now be scattered over the arboretum in Golden Gate Park. These words would never have been published. I would never have been able to give anything important back to Paul or the world.

Although maybe what I'm writing now is of little value. Maybe sitting here typing away at this very sentence in my study in San Francisco, struggling with every word to say exactly what I mean, is pointless. I don't think any of us can be sure of the worth of what we do.

∞

Paul and I live now in a tiny Victorian carriage house we bought on Hartford Street, one block east of Castro. My globe sits in the corner of our bedroom.

I haven't seen Jay in eleven years. I don't really miss him. Or more to the point, the Jay I miss pretty much all the time no longer exists.

I call my mom once a year on her birthday. She refuses to talk to me about my new life. Paul and I did try to visit her once on Long Island a few years ago. It was at the time of the O. J. Simpson mess, and we had everything planned, but when I called her from the Miracle Mile Motel in Manhasset, she said, 'I really think it best if you don't come over, Bill.'

'But you knew we were coming today,' I protested. 'We rented the car and everything. Jesus, we flew all the way from San Francisco to see you.'

'I didn't have time to cook,' she said. 'I've been watching O. J.'

'I don't care about the food. I just want to see you.'

Silence. She wasn't going to meet me half-way, was still punishing me with her silent judgments. So I said, 'You don't want to meet Paul, do you?'

'I never understood why you left Alexandra. She was a gorgeous girl. The best thing that ever happened to you.'

'I'm with Paul now. I love him. He's a great person. You'd like him.'

'Your father would not approve.'

'Dad's dead.'

More silent disapproval from Mom. It seemed to be weighing down my hand, my heartbeat, even the sunny parking lot out my window. 'Mom, we know what Dad would think, but what about you?' I asked.

'I think something went very wrong with you that time you went into the hospital. I think you sort of cracked up. I think maybe this man is playing on your weaknesses.'

I couldn't come up with anything heartfelt or even mean to say after that, so I just told her that I'd give her a call when we got back to San Francisco, to let her know we'd arrived home safely. I know exactly how she replied to that because I wrote it down out of disbelief on an automatic teller receipt I'd had in my wallet.

'I take the phone off the hook when I'm watching TV. You won't be able to reach me even if you try,' she said.

She was right, of course, and I know I'll probably never see her again.

∞

I'm part owner of Wheels on Fire now. Paul still works as a graphic designer for the *San Francisco Chronicle*. He also designs covers for a series of history books Neptune Publishers started putting out a few years back.

Even gay friends say we're crazy living in a mostly gay section of the city, but I like it that our neighbours and garbagemen and even the cop on the corner all accept that they're hybrids of sorts. I like it that they think sex is good. Paul says it's like living in a lavender Twilight Zone.

Our house has a garden with southern exposure where I can cultivate flowers. After my life with Peter, that seemed essential.

∞

It makes me happy to see Paul wearing colourful clothing from South America, that he sings songs by the Rolling Stones in the shower, that he occasionally runs down the street for no reason at all. I'm glad that he reads books in bed for hours at a time and doesn't need to use a flashlight.

I like to cover myself with his long hair at night. I even like ironing his clothing.

He says we're both lucky.

Even when we scream at each other and say mean things, we know that. It makes a difference.

∞

Before I met Paul, it was only sorrow that ever made me feel part of an ancient heritage, that gave me the understanding that I was just like other people – part of a species of frail sensitive beings destined to lose loved ones and face illness, who must eventually walk alone toward death. But this joy at being in Paul's presence ... at times, while watching him sleeping in the moonlight or simply talking with him over bran muffins about a novel he's just finished, happiness moves me beyond my own time and place as well. People don't usually write about it, but this steady soft beating of joy, of transcendent delight, it's as if it's there all the time, right beside sorrow, always waiting for us to be still and quiet enough to feel it.

∞

Once, when it was pouring outside, Paul told me that he'd read when he was a kid that certain native peoples in New Guinea regard rain as symbolic of God's loving mercy.

That, too, reminded me of things Peter had told me, and I started reading about the Sufis – just as he had predicted. In a wonderful little book by an eighteenth-century Persian mystic named Shahar, I discovered that the Sufis believe that rain is meant to revive the heart that has become as dry and barren as dust.

Maybe that's why Rain had taken her name. Her presence in my life, like everything else that Peter scripted, had been meant, perhaps, to awaken my dormant capacity to love.

While reading one of the books for which Paul had done the cover, *A History of British Piracy*, by John Case Navarro, I was able to find out more about the one man who had survived the ill-fated attempt by Majorcan Chuetas to escape persecution in the seventeenth century. It turns out that he reached the Welsh coast aboard a British pirate vessel and that his name was Peral de los Santos – the Spanish equivalent of two of Peter's father's Portuguese names, Pereira dos Santos. So maybe he was a distant ancestor of theirs. Which would mean that there was indeed a connection between Peter and Majorca, as I once imagined. Though it's much more likely, I suppose, that Peter knew all this from his study of Portuguese history and made up his father's names to fit the story. He wanted to confirm my hunch about his ties to Majorca. Maybe he was even using names to get me to make connections between different people and disparate events, to tug me beyond my usual ways of thinking. I've heard of Jewish mystics – of kabbalists – doing that sort of thing. Maybe he'd studied with one in Brazil. Maybe that's what his friend William was.

Over the years, I slowly scripted an explanation for what had happened with Peter and me.

I figured that he had come into my life expressly to revive

my emotions; they were what he valued most, inside objects and in people. He staged everything for that reason.

I told myself that there were so many hints I should have picked up on: all the troubling stories he told me; the amulets; his terrible illness when Maria was stolen; Rain's 'murder.'

When even our lovemaking failed to break my armour for good, when I refused to spend the night with him, he disappeared.

Sudden absence was to be the nature of his last effort on my behalf. It was how he would bring on my *winter*.

∞

I also figured that he was telling me that what I was most frightened of was my own androgyny, that I had to face it alone for a time.

He was right, of course.

∞

Thinking of Peter's stories – of Miguel and his magic worm, of Cecilia and her tyrannical dwarf, of Victor and Sarah and their etched poem of eternal devotion – I finally understood that these particular tales were meant to help me, to lead me by example. I saw that he was telling me that I could transform my own pale and repugnant interior life into a colourful source of wonder; could exorcise a good deal of my past and stop following anyone else's orders; could maybe even fall in love with someone able to speak my own personal language, who wanted to do a dance of life with me for as long as we both lived.

And I think I've been able to reach some of these goals – in part, at least, through the influence of his storytelling.

∞

I think he also chose to reach me in this particular way to cancel out the paralysing effect that my father's story of the Ethiopian newborn had had on me.

∞

Sometimes I wonder if Peter had everything planned from the very beginning. More likely, he made things up as he went.

Like Mara, he probably improvised.

Was it difficult for him to maintain the illusions? Did he enjoy them?

∞

There are no clear answers, of course.

So I started writing this book to see if I could make sense of everything – of Peter, Mara, Maria, Rain, Paul, me. Of how they'd revived me. Of life and death.

I discovered that this very act of reconstructing my past is what Peter meant by a mirror.

∞

He told me once that his mother thought of him as part angel, part devil. And maybe that's exactly what he was, a man of angelic darkness.

∞

I've looked at myself for many pages now. I'm not really sure what I've found. Everything seems both more complex and more simple than I first imagined.

∞

They say that first-time writers always begin with their births, and I think I have.

∞

Lying in bed at night with Paul, I often like to think that he and Peter and I and everyone else are all androgynous spirits – angels – who've been given earthly form in order to help our loved ones at their most difficult times.

Could it be true?